77 ° NORTH

77 ° NORTH

TP Wood

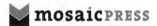
mosaicPRESS

Library and Archives Canada Cataloguing in Publication

Title: 77° North / TP Wood.

Other titles: 77 Degrees North | Seventy-Seven Degrees North

Names: Wood, TP (Author), author.

Identifiers: Canadiana (print) 20220257086 | Canadiana (ebook) 20220257159 |
ISBN 9781771616843 (softcover) | ISBN 9781771616850 (PDF) |
ISBN 9781771616867 (EPUB) | ISBN 9781771616874 (Kindle)

Subjects: LCGFT: Novels.

Classification: LCC PS8645.O63655 A617 2022 | DDC C813/.6—dc23

Published by Mosaic Press, Oakville, Ontario, Canada, 2023.
Second Printing - 2023

MOSAIC PRESS, Publishers
www.Mosaic-Press.com
Copyright © TP Wood 2023

ONTARIO ARTS COUNCIL
CONSEIL DES ARTS DE L'ONTARIO
an Ontario government agency
un organisme du gouvernement de l'Ontario

Funded by the Government of Canada
Financé par le gouvernement du Canada

Canada

ONTARIO CREATES

MOSAIC PRESS
1252 Speers Road, Units 1 & 2, Oakville, Ontario, L6L 5N9
(905) 825-2130 • info@mosaic-press.com • www.mosaic-press.com

To my grandfather, who fired my imagination.

ACKNOWLEDGEMENTS

First to my wife Debbie for providing the space, support and encouragement as I turned my thoughts into words. Thank you for your relentless listening while I chattered on about characters and plots, and your quizzical expression when some things just didn't make sense.

Susan Smith, who was brave enough to volunteer editing the earliest versions of the manuscript. Meticulous, insightful, an English language ninja, Susan never wavered in giving it to me straight. You made me a better writer.

My friend and author brother Andrew Lafleche, who opened that crucial first door to my publishing journey at Mosaic Press.

Howard Aster, who suggested I read the manuscript backwards (yikes!) to squeeze it one last time. And Rahim Piracha, website designer and patient guide through the world of publishing.

Add to that Jan Barrett and Anne Page, who sacrificed their time to read through the script. My poetry and novel writers' groups from the Canadian Authors Association, who helped toughen me to criticism, and define my style as a writer.

Last, but certainly not least, author Steven Pressfield. His book, *Turning Pro* was my constant companion as I wrote 77° North. I promised him a copy when published.

Here you go Steve.

TABLE OF CONTENTS

A NOTE TO THE READER:

There are certain voices throughout this narrative that warrant identification. First, is that of The Foundlings, the cosmic travellers who occupied the space at 77° North, which I have distinguished in *italics*. Second is my inner voice, that I now concede as the intonations of my tuurngaq, stated in parentheses.

Less obvious are the collective voices of PNs, the network of telepaths who connect with The Foundlings. There are no grammatical or font indicators to identify them. I trust the pictures formed in the reader's mind will suffice as the seed of understanding for their new wordless and universal message.

Chulyin Nakasuk
Pangnirtung
October, 2039

1. PANGNIRTUNG

We are the Foundlings, cultivators of all that sprout from the place of origin. We scatter in many places. This is just one. We are not perpetual beings; only the force of regeneration, renewal.

We do not know the shape of this unfolding, only the power that exists within, the power to chart its own course. The seed sprouts when ready and that time nears. All things begin with the seed, this seed, the girl child rooted in mountains of ice, the one who cannot see her wings that she might fly...

They never knew I listened. How could they? Tucked under the covers, their muffled words drifted through the open door of my bedroom, sailing into the docks of my ears. Tone told me more than the words. The softer they spoke, the more I heard.

April light was returning, and I studied a smudge of colour glowing beyond the frost-painted window.

Whispers. My name, Chulyin. They were talking about me. I liked it when I heard them say my name. I felt safe. Special.

But her yellow, unblinking eyes distracted me. She thought I was special too, and I was frightened when she came, perching on the post at the foot of my bed. I tried to turn away but could not, pulling the covers over my head, shielding my eyes, the stench of decomposing fish replacing her stare. Pinching my nose, breathing through my mouth, didn't help. I tasted it, tasted her presence, a metallic tang secreted by her feathers sour on my tongue.

Molding a tunnel into the blanket to breathe, I observed the pink luminescence fade along with their kitchen murmurs, and an urge to scream, to fend her off overcame me, but my throat froze. The odour was overpowering, and I dissolved into the vapour of a dream.

I told Aanaq about Raven. How she whispered things I did not understand, showed me places I could see without opening my eyes. I told her how I wished Raven would go away. Leave me alone.

Aanaq sat by the window, where the light was bright. I didn't know it then, but her eyes were failing, something her hands refused to acknowledge. She knew the exact place to push the needle through the hide, tugging the sinew tight. She was making boots for me, although I secretly wished for a pair I'd seen in the Co-Op a week before. I mentioned this to my uncle Anun, and he chastised me for being ungrateful.

Aanaq tugged a stitch through the sole, then placed the boot gently on the table. "Pay attention to your tuurngaq," she said. "I want you to promise me something, Chulyin," and her face turned solemn. "When Raven comes, tell me."

"I'm afraid. I don't want her to come."

"Fear is natural," she said, lifting from the chair and coming to me, cradling my cheeks in her hands. "It protects us. Secrets are more frightening than Raven. Raven is your helper. Your tuurngaq. Raven has chosen you because you have great courage. Courage to feel the wind. To heal her wings and send her back to sky."

* * *

The wind was a constant in Pangnirtung. I was dubious about what courage had to do with it, or how I somehow modelled that sense of bravery. I knew the power of the wind, watching it one fall day smashing boats in the harbour, sending one out into the fiord, never to be seen again. How on earth could I possibly have such power?

I was ten when I had that conversation with Aanaq. There were days when I felt like the wind. Not the warm summer breeze that funnelled up the inlet on a July day, but the torrent that roared between the mountains, rocking the sea like a deranged pendulum. Raw power, unrestrained and cruel, obliterating anything that might stand in its way.

The wind's fury kept me sane, or so I convinced myself. Riding its furor, the currents that lifted me over what made no sense at ground level and the fiction of Pang and its inhabitants. Looking down would devour me, like a seal being torn apart by a starving polar bear.

I rode the wind above them all, and I learned to do it without Raven. It was easy with the people of Pang. I could distance myself from them, flying above them, observing, pretending to care, pretending to listen. It's how I protected myself. Shut out the words that would knock me from the sky if I allowed them to penetrate my ears.

Predators lurked everywhere. Especially at ground level with my wings tucked tight, and especially in the schoolroom of my grade seven class.

Four pimply faces accosted me one afternoon while I walked home from school.

"There she is. Where are you flying off to tonight, Chu—lyin?" Freddy Tingenek was their ringleader and a complete jerk.

"Shut up Freddy."

"Woah, tough girl. What are you gonna do? Cast a spell on me?"

The posse fenced me in, and when I tried to push through, Freddy chest-butted me, knocking me to the ground.

Luke Olikpak piped in, "Easy Freddy. She's just a girl. Her Aanaq. She's crazy. She's a shaman."

"Shaman oogley-boogley." Freddy brandished his finger in my face. "That's bullshit," stamping his boot beside my head.

"Maybe she's one of them too," Luke said.

Freddy was on a roll. "My old man shot a walrus last week. Looked just like her Aanaq. She's got more whiskers than the walrus and my old man put together." Freddy snorted like a walrus and they all roared with laughter. "And those stupid tattoos. Maybe we should paint your face, too."

I scrambled to get up, and they pushed me down again.

"How about it guys? Let's beat the shaman out of her. What you think about that?" Freddy threatened.

I struggled to my feet, defiant. "Just try it. Maybe I'll put a curse on you Freddy. All of you."

They laughed, nervous.

"Listen to her big words." Freddy lurched forward a single step, then froze.

"All of you! You'll be sorry!" I bellowed, spitting at him.

From behind them, my cousin Fearney charged toward us, unleashing a war cry that scattered them like lemmings from a hungry wolf.

"What were those idiots doing?" he huffed.

"Who knows?"

"Jerks. Don't listen to them," he said. "You alright? C'mon. I'll walk you home."

I connected somewhere with Fearney on his mother's side. He was what some of the other kids called 'not too bright', but they would never say that to his face. He was tall and strong and although we were both in the seventh grade, he was two years my senior. Fearney had appointed himself my personal bodyguard and intervened a few weeks back when the same crew blocked me from my locker. I never asked for his help, but when he showed up, I sure didn't resist. He was my guard dog. Vicious to anyone who came too close. It was his duty, he said, to protect me. We were blood.

"I'd like to mash that Freddy's face in," he said, looking straight forward as we walked.

"Wouldn't hurt my feelings."

"Brave when he's picking on girls."

"I can take care of myself."

"I know, I know," he backpedaled. "I was just trying to even the odds. Can I ask you something, Chu?"

"Sure."

Breathing deep he asked, "Can your Aanaq really turn into things?"

"What do you mean?"

"You know. Things. Like animals. Or dead people."

Snow crunched under our boots.

"Never mind," he broke the silence.

(What would it hurt if I told him? Just a little?)

"No, no. It's okay. She can turn into a Fox."

"Wow." He stopped and looked straight at me.

"Well, no. Not in the sense she is a Fox. It's her spirit guide. Her tuurngaq. She does it in her head, you know? Then she can go where Fox goes. See what Fox sees. Get it?"

"Kind of," tapping his chin. "I wish I could turn into a hare."

"A hare? What for?"

"They can sit so still. Blend right in and they're–invisible. I watched one once for an hour. Never flinched."

"You watched a hare for a whole hour? Why?"

"I dunno. I just did. I wanted to see how long it could sit."

"You're crazy."

"Yeah, maybe," then, "BANG," he hollered so loud I dropped my books.

"And they can run like hell!" He sprinted off, laughing hysterically toward his house.

No doubt about it; Fearney was touched. I thought about him standing there watching that hare. What a scatterbrain. Even Freddy, as much as I couldn't stand him, had a measure of common sense. I didn't like what he had to say, but I couldn't deny there was truth in it. It just struck a chord in me, that's all. It was none of his business if my Aanaq was shaman. I'd never admit it, but I was secretly embarrassed because, although Freddy didn't have a clue, he was talking about me too, indirectly. It was easier for me to be indignant about what he said about Aanaq.

I kicked the gate, and the hinges groaned, barely budging in the cold and rust. We were two people disguised as one, Aanaq and I. She, in her private little shaman existence, fading away into a past that no one wanted to remember. And me, acting dumb, like I didn't know what was going on and wanting to punch Freddy for his audacity in bringing it up.

I pushed the door, which banged against Father McMurtry's giant leather boots. He was here for his Tuesday tea with Aanaq. They were an unlikely pair, my Aanaq and the Father. He was the priest at St. Luke's Anglican Church and decided, long before I could remember, that Aanaq was saved about as much as he could save her. I never heard him preaching or attempting to coerce her into being anything other than what she was. Whatever discussions they had regarding religion had long passed. Father McMurtry was perceptive enough to see her value. Somewhere along the way, she had conceded to him as well, a picture of Jesus hanging on our kitchen wall.

"You've a good heart, Mary," he would tell her, "And a good heart is a good heart no matter what you believe," and they would laugh. Aside from my uncle Anun, he was the only one I knew who could make her laugh.

Even if Jesus couldn't bring them together, they had a common denominator that did. Gardening. Aanaq had become quite skilled as an indoor gardener. Pots of African violets sprouted from every window shelf, making their way by a mysterious floral osmosis on to every table in our house. She cultivated them under the watchful eye of Father McMurtry, into a harvest that splashed the whole place in colour. The Father gifted her with a set of grow lights to compensate for the long Arctic winter, ensuring a bountiful display of blooms all year long. They were engaged in a deep discussion about one of her variegated species and its refusal to flower when I barged in.

"Good afternoon Chulyin." He perked up when he saw me. "I think we've solved Aanaq's botanical problems." They laughed. "I'll give her back to you now."

As he prepared to leave, he pointed to the portrait of Jesus and said, "He watches over us." Father McMurtry said this without fail before every departure.

Aanaq nodded, pressing her palms together. "Amen."

Every Tuesday before Father McMurtry arrived for tea, Aanaq would retrieve the picture of Jesus she had stored in the drawer and hang it on the nail that had been waiting for it all week long. It was a ritual, like their tea and conversation. When he left at precisely 2:30, she would watch him latch the gate—which seemed redundant since there was no fence extending from the posts beyond it—then she would remove the Saviour, wiping the glass with a fresh cloth and place Him back in the drawer for another week. It was like the resurrection itself, Jesus rising from the dead so He could look down and bless their Tuesday conversation.

I thought maybe Jesus was a gardener too. Especially when the Father would talk about sowing seeds and how some took root and flourished while others didn't. When the flowers and the Father came, so did Jesus. I just thought the Saviour knew so much about these plants Aanaq brought

Him out as an expert gardener. What I never understood was why, as soon as he left, she would store the expert back in the drawer. The flowers bloomed if He hung on the wall or not.

I never mentioned to Father McMurtry that Aanaq took down Jesus' portrait every time he left. She never told me to keep quiet about it either, I just intuitively knew.

One day, I asked. She was watering her violets, careful to position the spout onto the soil under the leaves. Father told her getting water on the surface of the leaves would cause brown spots. She believed him. "Why do we put Jesus away after Father leaves?"

"We're finished with Him," she said plainly.

"But doesn't He help you with your violets?"

"They help each other."

"How?"

Aanaq put down her watering can and moved to the kitchen. "See the violet?" she said, pointing to one in full bloom with deep pink flowers. "That's Jesus smiling." She removed the picture of Jesus from the wall, holding it up for me. "He doesn't smile here," she tapped on the glass, "but He smiles there."

"Then why don't you keep Him out all the time?"

"Because there's too much sadness in His face. It doesn't change. Look."

She walked over to the window and picked off a fading bloom. "When the flower's smile goes, we can let it go. Another always takes its place." She let the shrivelled bloom drop to the table.

I never asked her anymore, but somehow understood that was the end of our conversation. I also came to understand the strength of Aanaq, the strength in her stillness, and her ability to hold her tongue. There was no need to question Father McMurtry's tuurngaq or why he never smiled. Jesus was just sad, and she was okay with that. And no matter how long we waited, He always looked the same when the Father visited, all the while her violets were ever-changing, like the land and the weather just outside the window.

Either way, I liked Father McMurtry. He always included me in their conversation, asking me how I thought and felt about the colours of the flowers, or the feel of the leaves and the miracle of the seeds and their roots while the snow whistled around us. Although I think there was method in his madness. Somehow, the miracle of the seed always led back to Jesus and how we were all seeds and how some of us took root and some of us didn't.

He spoke about miracles, much the same way Aanaq spoke about Fox. She would tell me how Fox came to her, how she could see through his eyes, and move into places where she could not go. Like the roots in the soil. It made me wonder what miracle guided me, if any miracle at all.

Aanaq was a regular at Father McMurtry's Sunday morning sermons. She pulled me along with her to listen to the miracles that his tuurngaq had performed centuries ago. I wondered at his reverence for Jesus and I would squinch my eyes, wishing Jesus would appear for me too, but all that came were pins and needles behind my eyelids. Then on our way home I would see her, Raven, perched on our gate, waiting every Sunday when we returned from church. I knew Aanaq saw her too. She would squeeze my hand and look at me, smiling.

2. GROWING PAINS

My father drowned in a fishing calamity a month before I was born; my mother committed suicide just after my second birthday and I have one memory of her. It blends like grey smoke curling into a slate sky.

We were at the sea, a vee of dimples sparkling to the mountains on the farther side of the fiord. She came so close she blocked the sun and her hands, cool, touching my face. When she breathed, I breathed, and we threw stones, laughing. I'm not sure why we laughed, but it was infectious and we danced on the rocks, squealing in delight. Then I was alone. The dancing continued, the sun sparkling in the harbour, the birds, all except for me, sinking in the cold water, where the rocks had teeth. Powerful arms scooped me up, covering me in blankets, carrying me away. The sun was warm, but I shivered.

They found my mother's body the next day bobbing far out in the inlet. She had stripped herself naked so she would float. A good omen, Aanaq told me later when I was old enough to understand. The sea would not devour her spirit. And I was the luckiest of all. I had escaped Qalupalik, the water demon who abducted children, and raised them as her own at the bottom of the ocean.

(A good omen.)

If there was an omen that came from my parents' deaths, it was my upbringing with Aanaq and my uncle Anun. Between them, I traversed two worlds.

Aanaq was my confidante. When I was small, she shared about Fox, the way Fox could hear between the words and thoughts before people spoke them. About her baby sister, Chulyin, how I was her spirit, her namesake, who died before I was born and now lived on the moon. Aanaq would ask, "Would you like to see your great aunt today?" and, of course, I always did. We would set a place for her at the table, invite her for tea, then close our eyes and she would come. It always began with my introduction. "This is my little orphan," Aanaq would say, then we'd have a grand time drinking tea, telling silly stories. When great auntie returned to the moon, we would share her tea and I would help Aanaq wash the cups.

All of this was my truth, until later, when school introduced other truths. Truths that convinced me my memories were lies, and our tea parties only the crazy imaginings of an old woman. She was a witch, they said, a creature stuck in a past world that didn't work anymore.

I did not want to be a creature of her past and that came to a head one afternoon at school when Freddy and his hoods cornered me in the hall.

"You want to be a witch? We're going to make you look like one," he said. "Let's see how brave you are now when your fat cousin isn't around to save you."

"He'll kick your ass," I hissed.

"Hold her arms."

Before I could react, they pulled me into the boy's washroom. I erupted, slamming Freddie into the sink. They wrestled me to the ground and I let out a yelp, a wad of paper towels stuffed into my mouth, muffling my cry for help.

The pungent smell of the magic marker, and the malicious weight of his strokes, slashing the pen across my cheeks and forehead. Resistance was fruitless. I closed my eyes, and within seconds they branded my face with the caustic pigment, then fled, leaving me under a urinal. I coughed the towels from my mouth and pried myself off the floor. In the mirror my pigtails hung down, one loose, unravelling in black strands that sprayed out in a static fan. Thick jagged stripes looked back from the mirror, and my eyes singed from the ink oozing into their corners, a lightning bolt of black traversed my forehead, striking my opposing ear.

I charged home, barging through the door and into the bathroom. Aanaq was in her tupiq. I gathered a cloud of soap and scoured their handiwork until my skin was raw. I heard her come through the door and she called, "How was school today?"

"Fine," I stammered back.

I never told her, but that day I expunged Raven from my life. I refused to talk about tuurngaqs or shamans or hosting visitors from the moon. A chasm opened between us. One that induced sadness in her. Rebellion in me.

Anun was my ballast. Whenever I went off on an emotional binge, he could pull me into calmer waters.

"No need to be a thug to get your point across," he would say. Then he'd wonder out loud if it was colic or a defiant disposition that brought me screaming into this world. He concluded it was the latter and labelled it as my indomitable will.

I turned to Anun for alternatives. He was my compass in uncharted waters, and, as I learned more about the world beyond Pang, I distanced myself from Aanaq. That's not to say I dismissed her values. They merely became incidental considerations. I saw Anun as the bridge, straddling the gap between her ideals and my future. He was my salvation, and with that, Raven blurred into the background like the hazy recollection of my mother.

* * *

There wasn't much to do in Pang when school was out. The light was endless, and we were free to roam wherever we wished. Fearney and I became inseparable that summer between grade eight and high school. We concocted a master plan to ambush the gang members that had sullied my face. He thought it best we even the score with them one at a time. It would make revenge sweeter, he said, and we could leave Freddy to the last. I liked the idea. Fearney was an expert at revenge.

Throughout that summer, Fearney would show up tapping on my window, waking me out of a dead sleep. I'd get dressed, real quiet, and slip out while Aanaq was snoring. He'd say he couldn't sleep, but I knew different. His dad was a big drunk and Fearney would scram when he was on a rampage. The old man was brutal. I'd seen the bruises. He showed up once with a gash over his eye, and it took twenty minutes to stop the bleeding. His father broke his baby sister's arm too, yanking her around. I told him we should call the cops, and he nearly had a fit. "That would only make things worse," he said.

The old man didn't care who he abused. He'd swat anyone who crossed him, and I found out firsthand. Fearney's mom invited me to dinner one night, and he cracked my knuckles with a knife when I took too many potatoes. Laughed like a lunatic after, rolling his head back, exposing the black stubs he had for teeth. Nobody said a word. They all just kept eating, eyes glued to their plates, their forks scraping on the dishes.

If Fearney's dad wasn't drunk, he'd be in gaol because of it. One night, I watched while four RCMP took fifteen minutes to wrestle him to the ground. On another occasion, he barged into one of Father McMurtry's church services, smelling like a brewery dipped in rotten fish. The Father was in the middle of telling us how Jesus wanted us to see planks in our own eyes when he burst in, hollering at the top of his lungs that the Father was the plague of Pang. His outburst ended when Aanaq stood up and gave him 'the look', staring him right out the door. It was pretty entertaining. I thought Father McMurtry was going to have seal pups and cut the sermon short. Aanaq totally impressed me. Stronger than four cops.

Fearney had an older sister, Giselle. She was his cousin, really, from his aunt who died a few years back, and his mom insisted they take her in. The old man wanted no part in it, and only after one black eye and two visits from the cops, Giselle moved in to their already cramped accommodations, bringing the total to eight living in their two-bedroom shanty. It was the first time his mother stood up to his tyranny.

Later that summer, I saw her waddling with a swollen belly behind their house hanging laundry. Fearney and I had just commandeered his dad's .22, and we were on our way to the dump to blast anything that moved.

"Giselle. She's pregnant," I said.

"No, she's not."

"Come on. Are you blind?"

His face reddened, and he balled his fists. "What difference does it make? You always got your nose in something that's not yours."

"Just asking. You don't have to get so huffy."

"Mind your own business," and that was that.

Rumour was the old man knocked her up, but no one dared talk about it. No one wanted his drunken wrath raining on them, especially Fearney.

It was the end of August and uncharacteristically hot. We were down to our shirts returning from our daily excursion to the dump when I remembered Anun had stocked us up on ice cream bars. We ran back to fetch them, and when we rounded the corner to our lane, Fearney saw smoke coming out of Aanaq's tupiq.

"What's she doing out there?" he asked, pointing out the kitchen window, tearing the wrapper from his treat.

"Getting ready to turn you into a dog."

"Not funny Chu."

"I didn't mean it to be."

"My dad says she's evil."

"Your dad's an idiot."

"True," he said, biting into the chocolate coating. "Maybe she could turn him into a whale turd. I heard women shaman are more powerful than the men ones."

"Who knows? I don't go out there much." I lied.

He pointed out the window. "What's she burning? Dead bodies?"

"Ya. You're next."

The entire town gossiped about Aanaq's tupiq and what happened in it. Anun had built it for her, a solid structure to withstand the Arctic winter, but on the inside, it was her shamanic haven. Caribou hide lined the inner walls while a frame of whale ribs arched to the top, crisscrossing and bound with ropes. Standing inside felt like being in the beast's belly itself.

In the centre was a small fire pit and a portable altar assembled from wooden skids Anun had collected from the dock. A patchwork shroud of bear and fox pelts covered it. Near the back, a rack of shelves, strewn with objects she had collected, artefacts, amulets, passed down, she professed, by ancestors who still lived in them. Most notably, an assortment of bones, all shapes and sizes crammed on the upper shelves.

Aanaq's tupiq was her shrine to the past, to her shamanism, a shrine Father McMurtry's converts would have preferred didn't exist. They labelled her a demon, and at one point, hatched a plot to demolish it.

Dispatching a posse, Anun got wind of it and met them at our gate with his rifle. They slunk away without protest, no match for the gun and my uncle's resolve.

"What the hell?" Fearney's ice cream dropped to the floor when a scream erupted from inside the tupiq. We stared at each other for a split second, then bolted into the yard. Smoke poured from the canvass-flap door.

"Fire!" he roared and plunged in. I was seconds behind and slammed into him just inside. He'd frozen in his tracks.

Aanaq and Fearney's mom were there with Giselle. She was lying flat near the fire, her belly distended, naked from the waist down. Aanaq chanted softly while Giselle pushed, then shrieked like a wounded animal. Fearney's mom stood motionless while Aanaq warbled to her tuurngaqs and positioned herself between Giselle's thighs.

The baby came fast, and Aanaq had it in her arms, covered in blood and afterbirth. Fearney gagged and pulled away. It mesmerised me. The baby was quiet, motionless, and Aanaq instructed Fearney's mom to cut the cord, handing her a knife. She held the child over the smoke then raised him above her head, wailing, imploring the limp infant to take part in the world it had just entered.

Nothing.

Aanaq brought the baby to her face and placed her mouth over his nose, charging him with breath and incantations. For ten solid minutes, she implored the spirits to revive the child, to no avail. She cupped the infant's head, stroking it, then swaddled him in a tiny caribou cloth.

"Aaahhkk!" Fearney's mom wailed, slamming to the ground on her knees.

Giselle did not know her baby was dead. Their eyes met as Aanaq approached, placing the lifeless infant on her chest, leaning down, chanting softly, words I did not understand. They were sounds, sounds of spirit, of animals, the wind; the sun and the moon speaking, and when Giselle's eyes opened, she kissed her son for the first and last time on the crown of his head.

The fire's intensity increased, collecting in a ball of crackling energy that seared the air. Above the child, a sphere of light appeared, tethered to the tiny body by a silver umbilical thread. Aanaq's arms seemed to stretch beyond their physical form, extending across the room, cradling the tiny ball, guiding it to the fire, placing it in the crucible of light. She released it and the space infused with fizzling effulgence, particles, and motes, then— gone. The fire became fire again, and Giselle's weeping resuscitated the reality of what I had just witnessed.

Aanaq collapsed to the floor.

"Aanaq!" I crouched beside her as tears streamed down her face, and I could taste my own as they rolled over my lips, dripping from my chin. A blast of wind from inside the tupiq snuffed the fire.

"The child is free," Aanaq said, and we staggered to our feet. "Everyone to the house." We emerged into the surreal glare of infinite Arctic summer.

* * *

Later that month, they found Giselle in the highland tundra, just south of town. She'd snuck a pistol from the old man's collection and discharged it into her chest.

The day that infant died, Aanaq went into self-imposed seclusion. The event broke her. She imploded with the death of Giselle's son and ordered Anun to seal the tupiq. She refused Father McMurtry's Tuesday visits and sentenced Jesus to solitary confinement in the kitchen drawer. When she spoke, it was to chastise me for some trivial transgression or obsess over my whereabouts.

I couldn't blame her. Aanaq was no stranger to losing children. Three of her four offspring had perished. Anun, her youngest, and me, a copy of my mother's and her sister's resurrected spirits, were the last fragments of family left to her. Still, her grief placed secondary to my heightening sense of autonomy.

"She's driving me crazy," I protested to Anun.

"She's protecting you."

"From what?"

"I'll talk with her."

A week later, a large parcel arrived from Sumka Brothers in Winnipeg and I knew he had worked his magic. Packets of seeds, pots, tools and a 25-litre bag of fresh composted loam appeared at our door, along with their annual catalogue. There were gloves too, which she put aside because, she said, "this kind of dirt is for fingers."

I would watch her even though I pretended not to. She opened the seed packets, tapping the top to make sure no treasure stuck in the corners, snipping off the edge and releasing three, maybe four, of the precious jewels onto a piece of clean white paper. Her thumb poking the soil then releasing the seed, covering and tamping gently. She only used water from melted ice, something she stored in a large barrel at the back of the house. She said the water was her secret. More minerals and wizard power.

I knew the power in her hands. The way she rolled the seeds, feeling them, encouraging them. Her fingers possessed the miracle of the water, of soil, and the sun combined. I was never sure if it was the chemistry in her hands or the seed itself. She had that same power over me. A power I grew to resent, but never had the courage to confront. I loved her dearly, but hated the past that sentenced me to her world of dying memories. I vowed to sow my own future. I just didn't know how I could without hurting her.

Whether I liked it or not, I grew from her roots, a tuber that ran beneath the ground and shot up in another place. The same, but different. I was one of her cultivations. Even though I knew there was love in her hands, I wanted to disassociate with anything that obstructed my wild, twisting growth.

The kitchen became our demilitarised zone. We negotiated there, like the United Nations, countries with different ideologies, different viewpoints. I didn't want pruning or fertilisation; I didn't want to hear about plants and seeds, tender shoots or when they would break through the soil. I was far too intelligent, far too sophisticated for such trivial things. I was thirteen, grade nine, looming straight ahead.

Then Anun showed up with two gifts for me; a computer and the announcement we would leave on our annual pilgrimage to Mount Odin on my birthday. I could hardly wait. We set the date, and I marked the days off the calendar in anticipation.

Usually the group was large, between ten and fifteen, but this year it was only two. They were archaeologists from Leiden University in the Netherlands. They were an odd couple; her from Durban, South Africa, and him from Osaka, Japan. They had both been on separate archaeological digs and reconnected in Qikiqtani before heading back to Leiden for the fall semester. Qikiqtani. That's what they called it. It impressed me they used the Inuit name for our island.

Their tales intrigued me, especially hers, and I called her professor Sophie.

One night around the campfire, professor Sophie pointed to the sky and said, "They saw the sky better than we do."

"Who?" I asked.

"The ancients. Our far-off ancestors. They saw the gods and the power of creation. The spirits. Me? I just find bits of pots, look under stones and put together broken statues. And I think I understand. But I don't. All I see is leftovers. The things I dig up and hold in my hands. The actual story is up there," and she pointed to a bright star.

"Arcturus," she continued. "The magic is in the stars and the legends they produce. That's who we are. Not the statues or the pyramids. We're the fiction in the stars."

"Suvulliik," I said. "We call that star Suvulliik."

"See? That's what I mean. That's your story. Your name for that star."

"It tells me morning is about to begin. A new day. My Aanaq would send me out to see if Suvulliik was hanging its head. When the big one," I pointed to Suvulliik, "drops below the smaller one behind it, we start our day."

"Bravo," she said, clapping excitedly. "That's what we miss in the stones and the pots. The spirit of the stories and the hearts that tell them. We're seeds of those stars. Reflections of—what did you call it?"

"Suvulliik."

"Reflections of Suvulliik. See? You shared with me something greater than the star itself. A piece of yourself."

Suvulliik spoke to me that night as I drifted into sleep. And professor Sophie. Calling me to be the most famous archaeologist on planet Earth.

3. MS. STEVENSON

The day after our return from Odin, I met my grade nine teacher, Ms. Stevenson. A qallunaaq imported from Victoria, BC, she was an odd little creature. Literally. Half the kids in the class loomed over her, including me, but what she lacked in stature, she made up in spirit.

On our first day, she waited patiently while we bustled around, picking our desks, chattering and laughing. When all was relatively quiet, she addressed us in perfect Inuktitut. You could have heard a pin drop. From that day forward, she captured our attention and respect and as the semester progressed into darkness, she captured our imaginations, too.

Her full name was Emily Constance Stevenson. She had a knowledge of who we were as a people that was uncanny. She listened and encouraged our points of view and would stop a lesson if one of us had a story or an experience we wanted to share. She made us feel as if we were her teachers and this grew into a deep and mutual trust. Ms. Stevenson encouraged us to invite elders, and with a bit of prodding, she persuaded me to ask Aanaq if she would come and give us an account of tuqlurausiit, our traditional way of kinship and naming.

Aanaq thought it was a wonderful idea.

I was nervous. I overheard Freddy confiding with his sidekicks about a distinct possibility Aanaq would hex them. He shut up quick when Fearney and I strolled by, pressing his back against the lockers, looking sheepish.

Ms. Stevenson had us build a circle of desks on the morning of Aanaq's presentation. Aanaq breezed in and stood silent in the centre of the room.

Spinning slowly, her black eyes flickered while she appraised everyone, then plucked a leather disc from her pouch.

"E-six-seven-seven-four-six." Then she pulled up her sleeve, raising her arm, pointing at a faded tattoo on her wrist. "E-six-seven-seven-four-six."

The room held its breath.

"That's my name," she said. "The name Canada gave me when I was a little girl. Now I am Mary Nakasuk."

She scanned the room. "You," she pointed to a boy. "What's your name?"

"John Aglakti." He squirmed in his chair.

"Hmm," she reflected. "That is your paper name. Do you know what it means? Where it came from?"

"My mother says it was my great grandfather's name."

"Do you know birds?"

"Some."

"Do you like to sing?" she asked, a sly grin slipping across her face.

"Yes," he nodded.

"Your grandmother and I were friends. When you were born, you chirped like a Black-Bellied Plover. Aglakti means song maker. Your great grandfather was also a song maker. He carried that spirit and gave it to you."

A thirty-minute exercise turned into a full morning history lesson, unwritten in any book. Her knowledge astounded me. Ms. Stevenson led a charge of questions and by the time we finished, she had set up another session with Aanaq to share her knowledge with the entire school. It did wonders for Aanaq. A light returned to her eyes and she couldn't stop talking about the pretty lady with yellow hair.

* * *

Ms. Stevenson cried a lot. She would bawl when reading us a story or listening to elders. Once she had to leave the room when an elder told us a story about the RCMP shooting all his sled dogs. After, she told us it was okay to cry, that we didn't need to feel embarrassed to show our emotions. It made me feel squeamish and, frankly, I never saw the point.

We tried crying, Fearney and I, after class one day. We told each other sad stories, but we ended up laughing our heads off about the time his dad fell into the harbour, all drunk, shaking himself like a drenched polar bear when he finally pulled himself from the water.

One day in mid-December, Ms. Stevenson asked if I would mind staying after class. When the crowd dispersed, she began. "Chulyin, I want to ask you something. But before I do, I want you to tell me if you feel uncomfortable. Okay?"

"Sure."

"I want to ask you about your Aanaq." She checked my reaction. "She's a shaman, correct?"

I stiffened.

"I'd like to learn more about that."

"She doesn't say much to me about it." I deflected.

"I see. We can stop here if you like."

I wriggled in my seat. "No, I'm okay."

She remained quiet, and I continued. "She has spirits. Tuurngait. She uses them to help people when they're sick."

Her hands cupped on the desk, and she leaned forward.

"Fox talks to her." My tongue loosened. "She changes. Aanaq. When Fox talks, her voice changes too. She's Fox and sees through Fox's eyes. She goes somewhere else and Fox takes over. I don't know where she goes. It's..." I paused.

"Scary?"

"Yeah."

"Are you frightened right now?"

"No," I blurted indignantly.

"Good."

"She says I've got the power too."

"Why do you think Aanaq would say that?"

"I don't know. But I'm not interested. I don't want to talk to Raven."

"Who's Raven?"

She had me cornered. "My tuurngaq."

"I see. Does Raven want to talk to you?"

"Not anymore."

"Why?"

"Because I don't invite her."

"Of course," she nodded, and leaned back in her chair. "Chulyin means Raven though, right? Isn't that what your name means?"

"Yes. Aanaq says I was born with Raven spirit. And it was her sister's name."

"And you don't want that? Raven spirit?"

"I just want to be myself."

"Makes sense. Do you think Aanaq would talk to me? Maybe show me her tupiq?"

"She doesn't go there anymore."

Ms. Stevenson looked disappointed.

"I could ask her for you." I felt this would hasten the end of our conversation.

"Would you?"

"Sure," I said, and she thanked me and apologized for keeping me so long. I ran all the way home. The wind was howling, and my stomach grumbled hungrily.

I told Aanaq about my conversation with Ms. Stevenson. She got this queer look on her face, surprised that a qallunaaq would be interested in consulting her. She agreed to meet with Ms. Stevenson and I planned for the following Saturday.

* * *

We had a major storm the Friday before. It stopped abruptly late Saturday morning, leaving a brilliant canopy of stars speckling the January sky. Snow had piled so high a huge drift tailed off the front of the tupiq like a comet. Anun cleared the entrance and helped Aanaq build the fire. When Ms. Stevenson knocked on the door at 8 p.m., I bundled up and escorted her to Aanaq's sanctuary.

Ms. Stevenson's eyes were moons. She scanned the interior, then coughed from the cloud of smoke. An icy obstruction blocked the vent but was melting and a steady plop, plop, plop rained down into a bucket Anun had positioned beside the fire.

"Thank you for seeing me tonight, Mrs. Nakasuk," Ms. Stevenson said in perfect Inuktitut.

Aanaq was pleased. "Mary. Please call me Mary. My other names are too hard to pronounce."

"Oh no," Ms. Stevenson interjected. "Your language is beautiful. Music. Music that speaks of your land."

"Unless the wind blows everything away," Aanaq said, and they both laughed. "Leave us," she said to me.

A soft 'thank you', from Ms. Stevenson's eyes and I thought she was going to cry, and I hoped she didn't.

I wasn't sure how I felt walking back to the house. Jealous and pleased at the same time. Pleased because they both seemed happy. Jealous that they excluded me. Ms. Stevenson was mine; I wanted her all to myself. I didn't want to share her with Aanaq, and the more I thought about it, the more I wished I'd never agreed to have them meet.

It was a mystery what happened that night. She never asked to see Aanaq again, and I was grateful for that. But there was a change in her the entire class noticed. She became more detached. There were moments when she seemed distracted, as if she was somewhere else, or at least wanted to be. A quick barrage of questions would bring her back and she would be herself again.

* * *

My curiosity and passion for archaeology intensified. One evening, I stumbled across a PBS program about ancient Egypt. It transported me to the barges of Cleopatra, the tombs of Tutankhamen and Ramses, the Sphinx and the Nile, a magic river, ambling through the desert and stashing its secrets into the waters of the Mediterranean Sea. But it was their language that intrigued me the most. The symbols and pictures, tales in the hieroglyphs of pharaohs and gods, swelling my imagination like the river itself in a spring flood.

I could hardly wait to share my discoveries with Ms. Stevenson. She was as excited as me and told me she had taken a course in Egyptology while going to university. She remembered a book—The Cultural

Atlas of Ancient Egypt—and two weeks later it was waiting for me at Canada Post.

I immersed myself in learning how to interpret Egyptian hieroglyphs. I became, with Ms. Stevenson's encouragement, proficient at translating symbols painted on the ancient temple walls. We would meet in the small school library on weekends and pore over internet periodicals, speculating about secret tombs and mummies wrapped in linen and gold.

One afternoon she postulated, "Crazy, isn't it? How Egyptian civilization parallels yours."

"You're kidding, right?"

"No. I'm not."

"We've never built a single thing," I said.

"True. Not in physical form. You have living temples. Your elders. What they pass to you from generation to generation. Words and stories. Look at this," and she brought up an image of the great hieroglyphic wall at Karnak.

"That's Aanaq. She's your Karnak. Your record in history."

"I guess so." I chewed the end of my pencil. "I just never thought about it that way before."

She smiled. Then we ventured back to the Nile, the place I longed to be.

* * *

In September of my final year, our principal advised us Ms. Stevenson would not be returning. She had flown back to Victoria to care for her aging mother. Every sensation left my body. When the room emptied, I pried myself from my seat and, on my way out, the principal touched my arm and handed me an envelope. *Chulyin* swirled across it in her rolling script. I snatched it, then fled, past the dump, beyond the trail that led into the open tundra. I wanted to scream, to bellow my rage at her, but I just kept running. To get as far away as I could from the hole in my heart or anything that would have me think of her again. I ran, falling into a clump of soft heather.

I ripped open the envelope, and in it, a single folded page, crisp and perfect. It read:

To my most cherished student, Chulyin,

Thank you for being a bright star in my life. Although you think I was your teacher, you have taught me more than you could ever imagine. You may think me a coward for saying goodbye this way and you are probably right. I don't blame you. I just couldn't bear it myself and I apologize for my selfishness.
I want you to know how much I love your spirit and passion. Stick with your studies, dear girl. I know you will one day outshine dusty old Howard Carter and become a great archaeologist. Stay true to yourself and never lose sight of your dreams.

Love,
Emily Stevenson

I sat, fumbling with the page, listening to the men at the dock preparing to fish, the clang of a boat's bell, their laughter in the wind. Standing up, I stuffed the letter back into the envelope, feeling an object inside. It was a necklace, a circular piece of polished soapstone, a Raven embossed on it. Jamming it back into the envelope, I shifted a stone, tossing the letter underneath it. Clapping dust from my hands, I ran back to town, where I found Fearney at the dump with a rifle, cocked and ready to shoot the next available creature bold enough to show its head.

* * *

Grade twelve started off on a rocky note. I skipped the first two weeks, pretending I was off to school each morning, then walked all day north of town along the edge of the fiord. My truancy came to an abrupt end one afternoon when Anun was waiting at the kitchen table.

"Why aren't you going to school?"

"Because it's qallunaaq garbage."

"So, what are you going to do?"

"About what?"

"About when it gets too cold. About when you're working at Qikiqtani, selling trinkets for the rest of your life."

"Why can't I do that?"

"Because then you'd be stupid. Like me."

"You're not stupid." I snapped. "You're the smartest guy in Pang."

"Maybe."

"Maybe nothing. Everybody wants to be like you."

"Do you?"

"Of course. You get to do whatever you want."

"Maybe."

"Stop saying that! I'm sick of this place. I don't want to be here anymore!"

"Do you think walking out there is going to make that happen?"

"I can't stand that new teacher."

He laughed out loud. "You haven't even met her."

"Him," I snorted.

"Okay. Him." He paused. "You want to make a difference, Chu? You want to get out of this place?"

My eyes shot fire.

He stood up. "Aanaq tells me you spend too much time on the Internet. Wasting time. Looking at pictures."

"They're not pictures. They're hieroglyphs."

"I know what they are," he said, tossing a thick manila envelope on the table. "Look. Maybe something in there might change your attitude." He came over and hugged me, then vanished out the front door.

Inside the envelope were curriculum documents of archaeology courses from three Canadian universities. He had compiled a list that focused on Egyptology and the study of ancient languages, circled in red with the prerequisites for entry highlighted by each one.

Next day, I returned to school.

Anun's pep talk crystalized my resolve. Still, I wasn't immune to the everyday drama that unfolded in Pang. I endured protracted blocks of boredom, interrupted by flashes of violent insanity that broke out in the community from time to time. One of these erupted in February when Fearney's father came home drunk and beat his mom. Broke her nose and cheekbone and they had to airlift her to the hospital in Iqaluit. The RCMP arrested him, but his mother never pressed charges. Fearney quit going to school after that. I knew he stayed home to protect them. He told me after the incident; if that asshole ever touched his mother or any of his siblings again, he would kill him. And I knew he would. I even told him I would help. He just nodded and hung his head.

* * *

Traffic to Aanaq's tupiq ramped up once more, much to the chagrin of Father McMurtry. Maybe it had something to do with her elevated status as a knowledge keeper, something Ms. Stevenson had promoted through having her speak at school. She became a celebrity, and I was fine with that. It kept her occupied, leaving me to my own devices, surfing the net, touring the Ziggurat of Ur. The Sumerians became my heroes, the inventors of writing, and I absorbed myself in the logograms, the cuneiform syllabary of their ancient tablets. High school was less than challenging, but I heeded Anun's advice and dug in, applying myself in preparation so one day I would stand at the base of the Sphinx or the Great Pyramids of Giza.

Aanaq pressed me less and less about developing my shamanic abilities, which was a welcome relief. The visions diminished in frequency but never completely vanished. Sometimes I would hear voices in the rocks and the darkness, but mostly it was Raven. I would think I heard her, but was never sure if the sounds were coming from her or if I was creating them in my head. It wasn't so much the words as it was the feelings. Raven played tricks on me, cackling, like she knew a secret that I had to figure out.

Over time, I developed a strategy to shut Raven out. Before I went to sleep, I would envision myself at the dump, rifle in hand, waiting for her to show. When she did, I would take aim and fire. When the bullet hit, she would vaporize. I never told Aanaq about this. I was afraid of her reaction, that if I told her, I would be disrespectful. I kept it to myself. Sometimes words could be more lethal than bullets.

4. ANUN

My first memory of Anun was riding on the back of his snowmobile. I was four years old, and he had built a seat for me from an old milk crate fastened in place with bungee cords. Aanaq was beside herself, imploring him not to take me, but he laughed and hugged her, plopping me into his home-made safety contraption. Firing the engine, we were off, sailing over the snow, me clinging to his back, squealing. We rode to a high outcrop above town, where we stopped and gazed down at the twinkling lights. Pointing excitedly, spurring me to wave and shout— 'Aanaq, Aanaq, here we are!'—and I did, believing him, never seeing her, pretending I did.

Anun was my best friend. Funny. He listened, never judged, and he made me see things in different ways. I was safe with him. We had a mutual understanding, a connection that didn't need words. Our eyes would meet and they would say it all.

When I did use words, Anun taught me how to use them selectively, although this was challenging with Aanaq. He would listen when I argued with her, sitting quietly with his arms crossed. Then his look. 'What are you doing?' his eyes would say. Afterwards he would tell me, "Choose your battles, save yourself."

Excellent advice. When I followed it.

Anun taught me how to adapt and shift with conditions. He showed me how to create a better place for myself on the inside; the way I saw things. I'd get caught up complaining to him about how the past trapped Aanaq, and how she tried to force it on me.

"Relax," he said. "Add the two things together. Your way and hers, old and new. We don't have to disappear along with the ice. We can live and carry ourselves with dignity." And with a wink, "Take some money for doing it, too." Anun integrated those same traditions into a viable design for living, incorporating them into our new reality, the one where qallunaat wasn't about to disappear. They were here to stay and survival meant adapting to our new conditions.

I asked him about Aanaq one evening, about her being shaman, about why she pushed me so hard.

"Choose what you will Chulyin. Your life will unfold exactly as you decide," he said.

"Why can't you give me a straight answer?"

"Because there isn't one."

I was angry. Confused. Resentful I had to figure this out for myself. I wanted him to give me the answers, but he refused.

Where he abstained from directing my choices, he compensated by filling in the blanks from the past. Anun was a treasury of family history, especially about my mother. She was his eldest sister, and he adored her. Buniq was her name, but he called her Bunny.

"What do you remember most about her?"

Without hesitation, "The day you were born. Bunny was so fat when you were in her belly. I teased her. 'I can hear a walrus in there!' Aanaq made her a special top to wear because nothing else fit. She hated it. Said it was scratchy. But that was her way of refusing Aanaq's attention. They were always arguing. Oil and water. Sound familiar?

"It was hot the day you were born. We were walking Bunny to Aanaq's tupiq when she collapsed. You were on your way and there was no stopping you. Aanaq checked and said she could see the top of your head poking out. I made a joke—'does it have tusks?' Nobody laughed.

"Then the strangest thing. Ravens. Ten, maybe fifteen, squawking, hopping all around and flapping their wings. I tried to chase them off, but they swooped back down, diving at Bunny. One clawed her neck. Left a nasty gash.

"In that instant, you arrived. Aanaq handed you over to Bunny and said, 'this is Chulyin. The spirit of Raven is in her.'"

"Aanaq named me?"

"Sure did. You come from a long line of Chulyin's. All the way back to your great-great grandmother."

* * *

In the spring of 2008, Anun formed his company, Qikiqtani Quests, an adventure touring enterprise offering excursions into the Baffin wilderness. Qikiqtani brought money into Pang and our kitchen table became the hub of his budding enterprise. Anun's childhood friend, Michael Koonark, became a household fixture as they strategized the direction of the fledgling company. A computer squeezed out Aanaq's African violets, and even her sewing migrated to the living room. Anun spent hours organising tours and promoting his company, bringing an auspicious change to our four walls. Aanaq doted on him. At first, I was jealous, but he would wink at me, smile and say—'hmm, I think I'm hungry'—and she would fly off into the kitchen to make him something to eat, and we would have our time.

Qikiqtani Quests produced two profound effects. First was the economic impact on Pang. Satellite businesses sprang up with the influx of wealthy qallunaat. Money triggered a release of optimism, something leached from us over six generations. Hope returned, along with a sense of purpose.

The second effect was on me. I remember looking at the mountains across the inlet; Anun loading boats with supplies, the buzzing of the adventurers, then the purring of the boats, eventually swallowed in the fiord's mouth. By the time I was seven, Qikiqtani had been operational for almost four years, and that's when he started taking me on our annual excursions; a two-week odyssey that widened my perspective beyond the world of our tiny hamlet.

I saw Anun in a different light. He was a leader. A guide in our Inuit world where we were the masters, conservators of rock and tundra. He told the visitors of the great white bears, little auks, their spirits and the spirits of the mountains and streams that flowed from them. I never realised the extent of his knowledge before our trips. He was the interpreter, the voice of the land and all that filled it.

Life changed the summer I graduated from high school. We were preparing to set out on our annual pilgrimage to the park when Anun surprised me with something completely different. We were spending the entire time alone. Just the two of us. I was in heaven.

Loading the boat, we steered into the eastern glare of the morning sun. Chugging up the finger of the inlet took the better part of a day to reach base camp, a site Anun constructed to store equipment and supplies. It was the hub where all excursions began before hiking into the southern tip of Auyuittug National Park. Mount Odin was our goal. A ten-kilometre trek along the braid plains of the Weasel River, snaking between the mountains, carrying the glacial melt from the upper park to the sea. I was ecstatic. The entire mountain was ours. Hunkering down at base camp, we planned to set out for the mountain next day.

The valley was ablaze. Fireweed, and the pale-yellow crowns of poppies tethered to delicate green shoots, defied the wind that threatened to yank them from their roots. Closer to the river, the Arctic cotton was in full bloom. Aanaq's voice resonated in my ears, 'don't forget the cotton', as she crammed three bags into my already overstuffed backpack. She used the cotton to make wicks for our quilliq, along with the softest pillows on the planet. In just over two hours, we arrived, unloading our packs on the north shore of Windy Lake at the foot of Odin.

We pitched our tent and spent the rest of the day puttering close by. Over the years, Anun had accumulated a large supply of firewood, mainly discarded pallets from Pang. A blaze was roaring by 10 p.m., and we curled ourselves around it. Fire in the nautical twilight was one of my favourite things.

I watched the orange flicker dancing across his ruddy complexion. "What was Bunny like?" I broke the silence.

A telltale smile. "You."

"Come on. What was she like as a sister?"

He shifted and looked straight at me. "Like you. Fiery. Opinionated. Sometimes too much so. Loved arguing with Aanaq."

"I don't love arguing with Aanaq."

"I think I drove her crazy. As a kid," he continued. "Following her around. She couldn't shake me."

"You were a pest?"

"I guess so."

"You loved her."

"I sure did."

"What happened, Anun? Why did she do what she did?"

"She couldn't cope."

"Cope with what?"

"The pressure. We went through a lot of—hard times."

"What about you? You coped." I poked the fire, shooting a spray of sparks into the dimness.

"I'm different. She was sensitive. Words killed her. She was w—" He stopped.

"Weak?"

He took a deep breath. "She struggled with the way things were."

"Is that why she drank herself to death?"

"I don't know Chulyin. I don't know why any of us do what we do." He leaned forward and stared into the fire. "Maybe it's boredom. Or fear or grief. Lack of purpose. I don't know. But I know this. She is in you and I see that every single day. In your eyes and the way you fight. Fight for what you believe," tapping his fist over his heart.

"I won't be weak like her."

"You're too bloody stubborn," and we laughed, our jubilation echoing in the cavern of sky and twilight swelling around us.

* * *

On the fourth day, Anun went off to hunt for hares. I stayed behind, exploring the valley, collecting cotton. I had moved some distance from the river when I noticed a presence drawing me to a ridge that opened on to a craggy plateau. Scrambling to the top, I noticed a patch of ground off to my left that seemed blurry.

(Odd.)

Straining my eyes, I rubbed them, thinking the physical pressure would relieve me of the illusion, but the blur persisted. Moving closer, a pastel aura swirled tight around an enormous boulder that was black and uncharacteristically smooth. A shaft of refracted light extended straight up from the rock, piercing the blueness. Complimenting the visual display, I experienced an astounding sense of benevolence flooding my torso, calling me forward like a trusted friend. At the base of the stone, purple fireweed sprouted like a bald man's fringe, and all around a mat of green and yellow lichen, moored me to the familiarity of fall tundra.

The aura that had spun lazily was now animated by my approach. Reaching in, I penetrated the energy, swirls licking up my arm up to my shoulder, like a tide occupying a beach where it hadn't been seconds before. A giddiness accompanied an immediate shift in perception, like bubbles of surf rolling along the sand. My vision became more acute, enhanced. The rock under my feet coalesced with my boots, conniving, trading places—rock to leather, leather to rock—unconcerned with distinctions my mind might assign them. Labels seemed absurd, irrelevant. Who was I to judge mountains, rivers, flowers, or sunlight as something outside of myself?

I removed my arm, and it tingled, colours dripping from my elbow.

At the edge of the boulder, on the mane of fireweed, Fox. Scrutinising. She scurried a few paces, then turned, impatient.

"Come. This way."

I stood motionless. She returned to the same spot and rose on her haunches. I took a single step.

"About time."

Fox scampered over the tundra toward the wall of the mountain. I hurried to follow, losing my guide, then finding her, or her finding me, peeping around a tuft of heather, waiting for me to catch up. Fox evaporated again, and as I circumnavigated a craggy outcrop, I spotted her sitting beside a similar chunk of black rock. This one was unpossessed of energy and considerably smaller. Still, I approached it, thinking I could slip my hand into it like the boulder, but it was solid. Heat radiated from its polished surface.

(The sun?)

No. We were in shadow, the sun passing west behind the tail of Odin hours earlier. The stone tugged me to my knees, and I placed my cheek on it, and then my ear, closing my eyes.

What was I hearing? Something in the distance ebbed from the stone, beckoning from beyond my ears. A rush of wind, Raven's wings, and I oscillated in the blackness. Then, the delicate onion skin of Aanaq's hands.

Eyes shooting open, I bolted up.

Fox, head tilting, studied me, then scooted out of sight into the tundra.

Aanaq's touch tingled, lingered, but the timbre around the boulder had vanished. The sun dipped below the horizon and I hastened back to camp. Anun would be there roasting a hare and I could tell him about my strange experience. But when I returned, the camp was empty and the fire cold.

Odin loomed over me, rising straight from the jaw of the valley, a sheer vertical incline towering like a giant shark's tooth slicing into the sapphire dusk. The mountain bit into the thin air, tearing a piece from the sky, feeding on the light, consuming it in its insatiable silhouette. I was a morsel in its shadow, as it devoured the heavens and me along with it.

By midnight, he still hadn't returned. Worry crowded out my experience from the afternoon. He'd left his walkie talkie behind and I chastised him for it under my breath. I knew he could take care of himself, but this was uncharacteristic. Anun would never leave me alone. Unless? I didn't want to fill in that blank, and threw a scrap of hardwood into the pit, lighting the fire. A chill blew down the valley and I nestled close to keep warm.

(OK Anun. Any time now.)

* * *

The screech from a peregrine falcon jarred me from sleep. Flakes of ash had blown over me from the dying fire, speckling my face, and I licked them from my lips.

"Anun," I called out.

Nothing. I checked the tent to see if he had snuck in while I was asleep. Not there.

(Keep calm. Don't panic.)

Before I set out to search, I pulled a rifle from the tent and stuffed a box of cartridges in my pack. The bears were out.

He had mentioned there was a high ledge on the west side of Odin he wanted to explore. I retraced my path to the black boulder, then along the edge of a dry creek bed where Fox had disappeared the day before.

Distance takes on an altered perspective in the Arctic, its proportions shrinking in the finite field of vision. 'If you think it will take an hour, plan for two', Anun would say, yet as I ventured deeper along the western slope there was nothing to suggest a plateau, or a landmark where I could set my sights.

I'd been hiking for an hour when the terrain switched to sharp rock, debris from the mountain set loose by wind and snow and time. Walking was treacherous. I concentrated solely on my footing and it wasn't until I stopped for a drink I noticed two ravens, high above, losing themselves in and out of a vertical edge in the distance. I chugged some water and hurried toward the cliff jutting out from the base of the mountain.

(This is it.)

Hollering, "Anun!"

The sound shocked the silence, calling twice, three times, but my echo was all that returned. The ravens cawed, circling high above.

Fear summoned me, and I pushed forward, harder, at one point closing my eyes, wishing this was just a dream and I would wake up and he would be there, laughing. Me, just the brunt of one of his crazy jokes.

(Where are you Anun? Stop fooling around. Come to me right now.)

Ten metres away were the two ravens, one holding something in its beak. I flung a stone that careened off their rock perch, but the birds didn't flinch. Grabbing another, I ran toward them, hurling it with all my might. The stone chinked close to their feet and when I was within arm's reach they took flight, screeching, passing so close I felt the breeze from their wings brush my face. An object dropped from one of the tormentors' beaks.

I ran over and lifted Anun's talisman, a raven's claw, from the ground. I'd never seen him without it around his neck.

Poking the claw into my palm, I wanted to bleed, to feel, to wake up from the nightmare of my speculation. The ravens arced skyward. "Tell me where he is, you bastards!" I screamed, and the air, the birds, had no ears. A thick lump billowed in my throat and tears burst from my eyes.

Next day, I headed back to the boat.

I reached the craft and tossed my pack into the bow. We had dragged it up onto the stones and secured it with ropes to a rusted gear. Low tide had me dragging the boat across the stony beach, but in forty minutes, the stern bobbed in the frigid water.

(Gas.)

I ran to the shed and yanked the jerry can from the shelf. Pouring the gas into the tank, it overflowed, spilling into the hold, soaking my hands and coat.

(Get in the boat.)

I pressed the starter, and the engine fluttered to life.

(Drive.)

Reversing too fast, I spun with full throttle, taking on a large gulp of water.

The smell of gas. The high-pitched whine of the motor.

Nothing existed. No mountains, no sea, no light, or darkness. I was a piece of grey, blending with the rest of nothing. Feeling nothing. Being nothing.

A speck up ahead. A boat. I cranked harder on the throttle, but it had nothing more to give. My arms, my fingers cramped from pressing, squeezing it, but the rush of adrenaline numbed me, the boat in the distance, now larger, closer.

The smell of gas. The wail of the motor.

Closer and we were beside each other. It was Anun's business partner, Michael Koonark.

"Anun. He's gone. We have to go back," I hollered.

"Gone?"

"He went out three days ago. Never came back."

Michael's demeanour changed. "Pull up," at the same time tossing me a rope. "Tie her up and get in," he ordered.

"We've got to go back!"

"Get in Chulyin."

Michael radioed ahead and by the time we arrived back in Pang, a fleet of boats had assembled in the harbour. We refuelled and before we left, he told me to get rid of my coat and wash the gas from my hands. I tried to scrub it off, but the smell soaked my pores, an aromatic tattoo ever reminding me of that day.

Thirteen boats launched from the harbour. I squeezed Anun's amulet in my fist, hanging on for dear life, wondering if it was my life or his that was fading away. Michael led the armada that flanked us on both sides, an arrow piercing through the still water. The sound of the motors was low against the wall of mountains rising on both sides of us. It was sad, unhurried, a funeral procession without the body, without the confirmation of death. A sick inevitability rose in my throat. The camp at the end of the fiord, the hike to the mountain. I wanted the ride to end, to see him waving from the beach as we approached. Instead, the stark expression of Odin shrouded hidden somewhere behind the distant clouds.

We tied the boats and made haste to the camp under the mountain, where we split into four groups. Michael knew the terrain and remembered Anun talking about a spot he wanted to explore. He led us past the point where I had gone a few days earlier, rising higher, past the scree and on to the virgin rock of the mountain, traversing a shallow valley, then up beyond its ridge.

"That's it," Michael said, pointing to a table of rock jutting out from the steep rise that led to Odin's peak. Pushing forward double time, Michael motioned for two of the other men to scout ahead and ordered me to stay back with him.

Ten minutes later, they returned. Michael grabbed my arm. "Wait here."

I tore free. "Where is he?" I screamed. "Take me to him!"

They looked at Michael, shaking their heads.

"Chulyin," he said. "Stop!"

I bolted. Not far ahead, an orange jacket propped against the mesa. He looked so peaceful, content, and as I approached, I recognised how broken he was. The animals had had their way with him, his eyes plucked from their sockets, bits of flesh torn from his skull, a carabiner still clutched in his hand. He had propped himself up somehow, his back against the rock, his legs twisted and smashed.

The group caught up with me and one man attempted to pry me loose.

"Leave her be," Michael instructed.

I dropped to my knees and sobbed into the earth. "How could you do this to me?" pounding on his chest and that's when their hands lifted me free.

They wrapped Anun and carried him back to the boats, where they loaded his body and we made our way back to Pang.

5. ON THE ICE

The expiration of one called Anun compels prudence. It impedes the girl child's headway in accepting Raven, who directs our fate.

Raven possesses all potential and is the catalyst uniting possibility with correct choice, spawning ideal conditions for our release. Grief over the death of Anun interferes and redirects her choices, jeopardizing our success to leave this sphere to begin anew. If Raven is lost, potential expires.

We arrived here not knowing our origins, nor are we perplexed by this. There is a natural sequence to our migration and we acknowledge our progression is subject to laws governing probability. That same law guides how the girl child determines the outcome of our circumstance, through the power of her choices...

"You act like nothing happened."

Aanaq's hands moved without hesitation, weaving a thin strand of sinew through a hole punctured with the whisker of a walrus. She was singing when I stormed in, sound without words, music that pacified me as a child, but now rage kidnapped the memory. Hands continued sewing, adjusting the hide and aligning the holes, pulling the thread tight with a sharp flick.

"Don't you care?"

Placing the unfinished mitten on the table, she stared out the window.

"Why didn't you stop us from going to that bloody mountain?" I said.

"Would either of you listened?"

I knew the answer. "This place is a nightmare. Everything goes to shit. Why him? I'm dead already living here. It should have been me at the bottom of that mountain."

Shifting in the chair, her eyes penetrated past my fury. "Anun would not agree."

"Agree, disagree, who cares? Anun's dead. Opinions don't matter anymore."

"Anun understands your pain."

"Really? Did he say that from the moon, up there with your sister?" The moment the words passed my lips, I regretted saying them, but my tongue kept wagging. "This place is one big lie."

Aanaq was stone. "No lies. Only truth."

"Your truth, not mine."

Aanaq tapped the chair beside her for me to sit. "Do you remember when we went to the ice?"

* * *

The wail of the snowmobile. Bear's fur brushed my face, the smell neither hideous nor pleasant, a musky essence that once housed the animal, now housing me. Aanaq was beside me in the carriage. I was glad to be bundled— the soft animal coat impervious to the rush of air and spears of driving snow.

The motor died, returning voice to the wind. Muscular arms assisted me from the carriage, the moon shining bright above his shoulder, silhouetting an indistinguishable face.

"The pouch is in the igloo," the shadow said.

"And the bird?"

"Yes."

"Good. When will you return?"

"Three days."

"It may take longer."

"Perhaps. Does your son know you've brought her to the ice?"

"No. He is hunting."

The shadow gazed into the clear night. "The wind is coming. I will leave so you can begin."

The sound of the snowmobile roared to life, and he vanished into the darkness. The moon, almost full, painted us silver. Two igloos, one larger than the other, loomed before us. We walked toward the smaller one.

"Who was that?" I asked.

"My helper," Aanaq said.

"Why are we here?"

"For you. We're here for you."

"I'm cold."

"Yes. Let's go inside."

Aanaq squeezed through the tunnel, calling me to follow, and I obeyed. Inside was a grotto, dug deep into the snow, a single quilliq lighting the space, glowing orange on the curved inner walls. An ice block covered with seal pelts jutted from the rear of the chamber. On it, a shrunken Raven carcass with one wing.

Aanaq pointed to the remains. "This is Soolutvaluk. She is powerless in sky and longs to return. Soolutvaluk has been waiting. That you might make her whole again. Doing this will restore your own wholeness, too. You and Soolutvaluk are one." Her hands cupped my face, and the flame from the quilliq bounced in her eyes. "Raven is your tuurngaq. Now it's time for you to join with her spirit. Then you will both know the power of sky." She kissed my forehead and crawled from the igloo, covering the entrance with a large block of snow.

"Aanaq!" I scrambled into the tunnel, clawing at the obstruction until my fingers bled.

Nothing. I licked the blood from my frozen fingers and laid my head on my arm, a thick dullness numbing me. From inside the igloo, a presence tugged at my ankles, gentle, persuading and then—sleep.

My eyes shot open. Darkness.

(Where am I?)

A voice. My voice.

(The quilliq.)

I scrambled back into the chamber. The tiny flame hovered precariously on a parched wick. Along the wall's edge, I spotted a pouch. Inside was a tin of oil, and I replenished the reservoir, the flame surging back to life.

Movement. Was it gloom crowding about the flame or Soolutvaluk fluttering on the altar? The broken bird lay motionless on her seal skin bed, the flame from the quilliq an undeviating tear of yellow dripping from an invisible thread on to the tip of the cotton wick. Still, I detected something stirring, unsettled, slanting into the igloo from a corner I could not find.

From a perforation in the ice wall, she came. Raven. A speck at first, then a spectre from the shadow, perching on the altar, staring through me with amber eyes. Lunging, my fingers passed through her like smoke and I seized the carcass as compensation, flinging it against the wall. "It's your fault!" I screamed. "Fly away and leave me alone!" I picked up the remains, pitching it again, the bones crumbling, filling the air with bits of mangled feathers. A third time I hurled it and my foot knocked the quilliq, plunging the igloo into total darkness.

* * *

"The igloo. How could I forget? You left me alone." I said flatly.

Aanaq picked up the mitten and resumed sewing. "I was showing you the way. To who you are."

"No. That's who you think I am. Who you wanted me to be."

"I cannot force you to see the truth," resignation in her tone. "You choose your way."

"I don't want any part of this."

She shook her head. "It's not that easy."

"Why? Why isn't it? I choose me. Not some ghost from your past," shooting up from the chair, flipping it. "I hate this place. This—lie. You talk about truth, but there's nothing here but lies. You. Anun. Everybody pretending nothing's changed. I'm sick of it."

I charged through the door to the gate, no fence beyond the rusted metal posts, standing there like an idiotic sentry.

"Why are you here? You're a useless piece of junk!"

I kicked the gate, hinges tearing from their moorings, freeing them from their pathetic moan.

Running, my feet took me to the harbour. Too many people. Fishers were coming back with their catch and I spun, racing along the shore, lungs on fire, ready to explode. The tide was ebbing and I sprinted along the flat to the edge of the sea.

Anun's raven claw hung around my neck. I gripped it tight, tearing it off, then pitched it into the ocean.

"Die! Leave me alone!" My scream scudded across the water, lodging in the mountain's ears on the other side.

* * *

September sun in Pang is weak. Winter's darkness comes fast, but the onslaught that blows through the pass is quicker. By the time I returned home, the light had faded. I approached the wounded gate and automatically went to walk through it.

"Useless junk," I said, and circumnavigated it.

Aanaq had fallen asleep in her chair. Guilt poked, but I wasn't about to wake her to apologize. I'd do that in the morning.

Her singing woke me. A low trill and the shuffle of slippers on cold linoleum, bacon crackling, cooking for me. She never ate it. She had done the same thing the morning we returned from the igloo. Made bacon. I was famished that day and I felt my stomach grumbling now, along with an uneasiness about facing her. Hunger won, luring me into the kitchen.

Aanaq looked up from the stove. "I made you toast. Are you ready to eat?"

I nodded and sat at the table. A plate appeared, and I grabbed a strip of the crispy meat biting into it. "I'm sorry I spoke to you like that," I said, crunching.

She sat in her chair across from me. "Is it cooked enough?"

"It's perfect." I reached across the table and placed my hand on hers. "I'm sorry."

"I know."

Her ability to forgive exasperated me. To be so patient. But today I was grateful. Not so much that I wanted forgiveness. It was a lack of conflict I was looking for. I wanted off the hook, the hook that charged me with guilt.

She took the mitt she was sewing and forced the needle through the hide. "I never understood how you and your uncle could eat that," she said. "Meat in plastic packages."

"Changing times."

"Yes. Changing times."

"What are we going to do without him?"

"Live."

"I'm not sure I want to."

"What would he say to that?"

Her question floated past my ears. "I can't believe he's gone."

She turned and stared out the window. I wanted her to break, to cry, to see her pain so I might somehow find my own.

"He was a wonderful man. He loved you dearly."

My eyes welled up.

"You have a piece of him in you," she said. "Stubborn. Determined. Can you feel his spirit inside you? It lives. When you live, so does he."

"I don't understand any of this," I said. "Why this happened."

"Stop trying."

"I can't."

"There is beauty in mystery. Knowing that it's unnecessary to understand all things."

I pushed the plate away. "I can't accept that."

"Exactly. I gave birth to four children. All of them have died and here I sit. You and I. Would understanding why that happened lessen my pain?

"No," she went on. "I gather my pain. Bring it close. Embrace it. When I feel overwhelmed, I call to Fox. We face it together. I am never alone when Fox is near. My pain is my strength. Your tuurngaq will help you embrace your grief."

"How can a dead raven do that?"

"It's not Raven that's dead, but your will. Your will to accept your higher purpose."

"Higher purpose? Anun smashed at the bottom of a mountain? You taking me out on the ice, leaving me in that igloo? How? How does any of this serve my higher purpose?"

A flush of delight lit her expression. "That's a question I can answer. I heard you calling that night. Crying. Not wanting to be alone. I was there beside you when the quilliq went out. When your anger smashed Soolutvaluk. What you did not see was the product of your anger, your fear.

By tearing that carcass apart, you opened the door for your renewal. Do you remember when you came out three days later? Do you remember what you saw?"

"You. I only saw you."

"Close your eyes. See what you saw."

Closing my eyes, I was in her arms, my face buried in the fur of her parka. The night was windless, and I breathed her in, anchored in safety. All around us, croaking, clicking. Lifting my head, there were hundreds, thousands of them; Ravens, covering the tops of the igloos and standing at our feet. We walked through them, and they parted for us, undisturbed. Welcoming.

"They were there for you. You have the gift of wings for Soolutvaluk. And she has the gift of sight for you."

"To see what? There's nothing here but dead souls."

"You are a healer, Chulyin. You are shaman."

"No, I'm not. If I was a healer, Anun would be with us."

"You are not responsible for his death." Aanaq moved to the kitchen, fumbling in the drawer where Jesus lived, pulling out a pouch. "Do you remember this?"

"I—yes," taking the pouch and rubbing my fingers across the supple leather, the Raven sewn to it. "From the igloo."

"Anun made his own choices."

"And I'll make mine," handing her back the pouch.

It was the last time we ever spoke of it. His death. Raven. Me being shaman. My visions subsided after that and I poured myself into the ancient sites of Angkor Wat, Machu Picchu, the Moai statues of Easter Island. I travelled the world sitting at my bedroom desk, knowing once I left, I would never return.

6. INHERITANCE

Terrified, running, I could not turn to see. That would only make it worse. My lungs exploded, and I dropped to my knees, heaving. It was huge, clawing my throat, resisting, and finally... Raven, staring back at me. Anun stood on the tundra under the watchful eye of Mount Duval high above Pang, holding out his arm, and she flew to him, perching there, speaking in incomprehensible clicks. Then I am Soolutvaluk, shrivelling and single-winged, disintegrating into dust that blew into the heavens, surrounded by stars, and one brilliant orange glow consuming me.

I bolted upright, soaked in sweat. Aanaq snored softly in her chair and I crept into the kitchen. A beam of morning light nestled in her lap, her hands caressing it like she was keeping it from falling to the floor.

(He's gone.)

As hard as I tried, I could not expunge Anun's death from my mind. Waking, sleeping, dreaming—his absence haunted me like an event on the news, someone else's tragedy, but this was mine. I couldn't touch it, or more accurately, it couldn't touch me. I wouldn't let it. No, it did not confuse me. I would never hear his boots crunching over snow when he tramped to the door. It was more the sound of my own steps cracking over a thin layer of emotional ice that I couldn't calibrate. So what if I dropped into the sea? I'd welcome it. What's a little more heartache in a place like this?

Pain. Higher purpose. Aanaq was surely demented. If there was anything I wanted, it was to smash the pain out of existence. How could she lose everyone she loved and call it beautiful?

I skipped Anun's funeral. I told Aanaq the morning of his burial that I wanted to remember him the way he was. I couldn't possibly tell her how cowardly I felt, how guilty that I hadn't been there to help. When I told her I would not attend, she pulled my head to her chest, kissed me, and shuffled out the door.

One month to the day after I had found Anun at the foot of Mount Odin, my phone rang.

"Ms. Nakasuk?"

"Yes?"

"Ms. Chulyin Nakasuk?"

"Yes, that's me."

"My name is Josie and I'm calling from the Crawford Law Office in Iqaluit. First, let me offer my condolences on the death of your uncle."

"Thank you."

"There is some business Mr. Crawford would like to discuss with you. Your uncle Anun drew up a will, and he named you as one of his beneficiaries."

"A will?"

"Correct. Mr. Crawford has asked me to set up a meeting with you this Friday."

"I have no way to get to Iqaluit."

"No, no. He's flying to Pang to meet with you. Say 1:30?"

I agreed and ended the call. My heart sank. Lawyers now. He was giving the business to me and the last thing I wanted was an anchor tying me to this place.

"Who was that?" Aanaq chirped from around the corner.

"Some lawyer from Iqaluit. He's coming here on Friday to talk about Anun's will."

"That's nice," she said.

Friday afternoon at exactly 1:30 p.m., Richard Crawford rapped on our front door. Not that he had to. I heard the plane land and watched as he walked up our street from the terminal of what we called Pang International.

He was small and round, waddling as he ambled toward the house. His complexion was ruddy, as if steeped in a pot of scalding water, his nose bulbous, round like the rest of him, but redder than the flush of his cheeks. Burdened by the short walk, he laboured when he breathed, sucking in through his mouth, exhaling clouds of grey vapour through his nostrils. A walrus. I almost laughed but held myself back.

I opened the door. "Mr. Crawford, please come in."

"Thank you, my dear. Haven't been in Pang for ages."

He removed his coat, and I showed him to the table.

He began. "I'm sorry for your loss. I've known Anun for over twenty years. Tragedy." He pulled the file from his briefcase continuing, "He was very thorough in his arrangements around his business. And especially regarding you, my dear."

He stopped and peered at me over the top of his spectacles. "I feel like I know you, Chulyin," a softness swelled over him. "He spoke about you. Often. Your trips to Mount Odin. They were precious to him. You were precious to him."

He turned to Aanaq. "Your son helped many people. This place was withering before he started Qikiqtani Quests. And his legacy will continue. He has made sure there is something here for everyone in Pang. That's just the way he operated."

I fumbled with my hands.

"I know money and material possessions can never bring him back. But let me share with you what his wishes were."

"I don't want to run this company," I blurted out.

"No worries, my dear," Crawford said. "He knew that." He shuffled through the pages of the will. "Control of the company will always be in the hands of yourself and Aanaq. Michael Koonark receives 49% ownership and handles all daily operations of Qikiqtani."

I stared back.

"Anun set up an education trust fund for you when he formed Qikiqtani Quests. And enough money for both you and Aanaq to live comfortably." He removed his glasses and looked me straight in the eyes. "A trust fund worth over $200,000."

That fall they accepted me at the University of Toronto, with a full scholarship in the archaeology program. I sealed Anun in the museum of my memory, an artifact, an entire civilization of my life mummified under glass. Aanaq was right about one thing; he lived with me every step of the way. A fragment I revisited any time I wanted, untouchable in that silent place I shared with no one.

7. ASMED

Asmed Akbari materialized in a third-year psychology elective, loud and always laughing at inappropriate moments. He irritated me at first, but I soon looked forward to his classroom antics. Asmed was pure entertainment, comic relief in a course that dripped with boredom. His disruptions taxed the dusty professor, and by the end of the semester Asmed had gained celebrity status.

One afternoon, while coming out of the Robarts Library, we crossed paths. Hoping to avoid contact, I hurried my pace, but he nabbed me.

"Hey, you're in my psyche class," he boomed.

I nodded, hoping he would keep walking. He didn't.

"What do you think of Gustav?" referring to the professor. "He's tight," he said, twisting his fingers like he was wringing out a cloth.

I smiled. "He sure is."

"Be glad when it's over. That course is just a filler."

"Ditto."

"What's your major?"

"Archaeology."

"Oooo, digging in the dirt. What are you looking for?" Without skipping a beat, "I'm in poli-sci. Bullshit mostly." Reaching out his hand, "I'm Asmed. I was just going for a tea. Want to join me?"

"Chulyin." We shook hands.

"Come on. I'm buying."

Diabolos' Café was a short walk from the library. Ordering a couple of tea bags, he pulled a miniature silver teapot from his pack and handed it to the barista, instructing her to fill it half full with boiling water. Not the tepid bathwater that came out of the silver box. "Boiled with bubbles," he told her, wiggling his fingers, while the barista stared blankly somewhere above his head. When I ordered a dark roast, his face soured.

"Arsenic. You've got to get yourself off that," pointing to my steaming mug as we commandeered a table on the patio.

"Keeps me awake."

"Now this," he pronounced, pulling two juice glasses from his backpack, plunking them on the table beside his teapot, "is what you should be drinking. So, where are you from?"

"You wouldn't know if I told you."

He sat, waiting, leaning on the table.

"A place called Pangnirtung. On Baffin Island."

"Pang-ner-what? Where's Baffin Island?"

"Stick with Pang. Baffin Island, about twenty-five hundred kilometres north of here."

"The north pole," he said, ripping open the tea bags and dumping the loose leaves into the pot.

"Pretty much."

"This is the farthest north I've ever been. Or I'd ever want to go."

"Toronto? This isn't north."

"When you're from the desert, it is."

"Where you from?"

"Same thing. You wouldn't know if I told you."

"Try me."

"Tifariti. Sahrawi Arab Democratic Republic."

"You're right. Never heard of it."

"Not surprised. We're not an official country."

Asmed read the question mark on my face. "No worries. If you try to find it on a map, it's called Western Sahara." Decanting tea from pot to glass, then from a full arm's length above the table, he poured the scalding brew back and forth from glass to glass without spilling a drop. "I got all afternoon and I need to drink at least five of these babies."

Asmed wasn't kidding. Consuming four more pots, we talked all afternoon, discovering we were both fleeing toxic environments. Asmed's ordeal was war and oppression. Mine a slow death by what I described as cultural assimilation. We laughed about our divergent interpretations of our common denominator, Toronto, and its university campus. For me, it was stimulating, a ticket out of a place that suffocated me. For Asmed, the U of T campus was a sanctuary where he could strategize, without fear or interruption, the creation of a country and how might best to accomplish it.

When only sixteen, he created several shorts on the plight of Sahrawi refugees, one receiving accolades at the Cannes Film Festival. Asmed spoke with devotion about returning to his homeland and how he was going to promote solidarity among his people in their drive for political and cultural autonomy.

Lofty ideals played no part in my strategy. I had no intention of returning to Pang, or anything north. There was nothing I wanted to change or make better, nor did I delude myself into believing I had the power to do so. If there was change, it would be mine, by me, for me. This tidbit of information, however, I kept to myself.

Asmed walked with a distinguishable limp, and when I asked him about it, his demeanour shifted.

Taking a deep breath, he began. "In my country, there's a wall. We call it the berm. A twenty-seven-hundred-kilometre snake that splits us from the sea and divides our people. Stones, barbed wire and land mines. Hundreds of thousands of them. Buried in the sand.

"Father warned us over and over not to go near it. But we were kids. We didn't listen.

"My best friend Salim and I were hunting for lizards. We strayed too close to the berm. He was a few metres ahead when it happened. I was crouching when it exploded. His body flew back and knocked me against a boulder, snapping my ankle. Salim was dead."

"Asmed, I'm so sorry."

"No need. We were told to stay away. We didn't."

Looking up and smiling, "Another coffee?"

From that day forward, we became fast friends. Asmed shared his vision of how he was going to use his camera to educate the rest of the world regarding the plight of his people. There was a militancy about him that both frightened and excited me. Resolve fuelled by anger, a dark passion, hidden beneath the mask of a classroom jester. A militancy where he expressed a willingness to kill, to die for his beliefs, and when he spoke about it, he physically changed. A complexion already dark would tinge crimson, and a stare that could burn a hole in the back of your skull. It reminded me of Aanaq, her trancelike state, when she connected with Fox. But Asmed's tuurngaq was different. Ideals and dogma, guns and revenge drove his spirit in a fierce tenacity that incited the crusade for his people's self-determination. These changes would come. He decreed it so.

At first, his passion startled me, and I questioned my own motives for leaving Pang. Was I being selfish? There were moments when I felt a coward for not having a more noble blueprint for leaving. But those moments were fleeting. Truthfully, I wanted nothing to do with living in the past or the delusion I could alter the trajectory of Inuit destiny. I was doing this for me and if that was selfish, so be it. Resurrecting something already dead, be it homeland or belief, was beyond my scope of influence. Decisions had to be made. Moving into the future was my reality—my work, my archaeology, my place in the world. Dying for a cause? Noble perhaps, but better served by others more qualified. I wanted to live.

One thing was for sure: Asmed's friendship pulled me out of my shell. Through him, I discovered the value of university social life. We were both smart academically, but I was a serious introvert. I recognized the advantages of congregating and collaborating with my peers, although it was never comfortable for me. I relished solitude, but I learned that riding the coattails of Asmed's assertive personality produced distinct advantages.

He loved to party. I was selective about where I went with him, especially around the booze and dope scene. I couldn't, I wouldn't tolerate it and told him so from square one. I'd seen enough alcoholic insanity in Pang to last me a lifetime. Fortunately, it was the socializing that attracted him more than the drinking. Not sure if it was his Muslim beliefs, because he never openly displayed any devout religious practice, and he didn't use drugs, except pot maybe once or twice, and he said he didn't like it much. Made him paranoid.

There would be periods when we wouldn't connect, and others when we would be together for five or six consecutive days. Asmed usually found me, and I wasn't too hard to find, at my usual haunt in the sub-basement of Robarts Library. Peeking from around the stacks, he would just appear and I would pretend I never noticed while he dropped books or made squeaky animal sounds. I secretly waited to see his face and when he showed, we would be on our way, romping down Yonge Street, losing ourselves in all the craziness. One afternoon in the middle of exams, he commandeered me to a Blue Jays game. Said I looked like I needed a break and he was right.

During one of his political rants, Asmed mentioned a place just north of Tifariti, an ancient site littered with stone monuments, bazinas, and over a hundred caves with pictographs dating over ten thousand years old. Excavations had stopped in 2009, he said, because of political unrest. Too volatile, so the Sahrawi government banned any further archaeological activity.

"Why didn't you mention this before?"

"Didn't seem important."

"A ten-thousand-year-old goldmine in your backyard, and you figured I wouldn't be interested?"

"You want to go there? You want to see it?"

"How? You just said they've booted everybody out."

"I can get you in."

"Bullshit."

"No bullshit. I can do it." Leaning back in his chair. "I got connections."

* * *

Near the end of the semester, I was cramming for finals when a knock came at the door. It was Asmed, armed with a bottle of wine and a box with a frilly bow.

"What's this?"

"A gift."

I looked at the bottle. "You know I have a final tomorrow?"

He made a puppy face, and I moved aside to let him in.

"Half an hour," I warned. "What's in the box?"

"Open it."

He pulled the cork from the bottle and started pouring wine into a tumbler.

"Woah," I protested. "I need to stay awake."

He sat and pushed the box across the table.

I unravelled the ribbon, and inside was a photo album. He had put together a chronology of our time together, from the moment we first had tea at Diabolos' up to three days ago when he surprised me at Robarts Library.

"This is wonderful."

I looked up, and he was gazing at me, much too seriously.

"What's up?"

"Chu, I'm going home next week."

"Of course," I stammered. "You finished exams yesterday, didn't you?"

"Yeah. But. I'm going home for good."

"What about convocation?" My voice cracked.

"No. My plane leaves Friday."

"Then this is a reason for celebration," I rallied, raising my glass. "A toast to the newest Sahrawi poli-sci major."

"Cheers," and we clinked glasses. "I'm going to miss our conversations."

"Oh, come on. You talk. I listen." A hollow giggle fell from my throat.

"I'm going to miss you."

"I am a force to be missed," I said, avoiding his eyes. "I'm glad for you, Asmed. You'll be back home doing the work that calls you." I lifted my glass and drained it. "Now I have to get back to the work that calls me," and pointed to the books sprawled across the desk.

Asmed left, and I decided I might pour another glass. Staying awake just didn't seem so important anymore. Before I went to bed, I closed the album tight and filed it with the other volumes I would never open again.

8. WESTERN SAHARA

I didn't know why Charles Fenwick, U of T's Director of Archaeology, summoned me to his office. When I arrived, his secretary directed me to walk straight in. Dr. Fenwick instructed me to sit and for a moment just stared, then lifted a letter from the desk.

"I received this yesterday. From the Society for Libyan Archaeological Studies. They seem to be interested in you. Any ideas why?"

I shrugged.

He reached across the desk and handed me the letter.

I read:

Dear Dean Fenwick,

On October 20 of this year, the Society for Libyan Studies is sponsoring an archaeological investigation into the Neolithic rock art at Rekeiz Lemgasem. The site in Western Sahara lies north of Tifariti, in the Sahrawi Arab Democratic Republic (SADR). The provisional government of the SADR has secured a three-month window allowing an international team on site to catalogue and restore these precious artifacts.

Information comes to us that a student of yours, Chulyin Nakasuk, may be interested in participating in this project. We offer an opportunity for her to join our team. Please advise her to contact us at her earliest convenience.

Yours truly,
Omar Harbi, Director,
Archaeology Society for Libyan Studies

I looked up from the letter. "Asmed."

Charles shrugged. "Who's Asmed?"

I told him about our friendship and the conversation we had in the coffee shop over four years ago.

Charles leaned back in his chair. "I've looked into this place, Chulyin. Very dangerous."

I was still in shock, clinging to the letter. Excitement at the prospect of seeing Asmed. Taking part in my first real dig. In the Sahara Desert to boot. My mind was swimming with possibilities.

"When did you get this?"

"Yesterday. This Asmed must have extraordinary connections."

"His uncle. He said he's a colonel in their army."

"Interesting." He turned serious. "Chulyin, this entire region is a powder keg. Kidnappings. A UN peace keeping unit took fire just last week. Nobody knows from who."

I stared at the letter.

"This is your decision, Chulyin. The Chancellor has made it clear the university absolves itself from any responsibility regarding your safety."

When I looked up, he was studying me, like Fox on the day under the mountain when I was searching for Anun. There was a twinkle in his eye, and I sensed his approval, excitement perhaps for me, and a memory triggered for him that embraced the risk.

"I'm going."

"It's not university policy to support this," leaning forward into his desk. "But I do. That letter belongs to you. Keep it. Just ask Marianne to make a copy for my records. I'll advise the Society of your acceptance."

It took a full week to connect with Asmed.

"How the hell did you manage this?" I asked before I even said hello.

He grinned back like the Cheshire cat. "I told you. I got connections."

He'd filled out too. This was a man, not the boy I remembered from the U of T. He was rugged, unshaven, spun in white cotton, a red chequered keffiyeh wrapped around his head.

"You look content," I said.

"Hardly," he laughed. "This place is total chaos." Behind him, an open market teemed with activity.

"Thank you for arranging this."

"You're welcome. I'm looking forward to seeing you. On my turf."

"Doesn't look like turf to me."

He laughed again. "Agreed. But it's all mine."

We signed off, and he promised to keep me advised of developments regarding the dig. Things could change fast, he cautioned.

The next few months dragged on like an Arctic winter, and I stayed in close contact with Asmed. There was a delicate balance between the Sahrawi Ministry of Culture and the University of Algeria. The Sahrawis handled security, but the university subsidized funding for the entire project. Political posturing almost scrubbed the mission with the discovery that a junior archaeologist from the university owned a Moroccan passport. The wrinkle flattened when the university conceded to Sahrawi authorities and the young man bowed out.

During that time, I pored over every document I could find on Rekeiz Lemgasem. A Spanish team had amassed a mountain of documentation during the first years of 2000, their major focus on preserving cave paintings degrading because of erosion. Worse yet, was graffiti disfiguring several irreplaceable artifacts, damaging them beyond restoration. The team's goal was to collect enough data to have Rekeiz Lemgasem classified a UNESCO World Heritage Site.

Asmed advised me our contingent would comprise seven members, led by the author of the letter, Omar Harbi, head of archaeology at the University of Algiers. They assigned Asmed as videographer for the event. A clip from the dig would complement the documentary piece he was filming for an upcoming UN presentation, a thirty-minute audience to address the General Assembly later that year on the plight of the Sahrawi people.

On October 10, my plane touched down at Houari Boumediene Airport in Algiers. I felt as if I had grown a pair of wings with the plane, flying higher than I had ever felt in my life. I remembered one of my professors describing how he felt on his first dig, what he called a peak experience, where all the pieces of his life synchronized, and I understood what he meant. The wheels squealed on the runway. Africa. I was dreaming. It was my turn to explore. Discover. Pang was a million miles away.

As I weaved through customs, two things greeted me; a wall of heat beyond comprehension and Asmed's brilliant grin. I dropped my bags, and we embraced.

"You didn't believe me, did you?" he asked, as he picked up my bags.

"No."

"Let's get out of here."

We piled my luggage on a trolley, then navigated through a sea of travellers to a Chevy Suburban.

"I'm so excited, Asmed. I feel like I'm dreaming."

"That might change when we start into the desert," he laughed, as we pulled out on to the highway. "You must be starving."

"I am."

"No whale blubber here."

"Oh, I'm disappointed," feigning a frown.

"I'm going to give you a real Algerian treat. Tonight, you get spoiled. Don't get used to it, though."

We drove to Casbah, the ancient core of Algiers. I wanted to walk awhile before we ate and he agreed, saying it was the only way to experience the city.

Walls and doors cobbled and pressed the streets tight, creating passages like tiny rivers coursing through the delta of the city. The stones were shiny and foot-worn, polished from a thousand years of souls who had walked them. We squeezed through a crowded artery, then found ourselves in a massive courtyard. Three storeys of arches rose above us, splashed in mosaics, contoured by ancient art carved into the pillars that held the entire structure in place. Stairs, and plenty of them, reminded me of a sketch by the famous artist Escher, leading nowhere but everywhere at the same time. Laundry hung from balconies and shops while voices bantered, one bartering over a crate of tomatoes, and the Arabic, a staccato in my ears that somehow made me think of Inuktitut, and the cadence of my native tongue.

We turned into a corridor that funnelled us through a narrow lane, ending at an ancient wooden door. Asmed pushed through, and a gust of salty sea air delivered spices from a secret kitchen that reminded me how hungry I was. A gentleman with an immaculate moustache greeted us, leading to a table perched fifty feet above the Mediterranean Sea.

"I missed you." Asmed broke the silence.

"Me too."

"But you've been busy, yes? Your PhD?"

"For sure. But this? It's a breath of fresh air."

"Algiers? Fresh air? That's the first time I've heard that."

"You know what I mean."

He nodded.

"I'm finished with academia. I needed to get out. Into the field. Toronto was dragging me down. What about you? You said you were studying film."

"In Spain. ECAM, the film school in Madrid. Graduated last spring in documentary filmmaking."

"Wow. Fantastic."

"I want to make a historical record. For Sahrawis. For the rest of the world to see."

"Couldn't think of a better guy to do it."

"I've already filmed most of it. In the camps. Tifariti. I don't want my people to be cave paintings. We're not artifacts you look at in a museum. There's so much suffering. I want the world to know we're still out here and we could use some help."

"Was that a shot at my profession?"

"Of course not."

"Why didn't you tell me before you were making this film?"

"I knew you'd find out eventually. When they're handing me the Oscar."

The server arrived with a steaming aromatic dish.

"Tajine Zitoune," Asmed announced. "I ordered it when we came in. Best in Algeria. You'll love it."

I dove in to a rich stew of chicken, mushrooms, olives, sopping the gravy with a slab of traditional flatbread Asmed called kesra.

About halfway through, he said, "There's a military transport leaving for Tindouf on Saturday. I've organized for us to be on it. We're lucky. My uncle knows the Algerian Captain who coordinates aid runs with the UN."

"We're not driving?" He sensed my disappointment.

"No. This gets us there quicker. Safer. Besides, we'll have lots of driving ahead of us to get to Tifariti."

The debate closed. I couldn't keep the spoon out of my mouth.

* * *

We left after midnight Saturday morning for the military airport outside Oran. Asmed said it was best to get there early because aid flights took off the minute their cargo loaded. He was right; we arrived just after 4:30 a.m. and the crew was performing their last check before takeoff. We crammed into the Algerian Air Force cargo vessel, along with a Spanish doctor and two UN aides from Bangladesh commissioned to document supplies once we arrived in Tindouf.

Three hours later, we were rolling down the runway in Tindouf. The sun lurked above the horizon and when the door opened, a blast of desert heat promised a stifling day. The Algerian military quickly separated us from the three others going to the refugee camps. They drove us to the UN liaison office, where we were to record our overland route for our trek out of Algeria and into Western Sahara and the town of Tifariti. We spent the rest of the day with a meticulous Algerian customs agent who prepared our documentation for the exchange of responsibility to the Polisario, the official representative body of the SADR, once we reached the border. There, the Sahrawi army would escort us through the desert to the Republic's proclaimed capital of Tifariti. Asmed told me his uncle would meet us at the border for the last leg of our trip.

We left Tindouf before sunrise, travelling due west, our Rover sandwiched between two heavily armed combat vehicles of the Algerian Army. Thirty kilometres into the journey, we veered on to a dirt track leading into the open desert. It was the last paved road I would see for three days.

The sun had climbed high into the cloudless blue when we came upon an Algerian checkpoint. The commander in the lead vehicle spoke briefly with the sentry, and half an hour later we rolled into a heavily armed outpost where they ordered us out of our vehicles. A group of soldiers removed and inspected everything and after a few words and laughter, we were on our way. By midafternoon, we approached a stone barrier, forcing us into a narrowing passage that funnelled us toward what seemed an impossibly tight opening. Asmed squeezed us through, scraping the sides of the Rover only slightly.

"Say goodbye to Algeria," Asmed said. "We'll be on our own for an hour. This is as far as the Algerians go. My uncle's waiting for us just over there," and he pointed straight ahead into nothingness, shifting gears, heading due west into the Sahara.

The similarity of tracking through the desert and an Arctic icescape struck me. The feeling of incredible smallness, the monotony of not so much what the eyes were seeing, but what the brain could discern as distinguishable. I remembered Anun telling me once when we went hunting on the ice in the dead of winter. "Tricky," he said. "Don't let your imagination kick in. That spells trouble."

The sun burned its way across the sky like a white-hot branding iron, sucking the moisture from our bodies. Stopping to have a bite, I inadvertently touched the hood of the Rover, which was hot enough to fry an egg. I started out wearing sandals, but the sand was like walking on coals, and I quickly exchanged them for my leather hiking boots.

"I was wondering how long you'd last in those party shoes," Asmed said with a smirk, wiping his lips after gulping half a litre of water.

We came to a ridge of rock and sand, man-made, like the berm in Algeria, but this one was unkempt and abandoned.

"There," Asmed pointed, and we turned toward a deserted outpost. We inched through a maze following tire tracks, then found ourselves in a courtyard. Three Toyota pickups, machine guns mounted on skids and fastened to the bed, parked under a canopy. Nestled against the only standing wall of a dilapidated building were six soldiers. One rose immediately and ran to the Rover, embracing Asmed before he got out of the vehicle.

They bantered back and forth, and Asmed turned to me. "Seems my uncle has other business in Tifariti. Sergeant Kateb will guide us the rest of the way."

I sensed Asmed's disappointment, but that dissolved when we joined the group under the shade. It was after 4 p.m. when I learned we would stay the night, starting out fresh in the morning.

After a bite to eat, I slipped off to explore the compound.

"The walls are alive," Asmed warned. "Nasty things live here."

I assured him I would stay alert.

It was impossible to determine the compound's age, but there was no guessing about its function. A fortification built by hands, not tractors, one designed for defensive purposes. To keep invaders out. I scrambled to the top of the outer wall, the soldiers below talking, laughing. The enclave was a bubble bulging from a berm string that stretched into the tan waste of the Sahara from each of its rounded ends. Inside, smaller walls divided the fortress into ten compartments, an inner sanctum independent of them all protected behind its own embankment. A clump of dilapidated buildings stood in the northernmost section, a tower perched on one roof. I clambered down to make my way over and investigate.

Entering the courtyard, I stopped dead. A wave of anguish and I heard them. Voices choking in the sand.

—No escape—

On the shack with the tower, the door hung loose from a splintered frame, yawning, black and ominous.

—Run! Hide!—

I stalked into the darkness where a shaft of light illuminated a rickety ladder leaning against the rim of a trap door cut in the ceiling. The smell was pungent, stifling, like the congealed blood that smothered the docks with the entrails of butchered seals in Pang.

—Save us!—

I scampered up the ladder, gulping a lungful of air as I broke on to the roof. Voices returned, but they were murmurs of the living, not the dead, drifting lazily through the thin desert air from the compound below. Descending the ladder, I made my way back to camp. I'd had enough exploring for one day.

A soldier yelped as I neared the encampment, followed by a chorus of Arabic erupting from the entire group. They formed a loose circle around a stone, and as I approached, Asmed grabbed my arm and pointed to the base of the rock. "One of our little friends."

A horned viper, one of the deadliest snakes in the Sahara, peeked out from the rock the soldier was using as a stool. "Careful where you sit," he said to me in English, repeating it in Arabic, and they all roared with laughter.

* * *

We set out the next morning before sunrise. The sky was ink and the stars, unimpeded by clouds, sparkled silver in the last breath of night.

"Something happened back there." I said to Asmed.

"Where?"

"The camp."

"Did one of those idiots do something to you?"

"No. I mean before. I got this feeling."

"What do you mean?"

"When I went for my walk yesterday. That building with the tower. I just got this feeling of terror. Shock."

He was quiet for a moment. "There was an ambush about ten years ago."

"Their throats—"

"Were slit," he finished my sentence. "How do you know this?"

"I sensed it," I said, tapping my finger on my forehead. "The blade." I clutched my hand to my neck. "And their screams. Stuck in their throats."

"Fourteen. Murdered with machetes. My cousin was one of them. My uncle found them."

"It was quick." I interjected.

"I was a boy when it happened. My cousin. We played soccer. I wanted to kill every Moroccan I could get my hands on." He was quiet. "I'm sick of all this killing."

An onerous silence pervaded the cab of the Rover. Outside, the sun announced itself, percolating the cool morning air into shivering waves of heat.

He turned to me and said, "My grandmother sees things too. She told him not to go. Maybe you two can compare notes."

I kept Aanaq's shamanic abilities to myself for the time being.

"I'd love to meet her."

"You will. She's in Tifariti."

"Tell me about your film."

He smiled. "It's the voice of my people. The one ignored for fifty years."

"What's it saying?"

"Give us back what is rightfully ours."

"Your land?"

"What else is there?"

"Dignity? Maybe your pride?"

"Nobody could take away our dignity. Or our pride."

"I saw that in Tindouf," I affirmed.

"I want the world to see us. What we've endured."

"I believe you will, Asmed. I have faith in your ability. To tell your story."

"Faith is one thing. Support is another. We'll see how the UN receives what I have to say. We've been here before."

Three tires and one blown radiator hose later, we rolled into Tifariti. The Polisario had called away his uncle to an emergency meeting back in the refugee camps in Tindouf. Asmed could not contain his disappointment, even when a group of children cheered him on as the SADR's newest and greatest film producer.

"You're a celebrity," I said, trying to raise his spirits.

"Let's head to Rekeiz," he returned, ignoring my comment. "There's nothing happening here."

9. REKEIZ LEMGASEM

The drive to Rekeiz Lemgasem was magic. I felt outside of myself, a spectator to the night and the desert that swallowed me like a morsel in a dream. Carl Jung was right when he wrote about peak experiences, when possibility materializes into reality. Everything was manifesting before my eyes. Toronto and the sterility of my academic life faded into the darkness. Up ahead, the prize glowed.

(Rekeiz Lemgasem.)

The spirit of the Sahara sang in me. As we pulled into camp, fire lit the sky, and Anun flooded through my veins. Our trips to Odin. When I stepped onto the sand, I breathed him in, feeling his smile, the quiet approval of his eyes.

(You gave this to me, Anun. The power to be here.)

A town of tents huddled around the fire, a buzz of laughter and conversation filling the air. Asmed spoke to a soldier who escorted me to my quarters, where I dropped my gear, the smell of canvas permeating my nostrils. Rekeiz Lemgasem. I said it in my head, repeated it out loud, over and over, trying to convince myself I was actually here. Exhaustion pervaded my body, but sleep was the farthest thing from my mind. A knapsack with its contents spilled over the surface claimed occupancy of an adjacent cot, while a pair of tiny boots poking out from under a thin sheet that nearly reached the ground.

Laughter from the fire enticed me to explore. Three figures speaking Spanish congregated at the edge of a blaze, quickly switching to English as I approached.

"You must be the Canadian," a waif of a creature announced, extending her hand. "I'm Zaida. Your roommate."

"Chulyin," I returned. "I'm Inuit."

"Ah, Inuit. From high north. A place with lots of snow, yes?"

"Yes,"

"Snow. I never seen it. All I see here is sand."

"Kind of the same thing. Both deserts. One hot, one cold."

"I suppose." Zaida returned. "So sorry, these are Carmella and Victor. From the Spanish Archaeological Institute in Madrid."

"Careful what you say to this one," Victor warned jokingly. "Uncle Omar runs the show here."

"Professor Harbi is your uncle?"

"Yes," Zaida confirmed. "But don't hold that against me."

Carmella Diez and Victor Peña were part of the research team ten years prior, when political tension suspended the dig. Carmella was a geologist whose principal focus was on the preservation of the rock, the ancient canvas for the pictographs. Victor, a Palaeolithic zoologist, interpreted the wide range of animals depicted in the art.

After half an hour, I conceded to exhaustion and retired to the tent. My head was barely on the pillow when Zaida cruised in wide-awake, ready to banter. But polite as my eyes could be, they succumbed to sleep, her words drifting into the stillness of the desert.

When I awoke, she was still talking.

"Forty minutes and our meeting starts," she advised, lathering her face with a thick, foamy soap, splashing it away with what seemed an infinitesimal amount of water.

"It's all yours," she said. "Water's over there," pointing to a large plastic container. "I'm going to head over to see if uncle Omar needs me for anything," and she disappeared like a breeze that never existed.

Assembling in the mess tent, professor Harbi addressed us.

"It's a pleasure to have you all here," he began in impeccable English. "I extend my gratitude to Dr. Mennad Attar of the Sahrawi People's National Museum. For inviting us to help preserve this crucial site of North African cultural history.

"We're allotted a six-week window to expand efforts started in 2003 by the University of Girona and the Sahrawi Ministry of Culture. Rekeiz has been unattended since then and I am sad to report it has experienced significant deterioration. Some environmental. Most by vandals.

"Dr. Diez will concentrate on the preservation of the sandstone sediment. Dr. Peña will search for further evidence of bovine domestication. Shed some light, perhaps, on other quadrupeds that have defied classification.

"We are hoping professor Nakasuk can help us decipher the linear motifs uncovered in area 7b."

Professor Harbi turned and addressed me directly. "All we see are circles and geometric shapes. Along with some indistinguishable humanoid forms. We are looking forward to your interpretation, Dr. Nakasuk."

(Dr. Nakasuk.)

I felt my cheeks flush.

Turning to Zaida. "You will assist Dr. Nakasuk in her investigation. Professor Attar and myself will continue restoring damaged paintings and removal of graffiti. Last but certainly not least, our videographer, Asmed Akbari. Asmed will roam amongst all of you, collecting data and thoughts about the importance of Rekeiz Lemgasem." Speaking directly to Asmed: "I understand you will integrate these interviews into your documentary presentation to the UN later this year?"

Asmed was a million miles away. Zaida nudged him with her elbow.

"Ah, yes, yes. I'll be interviewing everyone. That's correct," he said.

Dr. Harbi continued: "We posted a detailed map outside the mess showing all the targeted areas. Everything is within walking distance of camp. I urge you all to go to your assigned areas today to familiarize yourself with the terrain. Take lots of water and cover your heads. The Sahara sun takes no prisoners."

The team exploded from the mess, crowding around the map. In minutes, Zaida and I were on our way to subsite 7b, crossing a stony flat to an outcrop of low sandstone hills. The rock face was both jagged and smooth, carved by a relentless wind and the rare deluge of Sahara rain that cleaved deep fissures at its feet. Combing the entire area while taking notes, we prioritized the sections we would explore first.

Next day, a convoy of military vehicles rolled into camp. At first, they were just a background presence, but by day three, their khaki uniforms were everywhere.

"Dining with them is one thing," Zaida said while we were scoffing breakfast. "But around the campfire? Something's up."

On day four the internet crashed, and they advised us all communications would be channelled through their military radio system. Asmed mysteriously disappeared with the arrival of the soldiers, and I mentioned this to Zaida.

"His video equipment is still here," she said. "I saw it stacked in his tent."

"Which he's usually lugging around," I added. "Maybe he's gone to meet his uncle."

"Maybe. I'll ask uncle Harbi in the morning."

That afternoon Asmed showed up at 7b.

"The happy wanderer returns," I said. "Where've you been?"

"Nowhere."

"Nowhere? Four days of nowhere? Filming at a secret location?"

"My film is a wash."

"What?"

"My film," he hollered, hurling a rock. "I'm not finishing it. They postponed the presentation at the UN."

"Postponed?"

"My uncle. He sold me out. Sold us all out."

"What do you mean?"

"He flipped. Defected to the Sahrawi traitors in Layounne. The Moroccans. And this gigantic corporation, Aquifor. They own the city and everyone in it. Everything we've been fighting for. Independence. Recognition. Aquifor bought him out."

I stared blankly.

"All these soldiers," he ranted. "They're here to spy on me. I'm guilty by association. He betrayed us. Set the whole thing up. I did a little homework and found out where he's been over the last few weeks. Meetings with the Moroccans and those Aquifor assholes."

Zaida was wide eyed, listening.

"Make your film anyway," I stated.

"What's the point? Besides, I can't."

"Why not?"

"They confiscated my equipment."

"It was there this morning," Zaida chirped in.

"Well, it's gone now."

A smirk crossed my face. "So what? Everybody in this camp has a phone."

"They've ordered me to stop filming."

"When have orders ever deterred you?"

A barrage of Arabic spilled from his mouth, and based on Zaida's expression were curses hurled at his uncle. "He was second in command of the Polisario! I'm pissed."

"All the more reason to finish your film."

"What's the use?" he snarled, spinning back toward camp.

* * *

Later that evening, I asked Zaida what she knew about Aquifor.

"One of the biggest food suppliers in Africa," she responded.

"Isn't that a good thing?"

"For most."

"Meaning?"

"Meaning the Sahrawi refugee camps get screwed. No food from their facility in Layounne comes to the camps in either Tifariti or Tindouf."

"That's insane."

"Sure is. Considering most of the puppets in Layounne's Aquifor facility are Sahrawis."

"What the hell?"

"Here's what I know. About ten years ago, Aquifor struck a deal to build this massive greenhouse facility outside Laayoune. Laayoune was the most important city in the Sahrawi economy. Now it's occupied by the Moroccan government. A select group of Sahrawis supported Aquifor because they line their pockets. This has caused a huge rift among their people.

"About three years ago, there seemed to be some progress. Sahrawis have families on both sides and they struck a deal to send a convoy of trucks across to Tifariti with food supplies. Thirty kilometres east of the berm, someone attacked the convoy. Nobody knew who, but there were lots of pointing fingers. Everything destroyed. Every morsel of food vanished and two UN soldiers killed."

"How does Aquifor fit in?"

"Interesting question. The Polisario speculate it was Aquifor who financed and orchestrated the attack. A total business decision. They're afraid if the SADR gets control, they'll get tossed out of Layounne. Aquifor's options are sweeter with the Moroccans."

I did a little homework over the next few days and found Aquifor was a multinational corporation that had their fingers in a lot of pies. Professor Harbi proved the greatest information source, and although he conceded that opinions and facts varied with the people who gave them, there was one thing all factions agreed upon: Aquifor was currently the third largest global enterprise, heading to be number one in less than five years.

Turned out I'd heard about them but not known it. They started out supplying high-end bottled water products, harvesting pristine ice melt from the Parrish Glacier on Ellesmere Island. I remembered helping Anun unload crates of Parrish Ice into the storeroom of Qikiqtani Quests.

Over a decade, Aquifor had mushroomed beyond what they called 'responsible water management', expanding with a real estate division that began gobbling up vast tracts of water-rich territory in the Northern Hemisphere. One article from The Globe and Mail traced the alarming speed with which Aquifor bought this land, through lease or outright purchase at depressed prices. The gist of the article implicated the company's expansion as an effort to monopolize global water supply, but a letter in the next day's edition by Aquifor's President, denounced the idea as preposterous. 'Environmental and humanitarian objectives drive Aquifor to ensure clean and plentiful water for generations to come,' he proclaimed.

From that model, Aquifor constructed massive food production facilities, highly intensive crops grown in greenhouses, the one in Layounne being the newest and largest. This was where the real estate arm appeared again, searching out and purchasing huge parcels of barren land where Aquifor could build their behemoth projects, then ship water to the site from their own private, secured sources.

The information on Aquifor was vast, but my time was not. Other than Asmed's resentment toward them, Aquifor passed from my mind, dissipating in the complexity of my work. More bothersome was Asmed's cloud of negativity that blew in wherever he showed up. Tolerating his mood for the first few weeks, I came to a breaking point one evening in the mess tent.

Plunking himself beside me, he immediately started complaining about the food.

"Why don't you stop moaning and do what you came here to do?"

"I wasn't talking to you. I was just commenting on this garbage they call food."

"Exactly. If you don't like it, get a job in the kitchen. You're not doing anything else."

"I never saw this side of you before, Chulyin. You were such a nice girl in Toronto."

"Victim," I muttered under my breath.

"What? What did you say?"

"You're a victim," bouncing my fork off the table. "Finish your goddam film."

The entire mess was staring at us. Asmed stormed out.

"Screw him," I announced, pretending to be pleased with my performance. Picking up my fork, I shoved a piece of lamb into my mouth, chewing, unable to swallow.

Later that evening, he caught me as I was going into my tent.

"Why are you are being such an ass to me, Chulyin?"

"You're the one being an ass."

"It was me who pulled all the strings to get you here."

"I'm grateful for that."

"Are you? You don't care about anything but yourself. Your little dig. Your PhD. Couple more weeks and you'll be out of here. Got what you came to get."

"Or maybe it's you Asmed. Maybe it's you feeling sorry for yourself."

"Maybe," he said, controlled. "Or maybe it's everything I've worked for up in smoke. Maybe it's our friendship. Up in smoke too."

"This has nothing to do with our friendship."

"That's where you're wrong. It has everything to do with it."

"Finish your documentary. That's something you can do."

"Of course I can. Do you think I'm stupid? What I can't figure out is you, Chulyin. You," pointing his finger into my face.

"I'm here to accomplish something, Asmed. You want me to stop everything I'm doing so I can pat you on the head? Make you feel better? For God's sake, finish your film. That's what you need. Not sympathy from me."

"You're right," he looked at me with—was it pity? Disdain? "Have a good night," he said and walked into the darkness.

Propped on an elbow when I entered the tent, Zaida surveyed my face rather than the book resting on her bed. "That was intense," she said.

"You were listening?"

"How couldn't I?"

I sat on the edge of my cot. "He needs to get over himself."

Zaida leaned back on the pillow and lifted the book, covering her face. "I'm sure he will."

After the lights went out, our conversation swam in my head. I replayed the dialogue, making modifications, extrapolations. The terrible news of his uncle knocked me off balance, but my emotional reaction? Who did he think he was, calling me an ass? I needed to make corrections. Refocus on my commitment, the very purpose of my time here at Rekeiz Lemgasem. To complete my PhD. Keeping my mouth shut, keeping my opinions to myself would best serve that purpose. Wrapping myself in Asmed's pity party didn't accomplish mine.

Outside, the crackle of flames and laughter from around the campfire spoke to an emptiness beneath my anger. Not so much for him or his situation, but to a hole in me that was better off sidestepped. There were too many whispers of loneliness echoing in it. Whispers that interfered with my aspirations. The dig would be over in less than four weeks, and I'd be on my way. No doubt Asmed would survive. He was a fighter. Like me.

* * *

We were five days from wrapping up our dig when it happened.

Zaida and I had just finished cataloguing a large array of handprints on the ceiling of an enclave when I noticed a crack on the back wall. The sun was dropping and a beam of light infiltrated the cave, illuminating the crevice and exposing an irregularity that would have gone undetected if not for the perfect angle of the sun. The sandstone was layered horizontal, but this showed an inconsistent vertical plane like a patch troweled from top to bottom.

I called Zaida, and we began removing the ancient plaster, widening the crack to where I could fit my hand through. A mud baked wall, about the thickness of my forearm, and beyond, a space. Chipping carefully to expand the opening, we shone the flashlight into a deep cavern. The narrow beam danced through a cloud of motes and onto the figure of a giraffe, pristine and perfectly preserved. The paint glistened red, and I thought for a moment it was still wet, fresh from the tip of the artist's brush.

"How deep is it?" Zaida asked excitedly.

"I can't tell," I said. "But it's spotless. We've hit something here." My voice was steady, but my heart was in my mouth.

Next day we returned with professor Harbi. Working for two painstaking hours, the team removed a portion of wall large enough to squeeze through. I wiggled in and dropped onto the ancient floor. Clicking on my headlamp, I was umbrella'd by a canopy of handprints spanning across the entire dome. Reaching to touch them, they receded from my fingertips, as if the stone was liquid and the handprints, leaves, floating on it.

Come forward.

The hands shrank, spiralling into a funnel, magnetized toward a black fist-sized orb, incongruous and imbedded in the ochre sandstone that surrounded it.

(Paint?)

Pressing the stone, tingles radiated to my elbow, like the day at Odin when I touched the black boulder. I jerked back and scanned the cavern with the flashlight. Riding the vortex of hands just before the dark orb were three tiny figures.

"I need a magnifier. And a ladder," I instructed.

Ascending the ladder, I brought the glass tight to the figures. Their arms stretched, distended and slender, fingers reaching forward, grasping for something only they could see. The trio were identical in pose, the leader larger than the other two, and at the centre of their chest—if the frail midsection of torso could be called a chest—a miniscule black speck. From that, a delicate strand connected them like marionettes to the core of the orb.

(A black hole?)

I killed the light.

From the core of all three figures, a surge of energy discharged into the chamber, swirling out the hole we had punched in the wall. Jolting back, I teetered on the ladder. "Holy shit."

"You okay in there?" Zaida's silhouette called to me.

"Yea. I'm good." I stammered.

Rubbing my eyes, pastels coiled around me, and I couldn't tell if the energy was twisting into the figures or outward from them, then realized it was doing both.

"Something wrong with your light?" Zaida's head bobbed in the river of colour gushing past her.

"No, all good."

(She can't see it.)

"I'm coming out for some air. It's stifling in here."

"Incredible," I said to Zaida, emerging into the desert blaze. "It's a mural. Never seen anything like it."

Dr. Harbi was in earshot and joined us. "What's your first impression, Dr. Nakasuk? What's your gut telling you what you saw?"

"The paint is so fresh. The pigments are brilliant."

"No, Dr." He made a fist and tapped it on his stomach. "Speak from here. Not your head."

"A black hole," I said definitively. "And a path of hands. Hands leading three travellers into it."

"Travellers?"

"Figures. Not human. Alien."

"You said travellers. Why?"

"Because they were on a mission. Marching toward it. Into a black stone."

"Obsidian?"

"I don't know."

"I'd like to get a sample of that rock. Have Dr. Diez examine it." Harbi said.

I hesitated. "I've seen stone like this before. At home."

"Let's see if we can chip a fragment off and have it analyzed," he said to Zaida, bypassing my comment. "I'd like to look at your three new friends."

Professor Harbi disappeared into the cavern, then Zaida asked me, "What happened in there?"

"What do you mean?" I deflected.

"I saw you just before the light went out. Looked like you saw a ghost."

* * *

That night I dreamed.

The black rock was a lens, a telescope, and I was being observed from the other side.

She can't see us. She only sees what she thinks.

I was Soolutvaluk, feathers, barbs and spines, my bones hollow. I tried to fly, but faltered. Protruding from my wingless shoulder, a quill covered with the downy silk of a hatchling.

Follow us.

The voice behind the lens beckoned, and the three figures dissolved into the aberration. I shrank, swallowed by the lens, while red hands clutched for me on the other side.

My eyes shot open and in that instant between dream and consciousness—a shadow—the same shadow from the igloo when Aanaq took me to the ice. A Raven's mask covered his head, and he watched me through the black rock, then melted like a spectre in the desert's morning heat.

* * *

The sheer volume of work cataloguing and photographing the mural eclipsed the dream and the event I had experienced in the cave a few days prior. Asmed faded too. He drifted in and out of my picture frame, our conversations laconic as he documented our discoveries. Perfectly fine. The last thing I needed was theatrics.

A few nights before our departure, the staff of the museum organized a celebration. We piled into vehicles and rolled into Tifariti, a bevy of multicoloured tents splashing the beige monotony of the desert.

Children swarmed us, pulling in every direction, spiriting the men to a soccer match where a dust cloud billowed from unseen feet, tracking the game's progress. They steered the women toward the tents, past a central court where a huge, unlit pyre waited patiently for the darkness. Coriander, saffron, and turmeric wafted from unseen cauldrons. In the pandemonium, I splintered from the others and found myself in front of a kiosk with a steaming stew bubbling over an open flame. Behind the makeshift kitchen, an old woman, rolling and flattening bread.

She was an oasis behind the clutter of pots tending a fire of her own, a bed of coals hemmed by a moat of sand, and a large convex disc suspended above it. In front of her a stone, impeccably smooth over which she flattened dollops of raw dough into perfect wafer-thin circles with an old steel pipe. Then she spun them over leathery fists, tossing them onto the scorching metal plate. As soon as the dough made contact, her hands flashed back to the stone, rolling another, then back to the plate, flipping, cooking the other side, folding it in half, then into quarters. After that, she flung them on to a growing stack. The entire process took less than a minute.

At first, I could only see her from the side, her hair smothered under a tattered cloth knotted at her ear. The tufts that did escape were twined and clipped at the back of her head. The cloth had colour once, I could see that in the patterns, but now it faded from the heat or time, I couldn't be sure. A robe draped heavily on her shoulders, equally faded, its burden compounded by a bulky metal collar strung around her neck. Globes of engraved metal and gems caught in a pewter mesh. I thought about the fishers back in Pang, their nets laden with the day's catch. Around her wrists, bracelets dangled, strands of gold and silver jingled as she pressed the dough, tinkling as it banged against the metal drum.

She caught me spying.

Her hands never stopped kneading her creations, eyes chips of coal. Tattoos zig zagged across her face, radiating from the bridge of her nose, fanning across her forehead, burrowing under the hijab that cut straight above her eyes.

(Aanaq.)

She rose and walked toward me. The vendor serving food unleashed a barrage of Arabic aspersions for leaving her post, which she completely ignored. Fumbling with one of her bracelets, she removed an ornament, reaching out to me.

I was in her grip, her skin rough and gritty. On her cheek, below her right eye, were three tiny tattoos.

(The figures in the cave.)

She curled my fingers around the amulet and released me, returning to her stool by the fire.

I stuffed the object into my pocket and felt a tap on my shoulder. Zaida.

"You've got to watch this," she said, her eyes saucers. "A camel race."

She grabbed my hand and started pulling me through the crowd.

"That woman," I said, resisting. "Cooking the bread. She had tattoos on her face."

"Lots of the older women do. It's tradition." She began tugging me again.

"No. They were tattoos of the figures. In the cave."

"Are you sure?"

"Positive."

She released me and moved back to the kiosk. "What woman?"

She was gone.

Zaida read the confusion on my face. "We'll come back. After the race," she assured me, yanking my arm, sweeping me into the buzz of the crowd.

We maneuvered our way to the front of a looping rope that designated the edge of the track. Six competitors prepared spitting, hissing beasts and lined them up behind a furrow plowed in the sand by the heel of the judge.

The riders bloomed in the colours of their tribes, all men, all young, except for one. He stood alone, his camel resting while the others scrambled. The judge announced the race was about to begin and the rider mounted. With a single click of his tongue, the camel rose, standing a half a metre above the rest.

Attendants cajoling the camels forward, the judge bustled back and forth, ensuring no hooves transgressed the starting line. Satisfied, he turned and nodded to a soldier wielding an M-16 and with a barrage of bullets, they were off.

Their speed flabbergasted me. A cloud of dust engulfed us and the entire south section of spectators. They catapulted toward the first curve where the tents precariously crowded the track, careening behind them, unseen, then pouring back into view, stampeding toward us.

The ground convulsed as they passed, the animals snorting, whips cracking their hind sides as they flashed by. Dust consumed us again while the crowd roared, cheering on their favourite rider.

On the second lap, the tall camel dropped behind the cluster.

"Watch him, watch him!" Zaida hollered excitedly. "He makes a trick!"

They slingshot past us into the last lap. Twenty hooves thundered by so tightly bunched they appeared a single mass, while ten metres behind, the wily rider paced his speed, and as he approached the tents, shifted to the outside of the track. The horde squeezed to the inside, but in the congestion a camel's hoof clipped a rope anchoring a tent. The structure tore from its moorings and vanished in a plume of dust, taking three more tents with it. Pots flew and bodies scrambled to dodge the carnage, exacerbating the fervour of the crowd, shrieking, surging past the rope balustrade, and on to the track to get a better look.

Three riders materialized from behind the carnage, storming toward the finish line.

"I told you, I told you!" Zaida screamed, oblivious to the shambles on the other side of the track.

The immense beast was in full stride now, its rider snug against its neck. The camel pulled away effortlessly, toying with its competitors, waiting to unleash its last surge. They crossed the finish line ten paces in front of their closest adversary.

In less than ten minutes, fires were extinguished, and the tents erected back on their poles, the crowd gathering around the podium positioned in front of the massive unlit pyre. Wagers were being settled and to the far left, a table set for the official tea ceremony honouring the victor. A group of children fashioned a makeshift laurel of soda cans for the camel, and when the judge attempted to hang it around the brute's neck, it spit and hissed at him, the crowd roaring with laughter.

The victor strutted to the table, waiting at attention. I had watched Asmed perform the ritual tea pouring ceremony a hundred times while we were at the U of T, but here I felt the genuine spirit of the tradition. The attendant pressing his forearm against the pewter teapot over and over while it nestled on a bed of coals, making sure the temperature was perfect, then decanting from glass to glass, the brew topped with the precise proportion of foam.

Perfect. They presented it to him. He lifted the glass with both hands, as if cradling a precious object, then downed the nectar in a single gulp. The crowd hushed. He wiped foam from his beard and when he clinked the glass on the table, a victory hoot rang from him, igniting the congregation. The pyre was lit and a huge flame burst into the desert dusk, sparks flying like comets into the chill evening air.

Zaida clapped and whooped beside me. I reached into my pocket and pulled out the amulet.

"What's that?"

"The old woman gave it to me."

It was dome-shaped, oblong. On the convex side, two deep grooves orbited a bead of metal, a nipple projecting off its surface, worn and polished, like a thousand fingers had caressed it before me. Imbedded in the outer rings, two single impressions punched into the ingot.

(Planets? Orbiting a sun?)

I flipped it over, my thumb feeling tiny grooves etched into the concave surface. I moved closer to the flame to see, and through the flickering light and bumping bodies in the crowd, I discerned three figures cut into its smoothness.

(The figures in the cave.)

At the centre of their forms a faint glow. I couldn't tell at first if flames from the pyre reflected from the surface, then a change in colour, a pinprick green that bled to the edges of the amulet, discharging into my palm.

A pressure on my shoulder. I spun, and she was before me, the ancient woman, her tattooed face and those black eyes, flames dancing inside them.

I startled back.

"Hey are you alright?"

It was Zaida. I scanned for the old woman.

"Did you see her?" I asked frantically.

She looked around. "Who?"

I stuttered. "The old woman."

"Which one?"

The one serving..." I stopped. "She gave me this," and I handed her the amulet.

"Amazigh art."

"Feel it," I heard panic in my voice. "Can't you feel it?"

She rubbed it between her thumb and forefinger. "It's a decoration."

I pulled it from her hand. "No. Look," and I flipped it over to the convex side. Polished metal.

She stared at me.

"Three figures from the cave. They were there. I saw them."

She took the piece, inspecting it, handing it back to me. "They're gone now."

* * *

We headed back to Rekeiz. As we drove away, I looked at the fire in the rear-view mirror, the dark shadows dancing.

(Is this sadness?)

I tore my eyes away and forced them into the small square of light from the headlamps shining on the road.

(Better. Nothing there but road.)

This place. My eyes filled with tears and I let them roll down my cheeks.

When was the last time I cried? I couldn't remember. Tears were such useless things. I know I had—cried, but in that moment, I couldn't recollect when or where. Tears of sadness, that is. What was there to be sad about? My first dig. A new discovery. I was on top of the world.

Asmed's face at the fire. I'd seen him there during the ceremony. He was laughing like when we were in Toronto.

"Are you sad we're leaving?" Zaida asked.

"Yes," and I began sobbing.

"Me too." She hugged my shoulder.

"I never thought leaving would be like this. I hate it."

"What do you hate, Chu?"

"This feeling."

"Is it Asmed?"

"No," I shot back. "I mean we're friends. And I was a complete jerk to him."

"Don't be too hard on yourself. He's intense."

"I know. I just feel so—guilty."

"About what?"

"I don't know. Not supporting him."

"Are you in love with him?"

"No." There was no impulsiveness or untruth to my answer. "He's a friend, Zee. That's all. But a friend who helped me more than you can imagine. We were tight at the U of T. He pushed me. To come out of myself. To be more open. If it wasn't for him, I wouldn't be here today."

"Have you told him this?"

"Of course not," and we laughed, breaking the spell of tears.

"Maybe you should. When are you leaving?"

"Day after next."

"Did you see that lunatic playing with the scorpions?" she said, changing the subject.

"I sure did. What is it about some people who just have to live on the edge?"

"Men. It's men." We laughed again. "Big versions of little boys. I think the world would be a better place if we took over."

As we turned into camp, she took my hand and said, "Tell him how you feel, Chu. You'll feel better."

Next afternoon, I received a thumb drive from Asmed. It was his documentation of the cave. There were at least a thousand photographs cataloguing every centimetre of the space, then a huge file that took forever to download. It was a 3-D panoramic representation of the entire grotto.

"Look what he's done." I turned my computer to Zaida.

"Amazing."

"I need to thank him," and I bolted into the courtyard to catch him before I left.

Professor Harbi was coming out of the mess tent. "Chulyin," he said as I approached. "I was coming to find you. How do your people say thank you?"

"Nakurmiik," I returned, extending my hand.

"Nonsense," moving in for a hug. "Na-kur-mik my dear professor. What you found here is invaluable. We are grateful," squeezing in for a second hug.

"I wish I could have given you a more concise interpretation."

"Patience, professor. Questions bring the answers. Tell me. Where do you go from here?"

"Back to Toronto. For now."

"If this site opens again, I'll be the first one calling on you."

"I'd be honoured to work with you again, professor. There's so much information. Asmed has catalogued the cave in great detail."

"Yes. He showed me before he left."

"Left?"

"To New York."

"New York?"

"Yes. Seems like his meeting with the UN is back on."

"That's, that's fantastic."

My throat was sticky. "I was hoping to tell him thank you. And goodbye."

"If I hadn't had caught him packing his truck, I'd have missed him too. Oh—one more thing. We've given your cave a name."

"7b dash one?" I joked.

"No. Chulyin—1. We're hoping you come back to find 2 and 3."

At dusk, I returned one last time to the cave. Zaida was chattering in the mess tent, and I slipped away unnoticed. Twenty minutes later, I crawled through the hole, engulfed in the cathedral of hands.

I looked up, the hands pressing on the arc of the ceiling.

(Here I am. Take me with you.)

Nothing. No colours. No feeling.

"Where do I fit?" The words extruded from my throat, a stranger speaking them.

(Leave.)

I gazed one last time at the treasure surrounding me.

(Odd. I never noticed that before.)

Black specks on the tips of the red fingers, some larger than the others. I moved in close and they were fragments of the black rock, consistent on every handprint, all leading into the vortex, the destination of the three travellers.

10. CAST FROM THE JUNGLE

The rear axle slammed into a pothole, catapulting our provisions into the mud. My head bounced off the roll bar and I saw stars, a temporary distraction from the mosquitoes feasting on me ever since we had turned off the main road into the jungle.

Two years had passed since I'd been in the field. After returning from Rekeiz Lemgasem, I honoured a teaching contract under my new title, Associate Professor of Paleography and Linguistic Studies. When the opportunity arose to explore a freshly discovered Mayan temple, I was sitting in Charles Fenwick's office.

"I'm going to Guatemala," I said.

He looked at his watch. "You're late."

"For what?"

"It's ten past nine," he tapped on the face. "I thought you'd have been here eleven minutes ago."

"They've found something interesting just outside of Tikal."

"I heard. When do you leave?"

"Tomorrow."

"What are you doing sitting here?"

Massaging the bump on my head, I questioned if it was such a good idea.

"Short, short," the driver showed, making a gap between his thumb and forefinger. "Small time," he assured us as we secured our gear back to the roof of the Rover.

Ninety minutes later, we arrived at a hole in the dense foliage, traversing the last few kilometres on foot. Somewhere on the other side of the jungle curtain, a crew with machetes was slashing a road to the site. The air was syrup, and when we squirted into a small clearing, a shirtless man motioned for us to follow. One last clump of trees, then a small colony of tents. He wagged his finger at one, nodding at me. Inside, there was a basin of fresh water. I splashed it on my face, rubbing it on the back of my neck, bites swelling into miniature volcanoes.

"Are the accommodations suitable?" I spun and a bronze face peered through the slit in my tent.

"Five-star," I said.

"The bellboy took the day off."

I moved toward the door. "Dr. Gomez?"

"Si." He extended his hand, and I noticed the softness of the skin.

(Odd for a guy chipping rocks all day.)

"How was the trip?"

"Delightful." I scratched my neck.

"There's calamine lotion on the shelf," he pointed, adding, "they don't seem to bother me."

"Or the fellow who brought me to the tent."

He laughed. "Mayan. They've got immunity to anything that bites. I am so grateful you agreed to come, Dr. Nakasuk. We have much to discuss." He was completely in the tent now. "Perhaps you could freshen up, yes? And we could meet in my quarters in a half an hour? And some dinner, perhaps? You must be famished."

I nodded.

"I'm three tents down," he pointed to the left. "I'll see what the chef can muster up," then vanished, machetes relentlessly chopping in the jungle. For the first time in a decade, I wished for an icy Arctic chill to cool my boiling skin, dabbing calamine on my neck.

Night arrived, and the drone of a diesel generator replaced the sound of machetes. Strolling toward Dr. Gomez's tent, a large fire blazed at the opposite edge of the camp, the smell of gasoline pungent, keeping the wet brush burning from the day's cut. I smelled my hands.

(Anun.)

The fiery heat of an unknown chili wafted under my nose at the entrance to his tent. "Knock, knock," I called through the netting.

"Come in, come in," he returned, bouncing up from a table of small artifacts he'd been examining. He wore a jeweller's lamp around his head, flicking off the light.

"Please, sit," removing the visor. "Tuesday night is kak'ik night. I hope you like it spicy."

I eyed the thick Guatemalan soup. "Love it."

"I'm assuming your trip was uneventful?"

"Mostly. Except for the mosquitoes. Almost as big as the ones back home."

"You have mosquitoes in the Arctic?"

"We sure do." I pointed to the table with the stone fragments. "What were you looking at?"

"Bits of a tablet we found at the base of the pyramid." He stood up and walked to the table of artifacts, retrieving a chink of black stone. "We found this today."

It was the hieroglyph of a raven.

I put down my spoon and took the stone, tracing the smooth edges with the tips of my fingers.

"It's a single glyph," he said, "but what's more perplexing is the rock. It's not indigenous."

I rolled the sample in my hand. "This rock seems to follow me around."

"You know its composition?"

"Not exactly. But it s like a sample we uncovered in Western Sahara. On a dig at Rekeiz Lemgasem." I neglected to mention the monolith at the foot of Odin.

"Did you have it analyzed?"

"I didn't. But I know who did. I can check." I rubbed the raven with my thumb. "This glyph. It seems atypical of Mayan script."

"It is," he agreed. "That's why we're eager to clear away the vegetation. To see what else is underneath."

"Let's see what tomorrow brings." I dipped my spoon into the bowl. "This is delicious."

* * *

Under the watchful eye of Dr. Gomez, workers had meticulously removed a stubborn net of fibrous tentacles that adhered to the structure, exposing the east face.

"I've seen nothing like it," Dr. Gomez said. "It's like the roots are feeding off the pyramid."

At that point, they had found no additional black material. The structure itself was typical Mayan engineering, but the hieroglyphs were another thing. Chiselled into the hundred denuded blocks, at least a single raven adorned each stone, one particular block counting twelve. They were all identical in pose but varied in size and the direction they faced.

"What do you make of it?" Gomez asked.

"Indeterminate," I responded, staring at the emerging pyramid.

Later that night I received a call from professor Harbi. "It defied classification," he said about the chemical composition of the black rock. "A meteor perhaps? Or some other unidentifiable interstellar debris?"

For the next four days, a tropical downpour turned the site into a bog. Work was impossible, and we hunkered down in our tents, praying for a break in the clouds. On day five, I couldn't stand it any longer and braved the deluge.

Mayan engineering is incredibly precise. The stones packed so tight the water ran in tiny rivulets along the chamfered edges where each block butted against its neighbour. It was a massive fountain, miniature waterfalls spilling down. The earth at the base of the pyramid was spongy, but there were no standing pools. I traced my fingers across the surface of a raven glyph.

(A tomb?)

Climb.

The blocks were perilous. The entire structure was in motion, and the combination of moss and algae created a film slick as grease. I started a cautious ascent. About halfway up, I stopped to catch my breath, resting my face against the surface of the stone. That's when I saw it. A channel in the vertical joint between two stones where the water disappeared. I followed the crease with my finger, up to the corner of the stone along the horizontal axis that was level with my eyes. The water disappeared there too, as if it was draining into the interior of the pyramid.

(A way in?)

It was my last thought before my foot slipped.

* * *

I was on the ice shelf. The sun, brilliant, and the dimpled sea stretched before me, dancing in a void blurred between sea and sky, constellations sparkling.

(Day and night at the same time.)

"Chulyin."

(Who's there?)

"Aanaq?" I called out.

She was before me. I couldn't define where the collar of her coat ended and her hair began, her face plump and perfectly symmetrical. Lines of tattoos sprouted from her scalp, collecting at the bridge of her nose into a single stream. Two parallel sets of three radiated across her cheekbones like the whiskers of a harp seal. Aanaq's expression defied gravity, rising in a perpetual smile, squeezing a glint from the slits that were her eyes. A parka hung below her boots, melding with the ice, its caribou hide taken when the animal was preparing for winter, when the fur was supple. A Raven embroidered in the centre directly under her chin, and below that, three Foxes, one larger than the others, flickering white and orange. In my hand, a Raven's talon.

(Anun?)

Aanaq disappeared and in her place an inuksuk, Raven perched on top. The stone marker sang in her voice, a throat song, calling her spirits.

"Come back."

I collapsed into the sea, sinking heavy as a stone, plunging into light.

"Can you hear me, little one?"

(Aanaq. I hear you.)

"She's awake." A voice addled in the fog.

I strained my eyes open, and a face peered down at me.

"Welcome back," it said.

I went to move and felt the gentle press of his hand. "Woah there girl. Easy. Do you know where you are?"

"I found the entrance," I said.

"Sure you did. Then you fell five metres and cracked your skull."

"What?" I tried to get up again, but a spin put me back on the pillow. "Where am I?"

"San Lucas Hospital. You've been unconscious for three days."

"How did Aanaq get here?"

"Who's Aanaq?" he said, listening to my chest with a stethoscope. "You had a visitor. Dr. Gomez left ten minutes ago." Draping the device around his neck, "Welcome back to the land of the living. You've suffered a mild concussion. No broken bones. Lucky. The ground was soft and wet when you landed."

"When can I get out of here?"

* * *

Two days later, I was back at the site, the goose egg behind my ear shrinking. The workers had cleared the entire south face of the pyramid, which I was preparing to inspect when a young student tapped my shoulder.

"Professor, there's a call for you," he said. "Urgent."

I made my way to the communication building, the only solid structure on the site. Opie, our communications officer, looked like they had stolen him from a farm in Iowa, his hair corn silk and his face covered with freckles. He was engaged in slaying gremlins on a large monitor, feet propped on the desk. Without looking up, he pointed to a headset on the adjacent table.

"Hello."

Dr. Nak-a-suk?

"Yes."

"My name is Maxwell Hursche. I'm the CEO of a company called Aquifor International and we—uh—we could use your help."

I stiffened. "I know about Aquifor. How is it I can help, Mr. Hursche?"

"Well, that saves me from preliminaries," clearing his throat. "I'll get straight to the point."

"Please do."

"Perhaps you heard about it on the news. There's a problem at our water production facility in Qaanaaq, Greenland. Something has temporarily interrupted operations that have brought production to a standstill. While our excavators were harvesting ice from the glacier, they struck a massive rock. The instant the blades made contact, all mechanical and electrical activity ceased. Our engineer on site has suggested the rock is emitting some kind of energy field that is disabling the equipment. Frying circuit boards."

"Sounds like you need a physicist."

"We've already recruited one."

"What does any of this have to do with me?"

"Dr. Nakasuk, the water harvested in Qaanaaq supplies several of Aquifor's global greenhouses, our largest in Morocco. The greenhouse in Layounne supplies half the produce for the European and African markets."

"Layounne. It's in Western Sahara," I corrected.

"You know your geography," Hursche continued. "Point is, we need to get the water flowing from Qaanaaq. If not, it could spell disaster."

"I'm not getting your point, Mr. Hursche. I'm an archaeologist."

"Precisely," he returned. "The stone is covered in some kind of writing. Runes or hieroglyphs. The government of Greenland has added another glitch suspending all activity at the site until we know exactly what we've uncovered."

"I'm in the middle of a dig right now."

"Yes, I am aware. Frankly, Dr. Nakasuk, we're baffled. When I asked who could help, it was unanimous. You."

"I'm flattered Mr. Hursche. But I have to decline."

"Now I have to stoop to bribery," he laughed. "This find could be the feather in your archaeological cap. Should you decide to join our team, Aquifor offers a seven-figure compensation package. Not that money would motivate you."

"Enticing. But once again, Mr. Hursche, I have to decline."

"Well, think it over. Give it a couple of days. This really is an opportunity of a lifetime for you, Dr. Nakasuk. I think it would be wise to take it up. We look forward to hearing from you."

The line went dead, and I removed the headset, placing it on the table.

Opie was leaning forward, slaying dragons, stamping his feet. I nudged him on the way out and he looked up. "Conquer the world yet?"

* * *

I was standing on a scaffold when the troops stormed in. They assaulted the camp in full battle gear, trailed by an artillery vehicle, with a miniature cannon mounted on a swivel turret. Seconds later, another Jeep cruised in and stopped at the base of the pyramid. The officer in the back rose slowly, surveying the situation, then leapt to the ground, strolling to the front of the vehicle. His left hand cradled his hip while his right caressed the butt of his revolver. Scanning the scene, he nodded to the driver, who scrambled to the back of the Jeep, retrieving a bullhorn.

I scampered from the scaffold and corralled instantly by a soldier who lined us up against the pyramid.

"You," he hollered through the bullhorn, pointing at a student. "Go with these soldiers and bring everyone here." He spoke in Spanish, then repeated his command in English.

"What the hell is going on here?" I protested, lurching toward him, and abruptly stared down a gun barrel. The soldier gave it a flick, and I retreated. In less than three minutes, we were all assembled in front of the pyramid, Opie being the last straggler, still wearing the headset around his neck.

"My name is Colonel Manuel Gonzalez," he announced. "The government of Guatemala decrees this site shut down. Immediately."

"What are you talking about?" I blurted out.

He pivoted, staring directly at me. "You are the one in charge?"

"You have no right to do this. We have visas and permission from the Guatemalan government to be here," I snarled.

"Revoked."

"Opie, come with me," and to the Colonel, "We'll see about this."

Two soldiers barred my way.

"Dr. Gomez is going to have your ass."

"Not today," his voice was calm, controlled. He motioned to his men, then said, "Escort them to the vehicles."

I charged forward, knocking one guard to the ground. Then my face was in the mud, a heavy boot pinning me down.

"This is not a request," the colonel said, zip-tying my wrists. "Would anyone else like to wear bracelets?" There were no takers. The soldiers loaded us into a lorry and we lumbered away from the ruins along the fresh-cut trail.

"What the hell's going on?" I said, wiping dirt from my eyes.

A student piped up, "I heard one of them say they're taking us to the airport."

"The airport? Has anybody seen Dr. Gomez? Anybody got a phone?" I asked.

"The took everything," another volunteered.

The student was right. When we arrived at the airport, they herded us directly on to the tarmac and divided us into smaller groups, until they had whittled us to a trio of Canadians. One of our guards ordered absolute silence, cutting my plastic restraints, while he bantered back and forth on a walkie talkie, waiting for instructions.

A student from Regina whispered through her teeth, "Is this a coup?" Her eyes were saucers.

"Why are they separating us?" the second student said, too loud, and the soldier hushed him, pressing his finger to his lips.

Twenty minutes later, they hustled us toward the south end of the departure facility. Rounding the corner, there was an RCAF Hercules transport rumbling a hundred yards out on the runway. An overly polite co-pilot speaking Spanish to the soldiers received us and pointed with his eyes for us to get up the ladder, pronto. Clambering up the metal steps, another Canadian uniform instructed us to take a seat and strap ourselves in. He retracted the steps into the fuselage and the moment the door secured, we lurched forward, taxiing to the end of the runway.

In minutes we were airborne, circling north over Lake Peten Itza, away from Mundo Maya Airport. The scene below was serene, so picturesque, a complete reversal from the events that had just occurred. As the plane reached altitude, the engines eased into a rhythm and the co-pilot emerge from the cockpit, his expression relieved, like he, too, was glad we were on our way.

"Any idea what this is all about?" he asked.

We looked at each other, incredulous. "Don't you know?" Regina asked.

"We came in last night delivering medical supplies," he said. "We were just going to refuel and go back home. Then they told us we had to wait. Fuel shortage. They filled us up this morning and told us some passengers needed to get back to Canada right away. Emergency. I was hoping you could fill in some blanks."

"They pulled us off an archaeological dig just north of Tikal," I offered. "The entire team. Twenty-two of us. Loaded us up and brought us here."

"Who's they?" he asked.

"The Guatemalan army," I replied.

"No coup?" Regina inquired.

"Coup?" the co-pilot responded. "They just told us we had to wait for fuel. Not uncommon down here. Everything else seemed status quo."

"Where we headed?" the other student asked.

"Canadian Forces Base in Trenton," he returned. "Sit back and relax. Let me see if I can dig up some more information for you," and he turned and headed back to the cabin.

No news came from the cockpit. The crew was silent throughout the duration of the trip and we spent our time speculating. Confused. None of it made any sense. We talked ourselves out, then settled in to our thoughts and the hum and vibration of the plane.

Four hours later, we circled and started our descent into Trenton airport. The sky was dazzling blue and the unfrozen lake gobbled up the brilliance of a white blanket that covered the rest of the earth. A scratch of grey, the runway, called us in and I lost sight of it as the plane levelled, taking us down for landing.

A gust of frigid Canadian air greeted us when we exited the aircraft. A trio of cadets hustled us to a cavernous hangar, then through a set of doors leading into a heated corridor. I was walking ahead with one cadet and when I turned to address a student, I was alone.

"What's going on?" I demanded.

My guide pointed forward. "Just up ahead, professor. Let's keep moving. They'll catch up."

"Catch-up?" gluing my feet to the floor. "I'm not moving until you tell me where they are. Where are the customs people?"

"This is a military base. We have special clearance." He gripped my arm, urging me forward.

I pulled away.

"Professor, please. Just up here on the left." A smile returned.

He asked me to wait in the hallway for a moment, then disappeared behind the door. The corridor was short, ten metres perhaps, and I hustled back to see if I could retreat into the hangar. Locked. Three cameras monitored the space and less than two minutes later, the cadet invited me in.

A dishevelled Charles Fenwick greeted me, along with an immaculately dressed stranger.

"What the hell's going on here, Charles?"

"Have a seat," he said, forcing a smile. "We'll brief you."

"Brief me?" I returned. "That would be nice. Considering I was in Guatemala less than twelve hours ago."

"I know, Chulyin, I know. Relax. Please."

The Versace suit spoke. "It was imperative for us to speak in person, professor."

I immediately recognized the voice. Maxwell Hursche.

I scanned back and forth between the two men. "What the hell is going on here, Charles?"

"Easy Chulyin. Mr. Hursche approached me with a proposal–"

"I've already heard his proposal."

"Circumstances have changed," Charles returned.

"What circumstances?"

"Your participation in this opportunity in Greenland," he said.

I shifted my gaze back and forth between the two men. "You kidnapped me."

"We understand how you feel right now, professor," Hursche said.

"Do you?" I blurted back. I turned to Charles. "They squashed my dig because this corporate power-tripper needs something from me?"

"We arranged with the Guatemalan military to help us—convince you—your services were more urgently required elsewhere," Hursche said.

I launched myself from the chair and stormed to the door. Locked. I spun and hissed at Charles, "Open the door!"

"Chulyin please. Ten minutes. If you want to leave after that, you can go. Please. Sit."

I plunked myself back in the chair. "Ten minutes Mr. Hursche. Shoot."

He took a sip of water. "It seems what we've stumbled on in Qaanaaq is unprecedented on two fronts. From a physics perspective, the energy emitting from this—monolith—has no recognizable footprint that science, to this point, can identify. Plus, we can't get close enough with conventional instruments to conduct testing. There's an atmosphere of energy surrounding the monolith like an invisible sphere, encircling above and below the ice surface. The force field extends a kilometre from the source. Entering the affected area neutralizes anything electrical. When we exit," he snapped his fingers, "everything pops back on. And it has its own weather system. It was -38°C today in Qaanaaq, with 90 kilometre an hour winds. Inside the bubble, no snow, no wind and a steady -5°C."

"Eight minutes Mr. Hursche. I still haven't heard what this has to do with me."

Hursche steamrolled ahead. "Our initial concern was to nullify the energy so we could get back to work. Then this." He motioned to Charles, who slid a stack of photographs toward me. "Our staff took these with a high-resolution camera from beyond the energy perimeter. At first, they considered the irregularities in the rock natural erosion anomalies—cracks, fissures, scars from glacial action. Then one of our technicians noticed a pattern in the markings. Like Druidic runes. More symbols than writing. What do you think?"

I glanced at the photos and pushed them back to Charles. "I think you have a problem."

"One that you can help decipher, we hope."

Charles couldn't contain himself. "There's something else. Mr. Hursche has committed a $20 million funding program for our archaeology department over the next ten years. Contingent on your agreement to join their team in Qaanaaq."

"Ransom," I replied to Charles.

"Incentive." Hursche rephrased. "And a strong call for help. Your expertise would be an invaluable asset, Dr. Nakasuk."

Both men were silent.

"Alright then," I stood up. "I thank you Mr. Hursche. But unfortunately, my decision is final."

Charles stammered. "We'll get back to you tomorrow, Mr. Hursche. I'm sure we'll work something out."

"I fear you're making a grave mistake, Dr. Nakasuk. Not only for your career. But for your people."

"And what do you know about my people?" I shot back.

"I know they could use a hero right now. This could be your opportunity to provide that."

Charles grabbed my arm and hustled me from the room to a black limo waiting in the hangar. "You need to rethink this, Chulyin," he said as we pulled away.

After a long pause, I said, "I already have. I've got nothing else to say to that sanctimonious son of a bitch."

"Go home. Rest. Take a week. I'll talk to Hursche and tell him you need a bit more time."

I nodded and fell back into the seat as an invasion of hulking snowflakes splatted on the windshield.

11. AANAQ'S FUNERAL

It was after midnight when Charles dropped me off. My belongings had been stuffed into a large duffel bag and loaded on to the Hercules in Guatemala. I rummaged through my pack and found my apartment key, sliding it into the lock. My tiffany lamp glowed softly, spilling light on the table below, casting a kaleidoscope on the wall behind it. Inside was stale air and loneliness.

(Must have forgotten to turn that off.)

My apartment was a tomb of artifacts, like one of my archaeological digs, before the shovels and rakes sifted through.

(Did I exist here? Have I ever?)

A puckered aloe limped over the edge of its terracotta pot. Impressive. Able to withstand the drought and my neglect. Dropping my luggage, I went directly to the kitchen and poured a glass of water, then tipped it gently into the cracked soil. Aanaq would be unimpressed. I never made it to bed, falling on the couch into a dreamless coma.

Pounding snapped me into consciousness. I staggered to the door, where two anxious faces greeted me.

"Professor, sorry to bother you. Dean Fenwick is trying to get in touch with you. He says it's urgent."

"Urgent?" I said, groggy. "I saw him last night."

"He wants you to call him right away."

I assured them I would and closed the door. Checking my phone, I saw Charles had called eight times and another number, area code 867. Pangnirtung. I called Charles.

"Chulyin I've been trying to reach you all morning."

"I heard. Your posse just left."

"I have some—bad news. Your grandmother. She's passed."

(Am I still sleeping?)

"How?" fell from my lips.

"I don't know. I got a call from a—" I heard him sorting through some papers, "Sylvia Etungat. Your grandmother's friend."

"Yes. Sylvia."

"I have her number—"

Interrupting, "I have it." I hung up and called Sylvia.

* * *

Michael Koonark was the first face greeting me when the wheels squawked down in Pang. He was a giant of a man, and his parka seemed to double his volume. And those black eyes, like the morning they looked when we found Anun at the foot of Odin.

"Michael," I broke the silence and buried into him.

"Chulyin. I wish things were different." His voice trailed softly above my head.

"Me too," I said, moving back to see him. "We've got to stop meeting like this," smiling, attempting to lighten the mood.

It was a five-minute walk to my childhood house. The air was frigid, and I sucked it into my lungs like life itself. I offered Michael a tea, and we sat at the table waiting for the kettle to boil.

"Where did they find her?"

"On the ice in the fiord. Fearney found her."

"Where is she now?"

"In her tupiq. Chulyin. She wasn't wearing any boots."

"She wasn't coming back."

The kettle whistled.

"I'll get that." Michael rose from the chair.

"No. Please. Let me."

I prepared the tea, then returned to the table.

"What do you need from me, Chu?"

"Exactly this," I returned. "Share a cup of tea with me."

I poured the steaming brew into his mug. "She knows I'm here."

He took a sip. "Would you like to see her?"

"No. I think I'll wait until tomorrow. She's busy. With Anun and her sister. With Bunny."

Stirring a spoonful of sugar into my tea, "How's Qikiqtani? Is the business well?"

"Thriving," Michael returned. "Better in the winter some years. This is one."

"That's good." Leaves on her violets were drooping. "Looks like these fellows could use a little drink."

* * *

It was early when I made my way to her tupiq. Suvulliik hadn't hung its head and dawn was still a few hours away. My feet crunched the snow, ricocheting between the sleepy dwellings, and I was certain the sound woke every soul in the entire town. At the door of the tupiq, I reached for the handle, glancing over my shoulder for eyes peeking through their curtains. Nothing. Pang was asleep.

Aanaq lay on an altar of ice at the centre of the tupiq, wrapped in a ceremonial parka, a soapstone clasp tight around her neck. A fox tail, brilliant, fringed the edge of her hood, unable to conceal a thick knot of silver hair that brimmed from it. Fox tail cuffs bore her hands, the skin translucent as frazil. Even in death she remained unchanged, her face furrowed, chiseled from the rock, the bones of the land. Aanaq was every fissure and crevice, yet in those flutings, a softness. A healing place.

I traced the arc of tattoos that spilled from her brow and slid down to the bridge of her nose. Faded now. The devil's stamp. I'd overheard a qallunaaq comment once when I was a little girl. I didn't understand. She was just my Aanaq. But I could tell from his tone those marks were reprehensible, that she was defective. And if she was defective, then so was I. We were blood. Her disfigurement was mine, only mine was invisible. Tattoos that inked my mind in an imposed ugliness I could not bear to challenge. I didn't know how.

Until today.

(She's beautiful.)

Her feet were bare, toes torn and black, consumed in frostbite.

(They took you as far as you needed to go.)

The parka she wore I'd never seen. Tailored not for function, but for ritual, her rite of passage through the in-between place, to the sacred ground of her ancestors.

In the centre, just above the lower fringe, a Raven. It was striking; its beak and head oversized, an orange orb gripped in its talons. Above it, two smaller spheres on either side of the bird, balancing on the crown of their own inuksuk. As I stared, they glowed, and I rubbed my eyes, thinking it was the flickering fire creating the illusion. Then they pulsated, their glow rising and falling like a heartbeat.

A web of light cast out from the orange orb like a crystal net, pinpricks appearing along the strands while a thick triangular causeway connected the three main beacons.

(A map?)

The impression jarred me from the altar and I stumbled on the ring of rocks that surrounded the fire. In the corner, tucked in the darkness, I detected movement. Squinting, I scanned the blackness. Then it moved again. I approached, bending forward that I might see more clearly.

(Nothing. There's nothing here.)

Turning back to the fire, I followed the smoke drifting lazily up. My mind climbed it like a ladder.

(I know this place.)

Odin. The black monolith. The cylinder of roiling energy. Suddenly I felt my body elongating, elasticized, stretching through the top of the tupiq, out under the sky. Three stars pulsed around me, one smoldering orange.

"When Suvulliik lowers its head, begin your day."

I detached my mind from the spectacle and looked into the darkened corner.

Fox. Her tail curled around her feet, front legs supporting her like a sphinx. Fire danced yellow in the slits of her pupils.

I turned to the ice altar. Aanaq resurrected, smiling, holding out her hand, and I moved closer. We looked up through the hole of the tupiq and our fingers touched. Odin towered above us, and the tundra, thick with lichen soft below. Aanaq's feet were bare and black, the spongy carpet oozing between her toes caressing the bone and wounded flesh. Sun and moon were simultaneous in the sky, a feint blue aura surrounding them and finding us too, bathing us in a cerulean mist. Below them, a bright orange glow.

(Suvulliik.)

"Aanaq!" I pointed to the star, but only Fox shimmered before me, like a chunk of brilliant white ice bobbing in the sea.

A whisper, 'Chulyin', and I turned.

A nukaq, her hair oscillating like kelp in a shifting tide. "Come on, come on!" she motioned, waving her arms, running toward Odin. My feet riveted and when I looked down, they were pieces of the firmament and the mountain that rose before me.

"FLY!" she exhorted.

My arms were wings, so black the deepest indigo leaked from them, staining the earth. I spread them and launched, circling high above the tundra, climbing, rising on the currents of air that lifted me effortless above the land. A patchwork of purple saxifrage and a sea of yellow Arctic poppies dappled below, waving in the breeze.

The nukaq's laughter called me earthward, and I spotted her on a stony outcrop surrounded by a thick cluster of pink Wintergreen. Diving, twisting my wings, I landed beside her.

"Look!" she said, pointing to the heavens, and in the sky were three stars, blazing, the lowest on the horizon seeping orange.

"Do you see?" excited as she spoke.

Facing the blushing orbs, she removed a pouch from around her neck, then reaching up, plucked the three stars from the sky, coaxing them into the satchel. Once inside, she fastened a thin sinew ribbon, twisting it through a buttonhole so they could not escape. She extended the satchel, gesturing for me to take it.

I reached out. What had been wings were now my arms and hands, and I received her gift.

(Aanaq.)

I was back inside the tupiq. Aanaq lay still and silent on the altar.

On the outside of the pouch, a Raven stitched into the hide. Unravelling the tie, I dropped three stones into my palm, all jet black, one larger and flecked with amber, rust and fire.

As I made my way back to the house, I saw her from the corner of my eye. Fox; her tail flashing white in a moment of silver, vanishing on a beam sent down by the sliver of a crescent moon.

* * *

I saw their silhouettes from the window, perhaps fifty of them, walking toward the house. Fearney led the pack. I couldn't distinguish him, but his gait was unmistakable.

"Hey Chu," he called, light from my door streaming across the pristine landscape of his face. He was plump and nervous and looked exactly the way he had the day I left for Toronto. Aging seemed optional for Fearney. His skin glowed adolescent, and whiskers were simply not welcome to take root in its tenderness.

"Look at you," I said, moving in for a hug.

"Never mind me," he returned, awkwardly releasing me. "This is about you." He motioned to the people behind him. "We're here for you."

"Thank you," I said to him. "Thank you everyone," to the crowd.

"We didn't know when you'd get here," He moved in close. "Father McMurtry has been pushy," he whispered. "I told him he'd just have to wait till you got home for the arrangements."

I knew what Aanaq wanted. A cairn beside her sister and Bunny, both buried on the north ridge under the watchful eye of Mount Duval.

"Don't let them lock me inside that fence," Aanaq said, referring to the cemetery at the foot of the airport runway. "This spirit needs to roam free."

Later that afternoon, I met with three elders, one I'd never met or heard of, Fanny Kilabuk, who had travelled all the way from Pond Inlet.

"Your Aanaq," she began, "we have been friends for many years."

"She never spoke of you," I said.

"No. We learned to keep our tongues silent."

"You are shaman?"

She nodded. "I helped Aanaq with your mother. So Bunny would not wander to the dark place." Her expression lightened. "I remember you when you were a little girl. You had the glow. Even now, the light of angakkuq shines."

"Thank you," I stammered, "but I—" The words would not come.

"Come," Fanny said. "Let's prepare her for her journey."

We entered the tupiq, and I braided her hair, tucking it neatly back inside her hood. The others surrounded her with fox pelts, gifts brought to her from hunters and wives of hunters. Reaching into my pocket, I removed the pouch and placed it on her parka.

"What's that?" Fanny asked.

"A gift. That helped me through the darkness once."

"Does your darkness fade?"

"Sometimes."

Fanny pointed to the Raven sewn on to the pouch. "This is your tuurngaq?"

"Aanaq would say so, yes."

Fanny shifted to my side, lifting the sac, handing it to me. "Perhaps this would better serve you. Aanaq's darkness is past, and she is on her way to greet those who love her with open arms. Keep this for your journey, Chulyin," squeezing my fingers around the pouch.

Fanny had instructed the men to remove a portion of the wall from the rear of the tupiq. "She cannot exit through the front," she warned. "It will hamper her spirit flight."

Outside, a dog team waited, restless, charged with energy. A group of men had positioned a bed of ice on the sled and with great care they transferred her to it, lashing it to the runners, securing her for her final sojourn.

The sky seemed cast in everlasting dawn, clouds high and wispy, guzzled in pink from a parched and infinite Arctic night. Michael motioned for me to join him on the sled. I felt inside my coat, squeezing the pouch, the stones clanking, rubbing together. His whistle brought the dogs to attention. Behind us, a squad of snowmobiles waited. Michael tugged the reins, and we were off.

Mushing north, the runners sung beneath us. Kalirrangit. The sound of the sled cutting across the snow, an Inuit word unique to us, to me. Then the snowmobiles fired up, their beams caroming off the ivory stage, our dogs charging forward, spurred by Michael's clicks and whistles.

We rolled up the ridge that looked down on Pangnirtung. Mount Duval waited patient as the snowmobiles circled, killing their engines. Silence returned, and no moon lit the sky. Four men approached and lifted Aanaq from the ice bed, laying her on the bare outcrop.

"South," Fanny instructed. "Her head is to the south to keep her from the cold."

One by one we placed stones around her, on her, building Aanaq's cairn, then rolling a white bolder, marking the position of her head. Fearney and Michael had come the day before and constructed an inuksuk. "For them all," Michael said, extending his arms to the stone graves housing Bunny and my great aunt Chulyin beside her.

Fanny spoke: "This is our time of grief. For our sister Mary Buniq Nakasuk. Daughter, mother," and she looked directly at me, "grandmother. Take her spirit in your heart and remember. Remember Mary. Remember who we are." Her eyes fastened on me.

Collapsing to the ground, I pressed my head against the inuksuk, whispering into the stones and the flesh beneath it. "Aanaq, I cannot receive this gift. That power dies with you. Pretending I am something I am not would only dishonour you." Reaching into my pocket, I removed the Raven pouch and lodged it into the cairn. Standing, I said to Michael, "Take me home."

I fell through the door. Across the room, Aanaq's chair, empty. She was there in my mind, sewing, singing, but I could not hear her voice. I lowered myself onto the seat, wishing her sound would come.

The chair's arms were worn from a lifetime of her hands. From the harbour, a wind erupted, and the house moaned.

A knock at the door, and it was Fearney. "You okay?"

"Get out of the wind," I ordered. "Sure."

"I thought you might want to talk."

We moved to the kitchen.

I shrugged my shoulders. "About what?"

"Your Aanaq," he responded. "About how you're feeling."

"What's to say? I feel shitty."

He tapped the table. "I missed you Chulyin."

"Me too," I quickly replied. "What about you? How's life been in Pang?" There was an edge to my tone.

"You know. Surviving."

"This place," I surmised. "Nothing changes."

"Are you kidding?" he retorted. "Everything has changed."

"Really? What's changed, Fearney? It's the same hell hole I left ten years ago."

"When did you become such a hypocrite, Chulyin?"

"Hypocrite?"

"That's right. Hypocrite. You come back here and act all high and mighty. Like one of them."

"I've never done that."

"You're doing it right now," he shot back. "Pretending you don't give a shit. You lie to yourself. I can see right through you."

"And what do you see, Fearney?"

"Someone afraid to see the truth."

"There's no truth here. When did you become a psychologist?"

"Change the topic. That's what you're good at. Talking your way out of how you really feel."

"I feel like this conversation is going nowhere."

"Sure you do. Do you have any idea how the people of this town talk about you? Or care?"

He waited. "No. You don't. Maybe you should ask. Or just open your ears."

He stood up. "I'm sorry Chulyin. I'm sorry about your Aanaq. Your uncle and all the crappy things that have happened to you. But hating this place won't make you feel any better. Pang isn't the problem. You are."

He left without another word.

Around me, Aanaq's violets withered over the edges of their pots. Any blooms that had existed, tufts of lifeless brown. I began collecting the dying plants, discarding them into the trash.

* * *

The next few days were quiet until a toothy Inuit showed up at my door. He was short, and a potbelly girdled his midriff. An oily sheen produced a reflectiveness that highlighted a complexion pockmarked with miniature craters. Presumably, I thought, from a childhood case of measles. He poked his hand forward, his teeth glistening like ice on a bright summer day.

"Ms. Nakasuk, my name is Isahah Agloolik," accentuating the 'hah' in Isahah. I reached out instinctively and shook it, the skin smooth and slippery like an Arctic char fresh from the sea.

"So sorry about your Aanaq," he said.

"Thank you," pulling my hand free.

"May I come in?"

"Of course," I stammered. "I was just making some tea," I lied. "Would you like some?"

"Yes. Please. That would be wonderful."

When I brought the tea from the kitchen, he was sitting in Aanaq's chair.

"I'm sure you're wondering who I am," he said, turning squarely to face me, jigging the tea bag like he was fishing at an ice hole.

"Yes."

"Let me get to the point. I... I mean, we... could use your help."

My jaw tightened.

"I'm the environmental strategist for Aquifor International and–"

"You can stop right there, Mr. Agloolik. I've already had this conversation with your boss. Twice."

"Yes, yes. I know. Please. Hear me out before you," he laughed nervously, "throw me out."

I crossed my arms and leaned back in the chair.

He slurped his tea. "Mmm. Peppermint," still fishing with the tea bag. "There's something else going on at the site in Qaanaaq." He pulled out an extensive file and shifted a stack of photographs across the table. "These images are invisible to the naked eye. X-rays, sonar, radar, everything. Until we got our hands on a cyclotron from our office in San Diego." He pushes more photographs toward me. "We set the photon beam deeper into the structure and here," he tapped on a dark spot in the centre, "that blotch. We think these are inner chambers under the surface. Constructed from, well, we don't know. And—who? Who built this?"

I studied the photos.

"Like I said, Dr. Nakasuk, we could sure use your help."

"All very interesting. No doubt you know my history with your company?"

"We're hoping we can circumvent our differences. Or at least put them aside for the time being. In the name of science." His toothy grin reappeared.

I nodded. "Science, yes. I appreciate that," I said, sliding the photos back toward him. "I have some things I need to clear up here. I'll let you know by the end of the week."

"I'm flying to Qaanaaq post haste," he said. "I hope you decide to take part in this, professor. We need you to decipher this. This is something where we, as northern people, can really make an impact. Show them what we're made of. I'll leave those with you," pointing to the photos.

"Right," I returned, nodding.

I watched him waddle down the street, heading back to the airstrip.

I pulled a photograph from the pile. On it were the three figures from Rekeiz Lemgasem.

12. GREENLAND AND AQUÍFOR

One week later, I was on a plane bound for Qaanaaq with Isahah Agloolik snoring across the aisle. Aquifor had sent their company jet to collect me.

Over that period, I had searched the internet to see if I could discover anything about what was going on at the Aquifor facility. For something they touted as being archaeologically ground-breaking, it was uncharacteristically quiet. None of the major news networks had picked it up, nor were there any murmurings within the archaeology community. All hush, hush.

I scoured the photographs Isahah left me. The parallels between the painting at Rekeiz and the impressions from Qaanaaq were uncanny. The limbs and torsos of the figures were proportionate, the only difference being the ones from Qaanaaq were not swimming in a sea of red handprints. Then there was Aanaq's bone collection. Her etchings were remarkably similar, sometimes exact representations of the runes depicted in the photographs.

I was grateful Isahah slept. The thought of chatting with him wasn't appealing. I didn't trust him. I was content to peer out into the Arctic night, something I thought I would never miss until returning to Pang for Aanaq's funeral. It's a darkness best experienced, especially when the moon is new and the universe of stars is unobstructed by any form of light. The artificial glow of the dials from the cockpit and the steady hum of the engines were the only reference that the world existed. That I existed. That anything beyond the glass portal was anything but void.

The pilot's voice, static through the speakers, interrupted Isahah's snore. "We'll be arriving at Qaanaaq in less than thirty minutes. Temperature is a balmy -41°C. Another day in paradise," he added.

As we approached, Qaanaaq glimmered below. It was a beacon in the darkness. The small hamlet in northern Greenland bloated with workers and immigrants fuelled by the thirst for water and the company that was there to harvest it. Ever since Aquifor began mining the ice, the town quadrupled in size. Twenty-five kilometres to the north, hidden behind a rise of rock and ice, was the Aquifor industrial complex. The production facility glowed brighter than the town itself, sending a stream of silver light straight up into the darkness.

The pilot's announcement woke Isahah. Rubbing his eyes, he jumped right into the conversation. "A helicopter will take us to the site."

From the plane, we darted to a massive tandem rotor helicopter. The blades were spinning, and the turbulence stirred the frigid air even colder, if that was at all possible. We boarded the craft where an official-looking colonel and two privates buckled their harnesses. The crew completed their pre-flight sequence while another team secured a huge skid of pipe to the undercarriage, which was being transported along with us to the site.

I had barely fastened myself in when we launched straight up. The copter jarred when the slack from the load tightened, and the pilot fired the rotors to full throttle. We inched skyward, propelling forward ever so slowly, north over a mountain of ice, leaving Qaanaaq twinkling in the distance.

The Aquifor production facility lay over a ridge, and as we surmounted the rise, a fan of incandescent light arced out like a renegade sun. I felt violated by it, the way it sliced through the astronomical twilight, washing out all but the brightest stars.

The site was five times that of Qaanaaq, a behemoth of steel and pipe. Arteries parallel and perpendicular, a sea of chaotic silver symmetry defying every notion of natural. Twenty-metre metal chimneys billowed clouds of steam and smoke, the snow around the facility taking on a brackish yellow tinge that stretched as far as the light permitted my eye to see. A city made of steel plate and girders, I-beams, scaffolds circumventing silos rising, stairs spiralling to the top, wrapping them like iron ribbons. This was a place of function, of single-minded purpose. That purpose culminating in a massive four-metre diameter catheter draining the facility, ending at a dock that leaned into the harbour, loading a colossal tanker. On the far edge of the dock was a huge dump, where three polar bears scavenged through the garbage searching for an easy meal.

The pilot set the pipe down, then landed the craft near the edge of the complex. As soon as the helicopter touched down, the colonel with his two soldiers rushed off. A uniformed Inuit motioned for Isahah and me to follow. The ground crew immediately retracted the blades, securing the helicopter with cables, while a forklift transported the cargo to the mouth of an open hangar. Wind howled, and I was grateful we were on the ground.

Entering an adjacent building, we stomped snow from our feet and passed through a series of security chambers, then entered—a tropical paradise. My senses reeled. I was back in the Guatemalan jungle, surrounded by hibiscus of every shape and colour. To my left, a huge pond thick with lilies and lotus, frogs croaking, and a waterfall spattering somewhere off behind a stand of palms.

I was in a dome, a holographic sphere of sun and sky, with clouds gently rolling by. Birds flew past and I couldn't distinguish if they were real or projections. The breeze was genuine enough, warm and shifting the trees, producing tiny ripples across the surface of the pond. I inhaled deeply and smelled the earth, the decay, the sweetness of fallen leaves and undergrowth.

"This is the common space," Isahah broke the spell. "Where you can come to unwind."

"Incredible," I said.

"Indeed. It's an engineering and biological marvel. Everything in here is exactly as you'd find it in its natural state." He pointed to a colourful toucan perched on a branch on the other side of the pond. "That's second generation. Hasn't got a clue what's going on outside."

I was speechless.

"A geothermal source pulled from under the fiord powers the entire plant. Unlimited energy for the entire facility. And this," he extended his arms, "technical wonder."

At that point, a young Inuit man clad in shorts and a T-shirt joined us.

"Are you a hologram too?" I asked.

"I'll let you be the judge," he said, and we laughed.

"This is Henry," Isahah said. "I'll leave you in his care for the rest of the tour. I have a meeting with Olivia in," he checked his watch, "twenty minutes."

"Olivia?"

"Olivia Pereira. Director of Operations. You'll meet her soon enough," and he was off, melting into the flora of the meticulous garden.

"Would you like to see more?" Henry asked.

"Maybe just my room, Henry, thank you. I'm ready for a lay down."

We exited the garden through a pergola covered with flaming red blossoms and into a corridor of stark incandescent light. Arriving at a door with my name on it, he moved in close to a device that scanned his eye, opening the door.

"There are instructions inside for you to program this," he said. "Straightforward."

The apartment was a miniature version of the park I had just left, complete with plants and a water feature trickling in the living room's corner. My luggage and computer sat beside another door.

"If you need anything, professor, just use this," he held up a small rectangular device. "It's a direct link to me."

"I'm Chulyin," I said, extending my hand.

He grabbed it and gave it a hearty shake. "Pleasure to meet you. I'll leave you now to get settled in. Dinner at six. Follow the smell. Don't forget," he picked up his device, "if you need anything at all, just use this."

The door clicked shut, and I walked into a bathroom with a huge Jacuzzi tub. Another room, next to the bathroom, was a miniature laboratory, equipped with every imaginable device and archaeological tool I might need for my investigation.

A soak in the tub and a quick nap brought me to just after five. Deciding to explore further, I retraced my way back to the not-so-common common area. The light was fading; the sun setting through the trees, angling down in a pastel yellow flush. On a stone bench beside the pool sat a tiny black woman. Absorbed in her thoughts, she never raised her head until I was directly in front of her.

She drew a deep breath through her nose and spoke, "I find the olfactory experience quite stimulating."

"Absolutely," I agreed.

"It just makes it—complete." She seemed satisfied with her assessment, then pointing to the image of the setting sun. "The visuals could use some technical adjustments, though. Are you part of the elite team?"

"I guess I am," I replied quickly. I reached out my hand, "Chulyin Nakasuk."

"Siti Okilo," she responded, not offering her hand. "No offense."

"None taken," I replied.

"They dragged me out of my lab and threw me on the plane," she said indignantly. "The sooner we resolve this nasty little problem, the sooner we can leave."

"Do you know what the problem is?"

"Not fully. But I'm working on it. Some kind of energy interfering with the computers and their ability to—compute. Like the software and programming goes in to this electronic amnesia."

"You're in I.T.?"

"Oh, lord no. Physics. Energy dynamics. What about you?"

"Archaeology. Hieroglyphics and language interpretation."

"There's a strange mix for you. Archaeology and physics," she said, then switched topics. "We have a dinner briefing in half an hour. I'm heading there now. Want to walk?"

We moved into the corridor, following the aroma to a set of frosted glass doors that whooshed open as we approached. Inside, Isahah and another man were in the middle of a heated conversation. He pressed forward on the table, visibly upset, towering over Isahah, who was leaning back, his chair on two legs. The conversation ended abruptly and Isahah immediately stood, visibly relieved by our interruption.

"Professors, welcome," he said, motioning us to take a seat at the table. "They will serve dinner shortly."

We took our place at a large oak table. "This is Atticus Day, our industrial and electrical engineer," Isahah said.

Atticus was still flustered, rubbing his hands like he was lathering soap.

From a set of swinging doors, two servers appeared carrying bowls of steaming potatoes, vegetables, and a succulent rack of lamb.

"Please," Isahah said, showing with a sweep of his hand for us to start. Siti piled two chops on her plate.

"I was hoping to have an informal chat before our meeting tomorrow," Isahah said. "Answer questions."

Siti responded. "Isn't it you that have the questions, Mr. Agloolik?"

"Yes," Isahah admitted, "we sure do."

"You're having an energy crisis and want us to solve it," she said, carving into the chops.

"Yes," Isahah returned. "Although it's a bit more complicated."

"How so? You're losing production. Money. What's more complicated than that?" she asked, chewing on a piece of meat. "Mmm. This is delicious."

"That's correct, Dr. Okilo," he said. "We want the plant operating at peak capacity. The water produced here sustains a food production facility on your continent."

"Touché," Siti responded, dabbing the corner of her mouth with a napkin. "How do you define the problem, Mr. Day? From an engineering perspective?"

"Simple." Atticus had regained his composure. "Neutralize the source that's creating the energy disruption."

"Sounds simple enough," she said, sawing off another bit of meat.

"I wish it was," he returned. "Problem is, there's no scientific reference point for this energy. It's ambiguous. The only thing we know is when our excavator contacted the stone, everything quit."

"Has anyone analyzed the composition of the rock?" I asked.

"We've tried," Atticus returned. "It defies classification."

"A comet?" Siti asked. "Or an interstellar meteor, perhaps?"

"Possibly," Atticus conceded.

"What about the runes?" I directed my question to Isahah.

"Every day, more and more of them are appearing," he answered. "Like they're growing from the rock itself."

He pulled a file of photographs from a briefcase, selecting a few, then sliding them across the table.

"They took these this morning," he said.

Welt-like distensions covered the surface of the stone, organized into blocks and sections. Another photo showed a fifteen-metre moat excavated around the monolith.

"All dug by hand," Isahah continued. "We thought we might dislodge it, but there's no bottom. The more we expose, the more prominent the runes become."

"Are those stairs?" I pointed at a rough zig-zag falling out of view into the ice from the face of the stone.

"We're hoping you can answer that for us, Dr. Nakasuk."

Siti positioned her fork beside her plate and addressed the two; "Has Aquifor considered enlisting a biologist?"

"What?" Atticus shot back.

"Mr. Agloolik suggested the runes seem to grow," she stated calmly.

"Well, not literally," Isahah interjected. "Perhaps shifting would better describe it."

"It's a bloody rock," Atticus rebuffed.

At that moment, servers emerged from the kitchen bearing a cheesecake smothered in strawberries.

"We grow the strawberries right here," Isahah said. "Our miniature food facility produces all the greens and fruit we need for the staff and employees. We even supply Qaanaaq with the surplus. Free, of course."

"Of course," Siti agreed. She wasn't finished her conversation with Atticus. "Could you please expand on what you meant by ambiguous energy?"

"That's what we need tou to answer," Atticus said.

"It's disrupting the energy flow?" Siti asked, stabbing a strawberry.

"No. Disrupting would imply a medium or a resistance. This is a vacuum where the energy simply—disappears. It has no effect on anything biological. Our doctor has been monitoring all personnel in and out of the affected area. Nothing detrimental. Even the polar bears. A family strolled through the restricted area this morning. The bears don't seem to listen," and he smiled for the first time.

"Case in point for a biological perspective, Mr. Day."

Isahah glanced at his watch. "Goodness, it's after 10. Let's finish this off for now. Olivia will provide more details in the morning."

"One more question," Siti said as we rose from our chairs. "Might I get a piece of that cake to go?"

Atticus launched himself out of the room with Isahah close behind. Siti and I strolled back through the corridor and into the common area, which was glistening silver from a huge full moon towering above. Our apartments were next to each other and just before she entered, she turned and said, "Mr. Agloolik is being deceptive."

I turned my eye from the scanner and gave her my attention.

"Mr. Day is too, but it doesn't set well with him. I feel truth from you," Siti said, opening the door to her apartment. "I'll see you in the morning."

"Enjoy your cheesecake," I said, and the door snapped shut behind her.

I plunked myself on the couch and lowered the lights.

Of course, Isahah was a liar. Lying was a basic strategy for corporate survival. And Atticus? There was no sense of politics in him, so his lies would be solely to further his own objectives.

Then me. What truth could this strange black woman be feeling from me? And why was I feeling like a charlatan? Something stirred inside me. I was less than honourable. A liar, not so much by design like Isahah, or fear like Atticus, but a liar by omission. Hiding my raw truth under the mask of all the things projected to be me. My titles, labels. Archaeologist. Expert. Explorer and adventurer, there for all to see, except for this unexcavated sense of fear that I refused to exhume.

(The feeling.)

No, Siti, you had it wrong. I am a liar. A manipulator of truth. My truth. Not with things or the science of the things I do, but in the art of who I project to be.

* * *

Olivia never showed up for our meeting the next morning. Instead, Isahah greeted us with an armful of documents.

"Please read carefully through the briefs and we will convene back here at 1900 hours," he said.

Siti and Atticus gathered their dossiers and left without a word. I sat and stared at him. I wanted to eat him alive.

"Is that it?" I asked with an obvious edge.

"For now," he said without looking up.

"Will the commandant be attending?"

"What are you so angry about, Dr. Nakasuk?"

"How much time have you got?"

"You've had a chip on your shoulder from the minute you opened your door in Pang."

"Oh, it's been there longer than that."

"You have a tremendous opportunity to make a mark here."

"What's that Isahah? Solve Aquifor's problems?"

He shook his head. "You don't get it," and closed his briefcase.

"What don't I get?"

"Opportunity. Right in front of your face."

"Like the opportunity you're taking? You want me to be a peon like you?"

"There's no use talking to you," and he started for the door.

"That's right. Truth hurts. You can play the corporate big shot as much as you like. But you're just an Inuit flunky as far as they're concerned."

He stopped in his tracks. "Is that what you think I am? A flunky?"

"That's what you are. Admit it or not."

He turned and faced me squarely. The smile had washed from his face and his jaw clenched. "You're no different from me, my dear. If that's what I am, then that makes you one too. Flunky for hire. Nothing more. Nothing less."

"At least my integrity is intact."

He laughed. "Really? You're delusional. You think because you left Pang behind, because you learned something about broken pots, you excuse yourself from who you are?"

"And who am I, Isahah?"

"An Inuit flunky. Just like me."

"You're a traitor. Everything you do here betrays what you call Inuit."

"And what makes you so different?"

"I'm nobody's peon."

"Yet here you are. I'm not interested in convincing you what you are or what you're not." He walked toward the door without turning. "Read the brief. Back here. 1900 sharp."

I stormed into the common area where Siti was sitting on the same bench, leafing through her brief. I attempted to blow past, but she looked up, pointing to the folder in my hand. "At least yours is nice and thin," she said, expressionless.

"I guess. You think they could have given us this last night."

"Thank goodness I'm a fast reader." She flipped through what looked like a hundred pages of mathematical equations.

"I'm ready to pack this in. Never wanted to come in the first place."

"Why did you?"

I hesitated, then plunked myself beside her. "Professional interests."

"I'm here because they offered me an astronomical sum of money. Money I can use to fund the research I'm truly interested in." She faced me and smiled. "I couldn't care less about Aquifor's problems. Other than it being an intriguing physics conundrum. I'd be sad if you left. I like you."

"I'm not leaving. They gave me a pile of money too."

"What's the trade-off for you, Dr. Nakasuk?"

"What do you mean?"

"There're hundreds of mathematical equations in here," she tapped on the folder, "and they all have to balance. That's what this is. Being balanced. The trade-off. Giving them what they want and making sure I meet my own needs."

"If you have that equation, please share it."

"I am right now," she said, standing. "Let's be ready for our precious Olivia. The sooner we can balance this mess, the sooner we can leave."

We walked back to our apartments and just before she entered, she said, "There's more going on here, Dr. Nakasuk, than what meets the eye. More for you than me. All that's required of me is to solve a little energy problem. You have a deeper mystery. One far more interesting than mine." Her eyes danced. "Or maybe I'm just a crazy black woman from Zimbabwe."

Before I could say a word, she vanished behind her apartment door.

The seventeen pages of my brief took me less than fifteen minutes to read. I was to catalogue and photograph the site, something any third-year student could accomplish. My words splashed back in my face. I was a flunky too, verified by the non-disclosure clause at the end of the brief. Aquifor would be the sole proprietor of all intellectual material collected and surmised from the course of my investigation. If violated, funding to the university would cease and all personal payments to me revoked.

How do I balance this equation, Dr. Okilo?

* * *

When we assembled in the conference room, another man had joined the party. He was weather-beaten, craggy as the island rock, not young, but I could see there was plenty of strength in him. His hands were bear paws, thick and calloused. On his left, the pinkie was entirely missing and his ring finger reduced to a stub, protruding out, imagining they were helping the other two as he twisted the cap from a Perrier bottle. I assessed this man would not be afraid of anything in the natural world, but here he fidgeted like a schoolboy in detention.

At 19:10, my anxiety heightened, and I was about to voice my dissatisfaction when a large screen flickered to life. A woman, immaculately coiffed, peered down on us.

She began: "Good evening. My name is Olivia Pereira." She smiled, unveiling her brilliant white teeth. "I'm the regional manager of our operation here in Qaanaaq. Please tell me your accommodations are suitable and you have taken the time to read the briefs Mr. Agloolik gave you this morning." Not expecting a response, she continued, "We have approximately ten days of reserve water at the African site. If production is not up and running within the next five days, the entire yield at our greenhouse in Layounne will be lost. Time is of the essence. We've organized special teams to help familiarize you with specifics. We're also expecting some additional support for your team, Dr. Okilo, who will fly in tomorrow."

The image switched on the screen, and we were viewing the site. "This is a live shot of the harvest area," Olivia continued. "The crews you see are currently rigging chains to the harvester so we can attempt to pull it away from that," a red arrow appearing, highlighting a black domed protrusion poking through the ice surface.

"I'd also like to introduce Ove Hoj, our Danish attaché in Greenland. Dr. Hoj is also the resident glaciologist and an essential member of our Aquifor team."

Ove sat frozen in his chair, hands folded in his lap, staring over our heads.

A distraction came to her from off-camera. She muted the sound and was back with us in seconds. "Seems I have to cut our meeting short. Does anyone have questions about your objectives?"

I spoke—"What's Aquifor's intent regarding the preservation of the site?"

She addressed Isahah, "Did you speak to professor Nakasuk about this?"

"Yes. We had a conversation earlier this afternoon," Isahah said.

"Cataloguing and photographing," Olivia addressed me. "Our intention is to maintain the integrity of the site."

"What does that mean? Maintain the integrity of the site?" There was an edge in my tone even I could hear.

Her eyebrow twitched. "Our immediate concern is getting the facility operational. Perhaps tomorrow, after your field visit, you'll be able to supply us with some data that can help answer that specific concern." Her teeth glistened, then her pixels vanished into the black void of the screen.

* * *

The world is flat.

I was dreaming.

In it, I was at the same meeting we had that evening. Olivia's briefing, all the same players, same room down to the minutest detail, Olivia's twitching eyebrow, Siti fiddling with her pen. Identical except for the topic. They were all adamant that the world was flat and I was the only detractor. I bolted upright when Olivia came through the TV screen and hollered in my face—'the world is flat!'

6:47. I had ten minutes to get to the cargo bay.

I slammed my feet into my boots and zipped up my coat. What if Copernicus was wrong? All science for nought, because someone found some corners to the world. Would it really matter? Flat or round? What if Olivia was right? It didn't seem possible what existed on the other side of the vacuum sealed door of this luxury apartment. A created paradise, perfect, yet so—falsified.

(This is the flat world.)

I tightened my boots and made my way to the cargo bay and the driver, who would escort me to the site.

Twenty minutes later, Roscoe Valdez delivered me to ground zero. A strapping 40-year-old originally from San Francisco, he was an amateur artist and a self-professed environmentalist, a fact he kept close to his chest. He whispered this last bit of information to me as if the vehicle had ears; the environment wasn't in the top ten concerns for Aquifor. Roscoe was an open book on the players and the corporate dynamics that drove them. His background was in people management, which, he also whispered, made him a bit of an armchair psychologist.

"This place. It's a petri dish for dysfunctional human behaviour," he shared. "It's amazing what you can learn if you keep your ears open and your mouth shut."

We rolled up to the perimeter of light. I felt like a predator on the hunt—not in the way of killing, but on the approach. Focussed and single-minded. I thought about Fearney and his story about wanting to be a hare. Unnoticed in stillness. I felt that here, veiled in its own quietude, something disguised in the stillness, my eyes powerless to discriminate its presence.

We stepped into the incandescence and walked toward the face of the glacier. It had a sullied off-green tinge, and I wasn't sure if it resulted from the unnatural lighting or some element that was infused within the ice itself. As we approached, the scale of the disabled ice harvesters became apparent. A colossal metal gear towering ten metres above us, a steel tread hanging limp and lifeless from its rusted cogs. Massive iron mandibles hung useless against the dome of the black rock that halted its progress.

"We excavate the ice in bites," he said. "Like strip mining. Only we go forward rather than down."

I looked into the trench dug around the structure. "How deep is this?"

"At least twenty metres to bedrock. Or that's what our last radar mapping showed before our instrumentation conked out."

He turned away from the glacier, fanning out his arm to a multitude of red flags scattered across the site. "The markers are fragments of that," and he pointed back to the stone. Roscoe had removed his hood and loosened the collar of his parka.

"Where's the wind?" I asked.

"Not here," he said. "We're in the eye of a hurricane."

(I'm not the predator. I'm the prey.)

My awareness shifted to my feet, a green lustre curling around my boots. Roscoe had vanished but his voice droned on somewhere in a lazy haze. I was inside a lens, my perceptual competence enhanced, giving me the ability to view from either side—a house of mirrors—reflecting on myself. Anun had taken me to a carnival on our trip to Halifax, and I remembered marvelling at my twisted shapes in the warped glass, duplicating into outlandish boundlessness. Except here, there were others with me, undetectable behind a veneer vested somewhere in the essence of the lens.

"Professor Nakasuk? Are you okay?"

"Yes," I stuttered back. "You were saying?"

"We've tagged several artifacts. But the biggest is right there," pointing at the solitary black monolith.

"What are we waiting for? Let's look," and we started our descent into the gully surrounding the stone.

13. THE ZIGGURAT

I felt as if I had entered a crypt. A sacred space that had lain dormant for a time I could not possibly comprehend, the same feeling I had entering the cave at Rekeiz Lemgasem.

But this was no crypt. This was a crucible, stirring and alive. I could hear it, tap, tap, tapping, an inquisitive beak cracking its eggshell from the inside, keen to join the world beyond. Pinpricks of heat permeated my coat like sunbeams concentrated through a magnifying glass. The sensation was not uncomfortable. In fact, it was quite pleasant.

With that physicality came a contradictory sadness, which intensified as I moved closer to the structure. Bunny. She was there, with me, more than a story from Aanaq or a projection of my fancy. Grief, harsh and remorseful. Then I recognized it was not my feeling of losing her, but her sadness towards me, seeing me now as a woman, the woman I'd grown to be.

Yet the energy was more than the just essence of my mother. It was wide, wider than my consciousness could assimilate, past the periphery of familiarity. I faced the dome. It was ten meters in diameter, rising five meters above the surface of the ice, the front portion exposed while the rest remained locked within the grip of the glacier.

Touch me.

I removed my gloves. There was an unnatural smoothness to it. Satin, neither hot nor cold. It seemed manufactured more than natural, metallic, but certainly not any kind of metal I was familiar with. I stroked the surface and there was a velvety sheen to it that left a wake like a boat does on the surface of a glassy sea. Crimson handprints exploded in my mind and I sensed them reaching up for me from inside the—ziggurat.

This was no rock. This was a temple, a sacred monument buried beneath a kilometre of ice, holding its secrets for uncountable aeons. My fingers discerned the structure, revealing its inner sanctum as if I had passed through a doorway now unlocked into a portico of memories. Memories not mine, but of the souls and hands reaching up to me, the builders and inhabitants of this undiscovered place. What I thought were stairs in the photograph Isahah had shown me earlier were a series of terraced rings that circled the ziggurat, culminating in a single point pressing the skin of my palm. The Ziggurat of Ur flashed into my mind, a shrine for the gods, rising to the heavens, and here I was at the pinnacle. Stepping back, I disconnected from the ziggurat.

"Look at this," Roscoe called, pointing to a stone identified with a marker. All along the surface were columns of embossed runes.

"Hieroglyphics," I said.

"Not my point. I've been out here every day sketching them. Those markings. They weren't here yesterday."

"Could you be mistaking the sample?"

"Impossible. I've got a photographic memory," he tapped his temple. "One-thirty-eight," he recited the number on the red flag. "We'll check my catalogue when we get back to the vehicle."

"What about the others?"

"Let's look," and we scrambled from the moat. Scouting the site, we discovered the same results.

"How many markers?"

"Almost two hundred."

"I want to talk to Dr. Okilo about this," I said. "Let's document these runes and get back to see if we can come up with something comparative."

When we returned to the facility, Roscoe excused himself to get to a meeting, and I headed back to my quarters. He had given me his drawings, along with a set of aerial photos taken a week prior. I spread them on the floor.

From the photographs, I noticed a pair of concentric rings radiating from the ziggurat. I took a pencil and connected the red flags and there were two inclinations circuiting the dome. I extended the trajectory into the ice behind the unexposed portion of the ziggurat and they formed perfect elliptical orbits.

Rekeiz Lemgasem. The talisman from the old woman. Rummaging through my knapsack, I grabbed it, a mild heat penetrating my fingers. The smoothness. I rolled the piece in my hand, then took it to the photo, rotating it to see if the impressions on the pewter ornament lined up with the stones in the aerial image. Placing the talisman over the dome in the photograph, I saw it. The two indentations in the pewter disc aligned exactly with the red flags, the nipple on the top of the amulet, the ziggurat. One impression was visible in the exposed section of the site, the other hidden behind the face of the glacier, perhaps ten metres beyond the wall of ice.

A gentle knock on my door. It was Siti.

"Am I disturbing you?" she asked.

"Of course not. I was just doing some homework. Come in. Excuse the chaos," I said, pointing to the photographs and notes strewn about the floor.

"I saw you today," she said. "At the monolith. I was passing by the security area that monitors the site. You were caressing the stone. What were you doing?"

My cheeks flushed. "Examining it."

"How did you feel when you touched it?"

"What's that got to do with anything?"

"Maybe nothing. Maybe everything."

"It was smooth. Like velvet."

"That wasn't my question."

I roiled. "Feeling? I don't know. Strange. Curious."

"I thought you might be praying."

"Praying? Hardly. This doesn't sound like a scientific inquiry."

"Oh, but it is. Humour me. Tell me how you felt."

I sighed. "It was like gravity. Tugging at me. Pulling me toward it. Gravity with light and…"

"Life?" She finished my sentence.

"Yes," I consented. "It wanted me to be a part of it."

"Like it possessed consciousness?"

"Yes. And this." I pulled up my sleeves and exposed my forearms. "I've been scratching since I got back. Then these showed up." On my wrists, thin welts ridged along my skin, replicas of rune one-thirty-eight Roscoe had pointed out earlier. "I felt like I was being watched. Observed."

"Perhaps you were." She leaned forward in her chair. "While I was watching, a charge of blue energy shot straight up from the dome. Then a pulse, like the aftershock from an earthquake, rippled out from the centre."

"Was any of it recorded?"

"I don't know. But I doubt it."

"What about the security personnel?"

"No reaction. It was as if they didn't see it. Let me rephrase that. I don't think they're capable. I want you to consider something. Something so preposterous it bends logic. What if you are the catalyst to neutralize the energy disruption? What if," and she tapped her finger on the photo of the dome, "that has been waiting for you to channel its power? And the only way that power can express itself is through our biology? Your biology? The biology of who and what we are as humans?

"What if what we are trying to quantify can't be measured in magnetic fields or mathematical equations? What if our humanness is the verification, the formula to solve Aquifor's energy problem? Every one of us knows love and sadness and joy exist. We don't need a machine to understand that.

"As a physicist, I can tell you quantifying unmeasureables is a slippery task. It's time we look beyond the blinders Mr. Newton imposed on us. Beyond the realm of conventional scientific protocol that buried human wonder in a test tube of elements and reactions.

"Don't get me wrong; I'm not dismissing the value of Isaac Newton. Or all the others following him. It's simply time for a new perspective. One that integrates human experience with the formula, whether or not we can measure it.

"It's the ether that holds everything together. Space. The container. Our platform of perception. My ability, your ability to see, to connect, to join in a way we have never been capable of doing before. A contorted reality our minds were neither ready nor capable of grasping. Until now."

"I grew up in twisted logic," I said. "My grandmother was a shaman."

"How wonderful," clapping her hands together.

"She would tell you I'm a shaman, too."

"Are you?"

"If I am, it's certainly not by choice."

"Spiritual gifts rarely are. Would you like to know the real reason I'm here?"

"Because you love the climate?"

"To conduct an experiment. To prove a hypothesis I've been working on for, it seems, my whole life.

"Electrogenetics. Biology and physics combined in a new paradigm of science. It requires a leap of faith, something that the established scientific community resists.

"I was attending a conference in Singapore on string theory and particle astrophysics when I met Miatzo Kai. At dinner, our conversation shifted to her research studying brain anomalies in clairvoyant subjects. I was being professionally polite, but when I heard 'psychic phenomenon' and 'the brain's capacity to transmit cosmic signatures' in the same sentence, my ears perked up. My physics training told me the celestial cacophony of cosmic radiation was a one-way street. From out there," she pointed to the ceiling, "to down here. It never occurred to me biology could alter the direction of transmission.

"Dr. Kai explained that while performing brain scans on her telepathic subjects, she identified atypical energy emanating from their hippocampus. MRI analysis revealed a tiny bubble attached to the anterior portion of the hippocampus present in all her participants. Dr. Kai also detected microscopic fibres radiating from the node into the prefrontal cortex and brain stem. 'I felt like I'd just pried open an oyster', she said, 'finding a beautiful pearl inside.' That's what she called it. The pearl node."

As Siti spoke, I felt myself fading into the space of the apartment. Like I had become a spider, inconspicuous in the corner, eavesdropping on the conversation. I was observing these two women through a set of compound eyes, multiple images of the same room. Siti's voice resonated from each hexagonal block, echoing through a thousand tubes, then collected in a single crystal clarity, amplifying both sound and meaning. I touched the back of my hand to confirm I was still there.

"We don't know how or why, but the development of this pearl node triggers an ability to communicate in forms beyond language," she continued. "Pictures. Visuals. Like the runes. And the PNs—that's what we call subjects with pearl nodes—can communicate at a rudimentary level, regardless of their native language.

"About five years before I met Dr. Kai, I was researching galactic muon and black particle emissions. Recording incoming cosmic radiation is routine. But we started detecting transmissions originating right here on Earth. My team couldn't make heads nor tails of it; when we tried to pinpoint the geographical locations, they would fluctuate. When Dr. Kai and I began correlating our individual data, we came up with some astounding observations. The pulse gradations conformed with heightened telepathic activity in Dr. Kai's subjects. I had made the assumption the energy was dark matter noise. Imagine our surprise when we discovered the source of the radiation was being transmitted from the PNs themselves.

"Measuring muon activity is one thing. Correlating mental connections between the PNs is another. Because there is no way to verify PN information, other than what they say they experience, their data is discounted. The problem augments in the scientific community's resistance to include psychic phenomenon as tangible evidence. With Dr. Kai's discovery of the pearl node, we have a biological reference point where we can launch our investigation into these energy fluctuations.

"There was a mammoth muon flux transmitting from Qaanaaq the day Aquifor lost power. Which brings me to where we are now. And you."

Siti leaned in. "The moment you touched that dome, a burst of PN neural activity erupted in every location we are conducting our tests. London. Montreal. Capetown. Tokyo. Every single PN reported a powerful rush of, let me call it, visual insight. Connection. Like a string of lights suddenly being switched on. And here's the thing. Every one of them reported seeing these."

She showed me a series of drawings replicating the runes Roscoe and I had observed earlier that morning.

"Look familiar?" she asked, a huge grin on her face.

A siren blared, rocking us from our discussion. In the corridor, Atticus sprinted toward the briefing room.

"What's going on?" I hollered.

"Get to the conference room. Now." And he disappeared around the corner.

Siti and I hustled to the conference room where Atticus had already joined Isahah and Ove. Seconds later, Olivia marched in with four lieutenants.

"We have a development at the site that requires immediate attention." She turned to one of her underlings, "Get someone to deactivate that bloody alarm," and he rushed from the room. The lights dimmed, and the wall became a screen showing multiple vantage points of the ziggurat. "Camera six," she snapped, and the wall was a single image of what appeared to be an undulating wall of water.

"Zoom in." The camera obeyed, narrowing on the ziggurat. It was glowing a brilliant orange.

"What is that?" she asked Siti directly.

"Fascinating," Siti exclaimed, perched on the edge of her chair.

"No doubt," Olivia said, unimpressed. "Perhaps you could offer something a bit more concrete? Camera three," and the screen switched, showing the entire face of the glacier.

My visit that morning allowed me to calculate the incredible scale of what I was witnessing. Stretching out approximately half a kilometre on either side of the ziggurat, the glacier was a shimmering aqua wall, transparent as if the ice had melted and was being possessed by an invisible harness holding it at bay.

"Anything at this point is pure speculation." Siti said.

"Then speculate," Olivia growled. "If that thing lets loose, it will wash everything, including us, into the fiord."

"That's assuming what we're looking at is water," I said.

"Okay, Dr. Nakasuk. What else might it be?" Olivia asked.

"Energy."

"Brilliant," she said, waiting. "Is there more?" then turning to Isahah. "Make preparations to evacuate all nonessential personnel."

"Can we get to the top so I can look from a different perspective?" Ove piped in.

"Assemble a team." Olivia shot back.

Ove bolted to the door, calling back to Atticus, "Come with me," and they vanished from the room.

Olivia turned to Siti. "I need more than conjecture, Dr. Okilo. Get me some answers."

Then to Isahah, "Back in my office. I've got the Danish Government breathing down my neck. And Dr. Nakasuk. I'm not sure what happened out there this morning, but this developed after your serenade with that thing. Give me a full report by 4 p.m."

"Dr. Nakasuk's expertise might better serve our purpose if she assists me," Siti interjected. "Deciphering these runes may help us solve the problem."

"Get on it," Olivia said, irritated. "My office. Five minutes," she rifled at Isahah, then flashed through the door.

As we rushed back through the corridor to our apartments, Siti said, "It's an illusion. I'll bet that thing is as solid as a rock."

* * *

By the time Siti and I met in the automotive compound, the evacuation was in full swing. Aquifor personnel were being collected and housed in the warehouse building until the helicopters returned from Qaanaaq for their second wave of evacuees. With the copters gone and the processing plant shut down, an eerie calm invaded the space, conquering the industrial clatter.

"Ready?" Siti snapped me out of my daydream. I jumped behind the wheel and fired the ignition.

"These runes. This event. You. They're all connected," she spoke with controlled conviction.

"You sound like my Aanaq with a physics doctorate." I attempted humour.

"You know a slinky?" she asked.

"Yes."

"It's like that. This energy. You start at the top of the stairs, flip it down to the next step and watch it go. Only this is a cosmic slinky, already in its own perpetual motion. An immaculate energy process independent of traditional laws of mathematics or physics. In fact, this slinky creates its own energy and can arc," she fanned her arm, "in space and whenever it lands, it creates a footprint or impression, duplicating the energy it brought with it."

She turned to me nonchalantly. "The signature of life. Ricocheting across the cosmos, stamping its feet wherever it lands. The footprint of— some might call it God. Right here at the edge of the ice. Remember the muon energy I spoke about? I would guess muons are pouring from you like water through a sluice."

My eyes were tunnels, and I squeezed my focus to the headlamps pulling me forward. Ahead, the spectacle we had witnessed on the screen towered like a captive sea in an aquarium. We pulled up to the perimeter of lights.

"I need them to shut down the lights," I said.

Siti picked up the microphone. "This is Dr. Okilo. I need the lights extinguished at the site."

Pause, then a staccato voice. "Did you say douse the lights?"

"Correct."

"I'll need to get clearance," the voice said.

"Turn out the goddam lights!" I hollered

Siti looked at me, amused, then compressed the microphone's transmit button. "I will take full responsibility for the lights. Shut them down, please."

"I just need—the night," I stammered, and in the next instant had it, the Arctic opacity swallowing the ruthless infusion of incandescent light.

I was awestruck. Spectacular night skies, aurora borealis, had danced above me my entire life. But this? It was outside the reckoning of my wildest imagination. Instead of above, this phenomenon lapped at my feet. An island of undulating transparency; ice or water, but neither. Stones from eons passed suspended in its invisible grip, and the visual clarity was unnerving, defying a firmness that could support the weight of a single feather.

"It's solid," Siti acknowledged, tapping her boot on the material. "Just like I said. We can walk on it."

I stepped cautiously, fearing I might plunge to the bedrock below. What was ice the day before was now a soup of aquamarine particles, the stones with markers blushing orange like embers. Edging forward, I slid my foot on to the elastic oscillation, the transparent material giving me serious vertigo.

We padded toward the dome. Whether it was a law of science or an indelible urge, the ziggurat dragged me forward with immutable gravity. It glowed brighter, like a log from which smaller embers had burst. As we approached, the scale became apparent. It was massive. Tracing the structure from peak to floor, it was smooth as far as I could tell, planted firmly into the island's core. If it was indeed an asteroid or a piece of extraterrestrial debris, it must have struck with great impact; the island's bedrock splayed out in a splash of hardened lava that cradled the foundation of the ziggurat.

"I feel like a spider walking on a web," I called to Siti. Silver threads sprayed when my foot touched down, connecting to the ziggurat. The two satellites orbiting the dome floated in the substance, offering a three-dimensional view, the one imbedded in the glacier fully visible and slightly larger than the other exposed on the plain.

Siti arrived at the dome ten paces ahead. Reaching out, she pressed her fingers to it, penetrating, and she pushed deeper, plunging her arm up to her shoulder. Looking down at her feet, she giggled like a schoolgirl. "What's holding us up?"

"You're the physicist. You tell me."

I joined her, immersing both my arms into the ghostly jelly. It was warm and when I retracted, I expected my coat and arm to be soaked. Instead, motes of green exploded from my jacket and hands.

"Aksarnirq," I said.

"What?"

"Aksarnirq. Spirits. Sky dwellers. An Inuit legend about the aurora borealis." I rolled my hands, hoping my fingers might find something concrete I could translate into words.

"This is beyond aurora borealis," Siti said.

Suddenly, the search lights blared back to life. The glacial wall shimmered and the particles that danced around us dematerialized. Three vehicles roared up to the perimeter.

A voice bellowed from a loudspeaker. "Dr. Okilo. Dr. Nakasuk. Return immediately." It was Olivia.

"They won't come out here after us," I said.

"Maybe they can't," Siti offered.

I looked at her, puzzled. "What do you mean?"

"Maybe this energy is selective. It likes us better than them."

I laughed and took a deep breath. "We better do what the princess wants. She might start shooting next."

Incensed, Olivia launched into us. "What the hell are you two trying to prove?"

"The runes," I said. "They're an instruction manual."

"What?"

"They're cosmic equations," I continued. "But they translate into unfamiliar concepts that Dr. Okilo needs to examine back in the lab." I had pocketed a fragment and held it out to Olivia. "See that rune? It's consistent with every fragment and the entire monolith is covered with them. They're dividing into fractals."

Siti jumped in. "I need to run this data through the computer. Could we hurry this along?"

"We need to evacuate pronto," Olivia sputtered. "Reykjavik has notified us of seismic activity right under our feet. We're lifting everyone to Qaanaaq."

"Impossible," I shot back. "How the hell can we make an assessment from forty kilometres away?"

"Not my issue. I don't want dead scientists on my plate. Dr. Okilo, come with me. Now that you've had some intimate time with that thing, I'd welcome your scientific assessment."

They chauffeured me directly me to the helipad. I climbed in and asked the pilot, "What's going on?"

"Don't ask me," he said. "I just drive the bus. Strap yourself in."

As we lifted off, I watched Olivia and Siti enter the complex. From above, the ziggurat was a star swimming in its own earthbound universe. I could see the other two satellites hidden under the ice, completing the miniature solar system. Ascending over the glacier's lip, we flew into a cloud of aqua particles permeating the helicopter. The pilot was oblivious, adjusting his instruments as they flitted about his head.

I looked down and at the edge of the glacier and I saw five figures camped under a dim glow of their own light. Atticus and Ove Hoj with three attendants.

"Fifteen minutes to Qaanaaq," he announced. "Looks like we got some wind coming our way."

14. A STORM BLOWS IN

Roscoe greeted me when we touched down in Qaanaaq. "This is a logistics nightmare," he said as I climbed into the vehicle. "They're packed into the church and the museum like bloody sardines. You're one of the lucky ones. Ove has arranged for you to stay with one of the locals."

"Locals?" I said.

"You know what I mean. Inuit."

"Yes," I said. "I know what you mean."

Roscoe was right about one thing. Qaanaaq was totally unprepared for the influx of humanity spilling in from Aquifor's industrial complex. Troupes of workers roamed the streets like truant school children.

We stopped in front of a battered shanty. "This is it," Roscoe said. "I have to get back to the zoo. Supplies coming in from our stores and I got to figure out where to put them."

I tapped on the door and a raspy voice directed me to enter. Inside, the darkness was thicker than the one I'd just vacated. A pungent smell of seal oil and I followed the sound of humming somewhere in the darkness. Beside a yellow glimmer, a quilliq flickered, its dim ribbon dissecting across his lap. Above, his torso melted into shade.

From the darkness, a voice. "Weathers' changing."

"Yes."

"You're Mary Nakasuk's granddaughter."

"I am. You know my Aanaq?"

He shifted in his chair, the light catching him for an instant. "She helped me once."

"You're from Baffin?"

"No," he responded. "But I visited there. Many years ago. Are you shaman?"

"No. I'm an archaeologist."

"Too bad. We need shaman here." His crooked finger pointed out the window. "See?"

I moved closer and from beyond the ice cap, a dance of green shot straight up into the sky.

"There's much misfortune. Our ancestors are speaking, but nobody listens." With great effort, he rose from the chair. "Would you like tea?"

"No. Thank you." I glanced at my watch and it was just after 1 a.m. "But I would love to close my eyes."

"There," he pointed to a cot barely visible in the corner.

"What do they call you?" I asked as I settled on the bunk.

"Taktut," he said. "There's a quilliq by your bed. With matches. For when you wake up." His voice drifted, as did I, into a dreamless sleep.

* * *

The walls quivered with the force of the wind. In the corner, an ancient oil heater moaned, fighting back the deep freeze breaching every chink of the structure. A yellow glow flickered on the floor from the furnace burners. I clenched the blanket tight under my chin, salvaging every calorie of body heat.

(Yellow eyes.)

I bolted up, groping for the matches, lighting the quilliq.

"Who visits you?" Taktut's voice drifted from the chair.

(Has he been sitting there all night?)

"I was dreaming," I deflected.

"It startled you."

"It was a memory."

"Sometimes memories cause problems," he affirmed. "Dreams can solve them."

Something about the old man disarmed me. "Raven. I was dreaming about Raven. I had visions when I was a little girl."

"Is Raven your tuurngaq?"

"My Aanaq believed so."

"Do you?"

"Sometimes I wish I did."

"That you believed? Or that Raven was your tuurngaq?"

"Both. I could use all the help I can get."

"Yes," he agreed, waving toward the window, the stream of green light obscured by a siege of horizontal snow. "The water people. They have caused great disturbance. Are you here to fix that?"

I was grateful for the shift in conversation. "The disturbance, yes. The water people?" I shrugged. "Not sure what I can do about them."

"Raven could help."

"Maybe," I returned delicately.

"Yes. We need shaman," he said, nodding.

A knock at the door. I opened it to a blast of snow and Isahah hollering against the wind. "Meet us at the church as soon as you can."

As I laced up my boots, I watched Taktut fade into the shadow, his face veiled behind the thin edge of darkness that separated him from the yellow glow of the quilliq. I pulled the door shut and made my way to the church.

When I arrived, I glanced through the crowd and spotted Siti, relieved to see her.

"When did you get here?" I asked.

"Last night. I thought the copter was going to end up in the sea." Then she said, "Two people died at the site yesterday."

"What?"

"We'll talk later."

Roscoe stewarded us to a narrow staircase that ended in the rector's office at the top. Twenty of us crammed in, Ove and Atticus, Isahah directing traffic and Olivia looking uncomfortable in the tight space, but as official as ever.

"Before we begin, let me report we've had a mishap at the site," Olivia launched right in. "Two of our personnel were killed yesterday. Right now, it's uncertain what happened. I can tell you they were both critically burned. Mr. Agloolik will give you the details as far as we know. Please." Olivia passed the podium to Isahah.

Isahah offered his best game face. "We suspect there was an energy surge from the structure that inflicted their injuries. We're not sure why they were near the site itself. They had left in the morning to take some last-minute ice samples outside the perimeter of the energy anomaly. We'll be sending their—uh—remains to Nuuk when the storm subsides for an autopsy."

Olivia interjected. "We're deeply saddened by this event. It does, however, give us greater resolve to get the situation under control."

"Who were they?" Ove asked.

"Lorenzo Flores. A colleague of mine from Brazil. And Kirsten Húnsdóttir. Our chemical engineer."

Ove sat still as granite.

Olivia continued, "We'll know more once this storm quiets down. Communications are out. And it seems conditions at the site are stabilizing."

"Stabilizing?" Ove stupefied by her comment. "Two people are dead. How is that stable?"

"I'm referring to the structure," Olivia shot back.

"The energy anomaly is subsiding," Isahah interjected. "It's returning to its original state."

"Nothing is stable," Ove countered. "The ice, or whatever it is you want to call it, is in constant flux." He turned to Atticus. "Tell them."

Atticus shifted in his seat. "There's room for interpretation," he tiptoed around Ove's call for backup. "For the moment, it seems to be contained."

Ove sneered at Atticus. "Bloody coward. I'd like to hear from the physicist."

"You are both correct. To a degree," Siti said. "The energy is certainly in transition. And for the moment is in temporary stasis, the operative word being temporary. Mr. Hoj and Ms. Pereira, I'm sorry for the loss of your colleagues. A terrible tragedy. I'm curious, Mr. Agloolik. You said a surge from the ziggurat caused their deaths?"

"Conjecture only," Isahah returned. "We found them ten metres from the—what did you call it?"

"A ziggurat."

"Yes, the ziggurat."

"Do we have security footage?" Siti pressed.

"Unfortunately, no. The entire network crashed an hour before."
"That is unfortunate, Mr. Day. Do you recall our conversation from our first evening?"

"Which part?" Atticus asked.

"About recruiting a biologist."

Atticus bristled. "I recall."

Then she dropped the bomb. "I believe we're dealing with a living entity. Correction. Entities."

"Ridiculous," Atticus retorted, turning to Olivia. "Are we going to listen to this? How is this kind of bullshit solving our issue?"

"Bravo!" Ove shouted. "Let the scientist speak."

"This isn't science," Atticus rebutted. "This is delusional."

"That's an interesting theory, Dr. Okilo," Olivia interjected. "But I have to echo Mr. Day on this."

Siti was unphased. "These are drawings produced by a global network of telepaths we have been monitoring for over five years. The moment Dr. Nakasuk connected with the ziggurat, our science team recorded these images. Exact replicas of this," and she slid Roscoe's sketch of the rune from two days earlier to Olivia.

"Coupled with that," she continued, "their telepathic connection increased exponentially the day your excavator crashed into the dome, concurrent with a massive burst of muons discharging from the ziggurat. An aberration, Mr. Day, since we here on Earth only receive muon particles from the cosmos. These are being transmitted."

"What are the little voices telling you, Dr. Okilo?" Atticus mocked.

"That whatever your excavator ignited is trying to communicate with us. Through the runes."

He shook his head and mumbled, "Blow the goddam thing out of the way."

"There's the solution," I said. "If we don't understand it, blow it up."

Atticus sneered. "What's your contribution to all this, Dr. Nakasuk? Should we make a pet out of it?"

I ignored his comment. "Dr. Okilo is right. The answer to your energy problem is interpreting the runes."

Olivia interjected. "Enough. I'm going to give you two forty-eight hours once the storm dissipates. In the meantime, I want two teams organized. Okilo and Nakasuk on one. Mr Hoj on the other. As soon as the weather breaks, you two," and she pointed at us, "will be on a chopper back to the site. Mr Hoj, I want you to analyze the ice beyond this energy peculiarity. Find us a new place to dig. If it's safe, we continue harvesting. Mr. Agloolik will use this as his office. If you have any further questions, please refer to him." She weaved through the crowd and disappeared down the stairs.

"We need to talk," Siti said.

"I'm staying at an elder's house on the edge of town. We can go there."

The wind was howling, driving against us, pellets jabbing our faces like hypodermic needles. Siti covered herself and clung to my coat as I navigated back to Taktut's. When we arrived, he was in the kitchen making tea.

"Taktut, this is my colleague, Dr. Okilo. Would you mind if we shared your kitchen?"

"I haven't had the pleasure of two women for some time," he grinned toothless.

He delivered our tea, then returned to his seat by the window. "What people do you come from?" he asked Siti.

"I am Maasai," she said.

"They must be proud. You stand straight. What medicine do you bring to Qaanaaq?"

"I'm a physicist."

"I think you make magic."

"Not magic exactly. Science."

"What's the difference?"

"Sometimes they seem like the same things," Siti agreed. "We're trying to understand what's happening at the production facility."

"What's to understand? The spirits. They are preparing to leave. And they need our help."

I squirmed, but it intrigued Siti.

"How? How do we help them?" she asked.

"By honouring them. Helping them fly. But we need a shaman for that."

"Do you know when they will fly?"

"Soon," he said, and looked straight at me.

Light from the quilliq revealed his pupils obscured in clouds of white, piercing me, leaving me soul-naked. I felt the heat from the teacup on my palms and from the periphery, Siti, waiting for the old man to give her more.

His eyes spoke directly to me—Now!

* * *

Raven flashed in the expanse of his eyes, and I was in them. She was roosting at the head of a table, stretching behind her, losing its form in the spot where their edges met, anchored somewhere on an obscure horizon. High-backed chairs fringed either side, looking more like thrones than dining furniture, perfectly aligned and ornately carved.

(Runes.)

A single ornament adorned the table; a large crystal bowl filled with translucent pea-sized pearls. Raven hopped beside it and plucked one out, placing it in front of a chair. In the distance, another Raven mirrored her movements, another and another, cascading back as far as I could see. She placed a single tiny globe in front of each chair and when there was one pearl left, she retrieved it and hopped to the end of the table.

My feet walked me to the edge where a chair appeared, and I sat. Raven tilted her head and plopped the object into my palm.

I'm at the sea and we are dancing.

"Look, look!" My mother calls out and she is standing in a gentle surf, bubbles swirling around her ankles. Reaching down, she dips her hand into the froth, then gently blows, the suds dissipating into the air, exposing the orb.

Raven's pearl.

"This belongs to you," she said, motioning me to open my mouth, then placing the object on my tongue, leaving me alone standing in the surf, the foam of a billion pearls caressing my feet.

Flutters on my tongue. I gape, and Raven discharges from my mouth, flying into the speck where the table disappears into nowhere.

* * *

"Perhaps we can honour both traditions." Siti's said. "Spirit and science. Wouldn't you agree, Chulyin?"

I was back in the room, and Taktut had returned to the shadow.

"For sure." I tried to tether myself to the room, my words.

"I think spirit make their own science." Taktut creaked up from his chair. "I'm tired. There's more tea in the cupboard," shuffling past us, leaving a strange hole in the darkness.

"I'm seeing things," I said to Siti when we heard the old man snoring.

"I felt you leave us for a moment," she said.

"It was Raven. And my mother. We were together. The bird put a pearl in my mouth. Then the pearl was—Raven."

"Taktut is right. The spirits create their own science."

"It was him. It was Taktut who opened the door. To the vision. Siti, he's blind. But when he looked at me, he showed me. I was seeing what he was seeing. The runes. The runes are alive. Spirits or life forms, whatever you want to call them. The essence at the ziggurat is on the runes."

"The pearl Raven gave you. It's your pearl node. Your gateway to communicating with them. They want to talk to you."

A gust of wind dislodged the door and in blew Ove Hoj.

"Where's Taktut? I brought him some supplies," and he began unloading groceries into the cupboard.

"Taking a nap. How long have you two been acquainted?" I asked.

"Long enough to know he likes cranberry tea. Mind if I join you?"

Ove's demeanour had completely changed. I thought he might have blown a cork earlier at the meeting, but now he was at ease.

"What do you think of Ms. Pereira?" he asked.

"Interesting." I was cautious.

"Mmm. Interesting indeed. I'm sick about those people. Kirsten Húnsdóttir. She was a student of mine when I was teaching in Reykjavik."

"Ms. Pereira is lying," Siti stated.

"You bet she is," Ove confirmed. "Something had alarmed Kirsten for months. About the water quality at the site. Pereira dismissed her. Kirsten was afraid. She said she stumbled on to something Aquifor did not want made public."

He reached into his pocket and retrieved his phone. "Here's an email she sent me a week ago," and he passed the phone to me.

It read:

I confronted Pereira today again about the ice. That it is not fit for human consumption. She laughed me out of her office and told me to get on with my job or face the consequences. I told her 'this is my job' and she said 'no, your job is to provide data that promotes Aquifor's corporate objectives'.

I sent a sample anonymously to a lab in Glasgow for analysis. They reported the water contains elevated levels of tritium oxide and asked where I got the sample. I never told them.

Mr. Hoj, I'm afraid for the safety of anyone consuming this product, or the contamination spread through the food Aquifor produces. Last week I refused to sign off on a shipment of water and Pereira threatened that more than my job was on the line if I didn't stick to corporate protocol. Since then, I've been demoted to the lab and banned from further field work.

I am going to notify UN-Water of my concerns.

I have sent a sample to your office as a safeguard.

"Tritium oxide," Siti said, thinking out loud. "Isn't that interesting?"

"What's tritium oxide?" I asked.

"A radioactive isotope of hydrogen."

"There's more," Ove said. "I've been doing a little research on my own with the help of my friends at NASA. We're mapping glacial shrinkage over the entire island and they pay close attention to the harvest at the plant at our request. Satellite images are showing increased tanker traffic. Thirty ships, to be exact. We were curious. Why? We followed them and they're being rerouted to a storage facility in Tenerife.

"Along with that, Aquifor has restricted my movements in the facility. Two weeks before you arrived, five suits from Aquifor showed up. All hush-hush. They were in and gone within 24 hours. I tried to squeeze some information from my contacts, but they knew nothing. I found out a separate lab was being constructed. Special access only."

"How does any of this fit with the energy fluctuations?" I asked, and the room went silent. "The water. Could this tritium oxide and the energy transmitting from the ziggurat be connected?"

"Possibly," Siti said.

"It's all connected," I said. "The runes, the ziggurat, the PNs and this crazy energy."

"And you," Siti added. "You're as much a piece of the puzzle as any of it."

"But it's more than that," I interjected. "These are energy impressions. It's the only way I can describe them. Directly related to the runes. It's a gravesite. A gravesite where the inscriptions are more than epitaphs."

"The energy transmissions started the moment you contacted the dome," Siti added. "You flipped on a switch."

"A switch to what?" I asked.

"A switch of biological energy. Emitting from your pearl node."

"Switched on energy?" Ove scratched his head.

My mind ignited. "No—it's not a gravesite at all. It's an incubator."

Ove pushed his chair from the table and folded his arms. "Of what? Extraterrestrial phenomena?"

"Would that be such a stretch?" Siti said.

"The runes are stamps of genetic impressions planted by our cosmic ancestors," I extrapolated. "These are their dormant energy patterns. Coming to life in the runes."

"Exactly," Siti agreed. "The PNs. Your PN. You are the hub for the entire process."

"We need access to that lab," I said. "Find out what Aquifor is doing."

"Not likely," Ove returned. "Atticus has it on strict security clearance."

"I'll handle Atticus," Siti said. "He's afraid of me."

"You're kidding, right?" I said.

She winked. "I played chess with him a few nights back. Kicked his ass."

It was the first time I heard a curse word from her mouth.

* * *

The storm raged for another thirty-six hours. The conditions outside provided a gap where I took inventory. From the moment Aquifor showed up, I had resisted every attempt to be dragged into something I never wanted. I resented Charles for his self-centred support of Aquifor's request to rent me like a U-Haul. None of this had anything to do with archaeological advancement. My distaste for Isahah and the corporate queen who jigged him like a cod on a hook triggered defiance. My solution? Run. It was my quick fix. I ran from Pang, ran from Aanaq, ran from anything that might breech the wall protecting me. But protecting me from what?

Then there was Raven. Those eyes. Staring. The fear. I felt it now and couldn't put my finger on what to do with it. Crush it, kill it. Running was so much easier. If I closed my eyes, she might go away, but I knew better. Raven never disappeared when I pretended she wasn't there. And neither was this. All the bells and whistles that brought me to this exact moment at this exact place. It was an impending doom. Like the world would smother me.

If I could only cry. Let the tears pour from me. Would that help me cleanse this guilt? Or the shame, the anger I was feeling? I've heard it, that tears can do such things, but not for me. I was an unbeliever. Yet something triggered in me when I touched the ziggurat, a charge I felt years ago when I came across the black stone at Mount Odin. There was a moment when I could have cried, but the tears never came.

I was preparing to return to the site when Taktut met me at the door. He cupped my face in his hands and turned it skyward.

"Look!" he said. The sky was ablaze with ribbons of green, aurora borealis dancing on a stage so clear, so calm, I could hear it crackling across the expanse above us.

"Our ancestors," he said, excited. "Not the others. These are ours. Calling you home," and he released me.

In the time to walk to the helicopter, a tear froze solid on my cheek.

15. SECRETS REVEALED

Siti and I were on the first wave to touch down at the Aquifor complex. It was a ghost town of ice and snow, no steam poured from the stacks, the crackling and hissing of the plant's industrial process silenced.

Emergency lighting illuminated the facility. It was surreal, like walking late into a theatre with the movie already playing, anonymous outlines settling into an unfolding drama. I shuffled past silhouettes of steel and pipe, a phantom audience waiting for the show to begin. Then it occurred to me. I was the drama, the star of the show. Nothing could get underway until I took my place. It was unsettling and equally exhilarating.

We entered the common area, which was playing out its morning ritual. The sun rising, a warm breeze blew as we passed by the pond. A trout broke the surface.

(Am I the projector or the projected? Who is the hologram and where does it start?)

Passing through, we entered the sterility of the corridor leading back to our apartments. "I need to get back to that ziggurat," I said.

"And I'm going to get into that new lab," Siti replied.

"How?"

"With the key," she said, pointing at her eye. "I adjusted her optical scanner. It thinks I'm Olivia."

"Clever. We need to move fast."

"There are guards floating around. I'll find them and keep them from the cameras. Give me fifteen. I'll meet you back at the vehicle compound."

Twelve minutes later, she hopped on the snowmobile and we were on our way. A ceiling of low cloud rolled in, amplifying the darkness and the solitary beam from the vehicle. The wind rose again, snow ricocheted off my visor, an onslaught of relentless white warriors.

"This weather might give us more time," Siti bellowed in my ear. I opened the throttle.

Darkness shrouded the site. It had returned to its natural state—ice and snow—the energy in remission from a few days ago. The protective bubble surrounding the ziggurat forbade the oncoming inclement weather, and we hurried across the flat. This time, when I placed my hands on the surface of the dome, the charge was different. I fell into the structure's essence; its gravity drawing me like a stream, trickling deeper into a secret world, eager to reveal itself to me. I split in two, a mitosis dividing my attention between the form connecting with the dome and the other percolating into the ziggurat.

Bubbles danced in a brook that took me deeper into a fluid consciousness, cascading down the surface of the ziggurat, then spilling me into a vast lake, mingling with the water. The surface became my receptor, a cornea collecting impressions extending beyond my limited comprehension. Whatever hovered above me, I hesitated to call it sky. It was blue and black and orange, an artist's canvas, simultaneously day and night. From it, a single luminous point, laser sharp, descended and gathered me into its beam, then one by one, punching holes in the canvas. Tens, hundreds, then thousands of them, stars but not, they breathed pictures, experiences. Some familiar, and others completely strange to me.

Guatemala. The jungle, a memory. I had risen early to walk, trudging west for an hour, then reversed, returning to camp. The sun cracked over the top of the trees, backlighting a million spiderwebs thick in dewdrops. A billion prisms reflected through the droplets, enveloping me.

But this was beyond the memory of sunlight and dew. This was shimmering life in its purest form. Living entities, the runes that materialized when I touched the dome for the first time. I reached up with what I thought was my hand, extending toward the original speck of light. The entire web trembled, the surface of the lake—me—and voices coaxing me not in words or language, but in experience.

Come. Play with us.

A swirl on the surface and the web disappeared, droplets exploding, colour settling into deep darkness. Above, I witnessed a figure pressing down on the dome and another shaking her, as if trying to wake her from a dream. A sense of urgency.

They need you up above.

(Aanaq? Is that you?)

We were in the kitchen in Pang, Aanaq, standing at the sink, her back to me.

Go now, child.

(Can we stay a little longer?)

No child. It's time to leave.

(I don't know how. I don't know how to get back.)

Follow me —

Fox, leaping up the steep incline of the ziggurat, urging me higher, waiting for me to catch up.

She needs you.

Gravity. The same force that tugged me down now propelled me up to the figures above. Fire invigorated the muscles in my legs, my arm straining, grasping for handholds in the towering steepness of the ziggurat. A sense of panic overtook me. Fox had disappeared, and I recognized the other figure, Siti, attempting to pry me from the dome. "Wait!" I hollered, but my voice was mute, hollow to the outside world.

Erupting from the ziggurat, I slammed into her like we had stepped on a landmine. We crashed in a heap five metres from the dome, Siti, unfortunately, at the bottom of the pile.

"Are you okay?" I asked, scrambling to my feet.

Siti looked up in amazement. "I was wondering the same about you."

"I'm fine. I think."

"I started calling, but you weren't responding. After the first hour, I thought I lost you."

"The first hour?"

"Two hours and forty-five minutes."

"It was only… seconds. When did the lights come on?" The incandescent glare invaded the sanctity of darkness.

"About fifteen minutes ago. Olivia, I presume."

* * *

We collected in the conference room. Ove had arrived from Qaanaaq and Atticus twitched in perpetual agitation. Isahah sat silent.

Olivia stood, pressing the heels of her palms into the table. "How did the seance go, girls? Is the rock talking back yet?" Then she addressed Siti as if I wasn't in the room. "But you? You are a goddamn physicist. I want facts and numbers."

"We're trying to give you facts," Siti responded calmly.

Olivia glared.

"You want facts that suit you," I said.

"Is that so? Give me a fact, Dr. Nakasuk."

"We're dealing with living entities." I stared straight back.

Olivia's eyes rolled, and she exhaled through pursed lips. "For the love of Christ." She turned to Siti. "You comply with this?"

"There is data that suggests it."

Her voice elevated. "Suggests? You're saying we woke a colony of sleeping aliens?"

I surveyed the room. Ove was staring into the wall, Atticus shifting his glance between Siti and me, unable to comprehend our proposition. Isahah twiddled his pen, a sheen of dew coating his upper lip that he wiped away with a handkerchief pulled from his jacket pocket.

"Is this what we're paying these people for?" Atticus broke in, directing his comment to Olivia.

"What are you doing with the water?" Ove asked.

"What are you talking about?" Atticus fired back.

Ove glared. "What are you doing with the water?"

"We're taking it to bloody Layounne. To feed the greenhouse. Which is withering."

"You're lying," Ove said, hushing the room. "Or at least ignorant." He turned to Olivia. "Is it true? Are you taking the water to Layounne?"

Olivia's simmer shifted to a calculated response. "You are correct, Mr. Hoj. We have diverted tankers to a storage facility in Tenerife."

"Why not use the water in Tenerife for the greenhouse?" I challenged.

"That's another complication." Olivia's tone was terse. "It's really none of your concern, but here it is. Three days ago, an earthquake ruptured our tanks at Tenerife. Which returns me to our current problem. Mr. Day needs his plant running. Dr. Okilo, I want science. Get this thing going. Or I'll find someone who can."

Then to me: "I understand your people have different belief systems. Leave a plate of milk and cookies for your ghosts if you like. I want water flowing through those pipes. I don't care if you use a Ouija board to decipher those runes."

Isahah was her last target. "Make sure our guests have everything they need. I have a conference call with Berlin," she said, looking at her watch, "in nine hours. I need to tell them something. Other than we're infested with poltergeists who want the water for themselves." With that, she marched from the room, Atticus toddling close behind.

"How do you tolerate that?" I asked Isahah.

Daggers shot from his eyes as he straightened a file of papers, tapping them on the desk.

"Mr. Agloolik, might I suggest something to you?" Siti asked.

Isahah shifted his glance between us, then raised his hands in submission. "If it gets the water flowing."

"Our aim is the same as yours," Siti said. "To solve Aquifor's problem. And I'm sure you'd agree this is no ordinary circumstance."

"You're the scientist, Dr. Okilo."

"Exactly. I ask you to consider this. We are on the precipice of a new science. Uncharted."

"If you're going to repeat more nonsense, this will be a short meeting," and Isahah started making his way to the door.

"Indulge me. Please."

He stopped, facing Siti.

"I'm spearheading a consortium of scientists linking human biology and physics," she said. "Our team has revealed data illustrating a new biological development in the brain that's producing the same energy patterns disrupting your production operations. Nothing like the scale you are experiencing here. Our initial experiments show only small electrical interruptions. Magnetic distortions. Aberrations in x-ray and radio waves. This tiny biological pea can emit and receive massive muon fluctuations, atomic particles of cosmic energy."

"You're losing me, Dr. What does this have to do with my production problem?"

I wanted to reach out and slap him. Slap him for his ignorance and resistance. The same incomprehensibility I found within myself. This was bigger than all the injustices of my life combined. The death of my mother, Aanaq, Anun, and my judgement shutting Raven out from being a possibility, a part of the solution. In that moment, I hated that man because I was his reflection, a leach sucking the life from whatever host it might attach. Isahah called his Aquifor. And mine? I was just a runaway with a fancy label—archaeologist.

"It's alive," I said, monotone.

"The shaman speaks." Then turning to Siti, "If this is your science, you're going to have to come up with something better." He moved to the door. "I'll reserve judgement about whatever you think that is out there. But here's a simple fact. If we don't get this water flowing, thousands, millions may die. And those are real living entities. We'll talk about your spirits after," marching out the door.

Ove broke the silence. "That's an interesting hypothesis. And I have some data to share about this water. First, Pereira is lying. There was seismic activity in Tenerife, but satellite images show no rupture or spillage from the tanks. I also received lab analysis from Copenhagen on the water sample Kirsten sent me. They confirmed unusually high levels of tritium oxide."

"What value would Aquifor see in that?" My question hung in the air like a thundercloud.

"Fuel. For a fusion reactor," Siti said. "Or," she paused, taking in a deep breath, "a weapon. Sold to the highest bidder."

* * *

After our meeting, I walked through the common area back to my apartment. I couldn't get the images out of my head. The ziggurat, pouring into me like dye in clear water, infusing every cell, collecting at the focal point of my mind. But what was I collecting? I wasn't sure. Sketches that hadn't quite made their way from the tip of the artist's pencil, and if this was an attempt to communicate, as Siti suggested, it was beyond my comprehension. The runes. They nagged my consciousness, yet while I melded with the ziggurat, the runes were absent. Or were they? Nothing in my professional life gave me a reference point. I needed a place to begin, a fixed point from where I could measure. But this was a moving target. How could I dovetail this together? Somewhere inside the runes, immaculate, like a great clock, gears meshing smoothly, springs and levers, all their pieces blending in a harmonious integration. I just had to assemble it.

(This is all a game.)

I laughed out loud as I walked past the pond. A flock of ducks V'd, projecting honks across the projected blueness of a hologram summer sky. Pushing through the doorway out of the common area into the corridor, Olivia arranged herself at my doorway, crisp and stern.

"Might I have a word?" It was a demand more than a request.

I unlocked the door with the blink of my eye. "Of course."

"What do you think we have here, Dr. Nakasuk? From an archaeological standpoint?"

I blocked her entrance. "I'm not sure I'd classify it as archaeological. Archaeology infers artifacts. These items aren't shards of pottery or tools left behind by some lost civilization."

"What is it then?"

"We told you."

"Yes, you did." She took a moment, collecting her thoughts. "Might you consider your interpretation skewed? By your personal beliefs?"

"Skewed? Hardly. I'd say enhanced. Might you consider something extraordinary is happening here?"

"Absolutely. But aliens?" She shook her head. "Isahah tells me you call yourself a shaman. Could that interfere with your objectivity?"

"Mr. Agloolik is misinformed. And my indigenous beliefs? None of your business."

"You call what you do science? Collecting broken pots and picking through ancient garbage? Seems more like an inventory exercise in dead people's crap. But I'm no expert. Pick up as much junk as you want over the next day or so. You're being replaced."

Olivia started down the hallway, then spun on her heels. "One more thing. I'm not sure what planet you steered Dr. Okilo on to. But if she doesn't get it together, she'll be on the same plane right along with you."

The door shut, and I flooded with the oddest sensation. It was more the absence of feeling that struck me than the appearance of it. Something inside stirred to call her a bitch, but my indignation sat curiously inert along with my anger. There was no need to plot what I might next say to Olivia, regardless of her opinions or objectives. I recalled the same clarity at releiz Lemgasem, in the cave, the ochre handprints, the mural of stars and those three intrepid figures. The hands that drew them equally real as Olivia and the experience at the ziggurat.

I was floating and needed a ballast. I walked across the hall and rapped on Siti's door.

She was garbed in full Maasai dress. Around her neck, a collar of brilliant beads, meticulous and ornately crafted in a plethora of colours orbiting her head, a brilliant black sun shining above it. Hanging beneath, another beaded necklace cascaded down to her navel, tiny discs of paper-thin silver suspended in an arabesque of glitter, the rise and fall of her breasts setting the ballet of light in motion.

"You're beautiful," I stammered.

"Thank you," she said. "I don't go anywhere without these," and we laughed as she stroked the beads. "Come in."

"I just had a visit from Pereira."

"Me too. She read me the riot act. Seems we're not performing up to standards."

"She's replacing me."

"Not surprised." We moved into the living room. "I need to tell you something. Before we went to the site, I notified Dr. Kai to monitor muon activity at the site and the brain patterns of five PNs. Two in South Africa. One in Japan. Two in Vancouver. We know our PNs can both transmit and receive muon bursts. But the transmissions up to this point have been erratic. We wanted to determine if a connection existed between the ziggurat and them. Through you."

"And?"

"As soon as you touched the dome, our instruments exploded."

"I'm a conduit?"

"Precisely. The energy was off the charts. All five PNs reported what they called a surge of seeing. Every one of them drew this." Siti handed me her phone. "These drawings are identical in scale and detail. None of the PNs claim artistic abilities. They said their hands manoeuvred across the page on their own accord."

The drawings depicted Raven, suspended above three ambling bodies, the paintings from the cave in Rekeiz Lemgasem.

I returned her phone. "The figures. I uncovered them on my first dig in Western Sahara."

She waited.

"My name means Raven in Inuktitut. She is my tuurngaq. My animal spirit guide." It was the first time those words had escaped my lips.

"What happened out there, Chulyin?"

I took a deep breath. "It's hard to verbalize. I just felt this overwhelming sense of grief. A million years of loss and sorrow. And joy. Joy I've never experienced. I was with them. They were showing me, sharing with me. Everything. Where they came from. Where they're going. All compressed in an instant. It was like I was riding a pulse, a wave right along with them. They're a collection, a colony. No, an entire civilization with a single voice, yet it wasn't a voice at all. They were just a presence." I stopped and nodded my head in acknowledgement with the feeling that verified the soundness of what I was about to say. "It's them. Their energy is disrupting the operation of the plant. They're preparing to leave."

"I want to show you something." Siti broke my spell, vanishing into the bedroom. She returned holding a polished stick with the curious knob carved at one end. "This is a rungu," she said, gliding her hand along the stick. "I've carried it with me since I was a little girl. The rungu is a symbol of the warrior in Maasai culture. Not for girls or women. Yet here it is. Between us now.

"They murdered my parents when I was a toddler. Our village burned to the ground. My adoptive parents heard of the atrocity and came to Narasha, the village where I lived, to see what they could do to help.

They found me there clinging to the rungu. If anyone tried to take it, I would wail like a wounded hyena."

She presented the rungu to me. "I found out much later it was my great-grandfather's. He was a powerful tribal shaman. His energy lives in it still."

I received the rungu with great care. The ebony was finger-worn and smooth as satin. A subtle charge pulsed into my skin, the way a magnet aligns iron filings.

The rungu was a single cut of striped ebony, an intricate pattern of blond and midnight swirls twisting up the funnelled shaft. At the top, a bulbous protrusion made a horizontal twist from its vertical axis. The walking stick gazed in every direction, and I sensed it peering outward, inward, observing. A beacon. It tapped directly into my heart and my mind's eye; a replica of my experience at the lake below the ziggurat.

"Raven. She's been with me since I can remember."

"I know. The rungu told me. This is the science these people could never understand. Look closer."

I examined the ebony knob, running my thumb over the smooth surface and felt a nipple, like the bottom of an acorn. Closing my eyes, I let my fingers see the tiny grooves and the minuscule pinpricks orbiting the hand-worn bump. My eyes shot open. "The talisman."

"I noticed it immediately when you invited me to your room a few days ago. The positions of the indentations are identical."

"I'm in a dream."

"Maybe you are. Maybe we all are."

"I—I've tried to resist this my whole life. These visions. Raven."

"Maybe it's time to see what the dream is telling you."

My thumb circled the tip of the rungu.

We ended our conversation, and I strolled into the common area. The holograms rose and fell around me. I close my eyes and envisioned the metal shell behind the illusions holding the cold at bay. The real world. Or so I convinced myself, dissecting me into four realities; the Arctic winter beyond the steel skin, the holograms, ziggurat, and the animated energy of the runes, all immersed in an unfolding drama. If there was a script for this play, I was the author. Because every choice I made, every step forced the appearance of the next piece of my unraveling puzzle.

Raven.

Aanaq was right. It was time for me to fly.

16. THE NANURLUK

Olivia was true to her word, and I was in Qaanaaq two days later, tapping on Taktut's door. The old man delighted in my return.

"The ice killers don't understand," he said, pouring tea. "They see only what their eyes tell them. They do not know our ways."

"I'm not sure I do either."

I sprinkled a spoonful of sugar into my tea, stirring, while the sky danced above the Aquifor plant. "Why did you come to Pang, Taktut? To see Aanaq?"

He faced the window. "Because of them."

"Who?"

"Sila. The spirits of light. Our common ancestors. They are the source, the seed, the beginning. Your Aanaq taught me qaumaniq. The gift to see what binds our form, our spirits. You have this gift too. Should you choose it."

"When I touched the dome. They were in me."

"Yes. Your seeing begins."

"But what am I supposed to see? I don't understand."

"Because you resist."

"Resist what? The old ways? Is there wrongdoing in changing how I live?" My words floated into the kitchen.

"You speak like an Inuit. Maybe you are here to prevent future wrongdoings."

"How?"

"I cannot say. What does your tuurngaq tell you?"

"I don't know. I don't listen."

He turned his head toward the window, watching a scene only he could see. "Perhaps we can listen together."

"I'm scared, Taktut."

"Your words sound like qallunaaq, but your heart speaks otherwise."

"I'm sick of the lying. Aquifor doesn't care about archaeological preservation or whether they tear this land to shreds. Or the people in it."

"They think we are ridiculous, stupid people," he continued. "They are ignorant of our true nature. There is power in their not knowing."

He stood up and motioned to the window, energy from the ziggurat churning the night sky. "The qallunaaq believe their knowledge is superior. To know what a polar bear does, one becomes the bear. To walk its path, to hunt, to see as the bear sees. Feel its hunger. They believe they know. To understand the bear, it must be here," and he tapped his fist to his chest. "Qaumaniq is our advantage. They cannot see like you or me. They cannot see the bear's true nature."

"That's gone Taktut."

"You have convinced yourself of it."

"No. It's true. What we had is dead. Everything lives and dies, including us and our ways."

"Maybe so. But something lives out there."

I felt heaviness pressing on me. "The tea tastes different. I like it."

"Do they know you can fly?"

"What?"

"Do they know you can fly?"

"I don't know I can fly."

"I was with you on the ice. In the igloo." He raised his cup. "Blueberry. I like it too."

* * *

Ove arrived twenty minutes later. Taktut poured Ove a cup of blueberry tea and shuffled to his chair.

"Something's going on," Ove said. "My contact at NASA just informed me of a cargo ship docked at Aquifor's port last night. Escorted by a frigate armed to the teeth. No flags. No identification.

"They've got their own bloody navy?"

"We confirmed its point of origin. North Africa. Layounne, to be exact."

"What are they up to?"

"Nobody knows. Aquifor pumps more money into the Greenland economy than the fishing industry. They've got free rein to do whatever they want."

"Sila calls you," Taktut said, the night sky blazing, snow reflecting its coral tinge. "You must go."

"Yes," I conceded.

"We can get you to the facility. Quietly. I'll get it organized." Without another word, Ove slipped off into the pink Arctic twilight.

* * *

We struck out from Qaanaaq with three teams. The sleds were light, which helped us make haste, and although we tried to convince Taktut to stay behind, he was adamant. "If you don't take me, I'll walk."

We steered straight for the tongue of the glacier lapping between the low-lying mountains. The ground was thick in January snow, packed hard from driving winds that crystallized the surface, the runners singing over the white highway. Moving undetected was paramount; dog sleds doubled our time, but stealth supplanted speed. An escalating magnetism pulled me as we trekked closer to the ziggurat. The others sensed it too, especially Taktut, standing erect, peering into the vision of his mind's eye. Even the dogs quickened their pace and their yelping subsided, cognizant of our need for urgency and silence.

About a half a kilometre from the glacier's edge, Taktut ordered us to halt. He stepped off the sled and walked forty paces, then abruptly stopped. Tamping with his boot, he bent down and scooped a handful of snow, smelling, tasting it, then shaking his head, moving to another location. After three repetitions, he found what he was searching for.

"Here," he announced.

While we unloaded supplies, Taktut continued stomping the ground, exploring with a metal probe, poking, testing the consistency of the snow. By the time we had offloaded the equipment, he had scratched a circle five metres in diameter with the heel of his boot. Some of the equipment was inside its perimeter, and he immediately told us to remove it. We lugged the gear outside the perimeter but when we put it down, he shouted "no", motioning us to move it farther back, until it satisfied a border comprehensible only to him.

The old man summoned us to the circle. From inside his coat he pulled a pana, a traditional Inuit snow knife the length of his forearm to the tip of his fingers.

"This was my father's. A gift from a great bull caribou."

He held it up, a shinbone stained in time, fashioned flat like a seal's flipper. It tapered thin toward the hand-held end, a series of three carved knuckles that fit between gripping fingers so the tool would not slide while cutting snow. Along the flat surface of the blade, two black parallel lines ran along the top rounded edge. From the handle, routing down just below the spine, a trail of three-pronged markings—raven talons was my immediate reaction—leading down to the widest part of the blade. The tracks ended in three circular impressions, bored into the bone, then inlaid with dark stones, one significantly larger.

Taktut took his pana and plunged it into the snow, slicing the first cut. The others retrieved their blades and block production began. He measured each by instinct, cutting them with the precision of a stonemason.

Inside, Ove built two platforms, smoothing the surface with the flat of his blade. Taktut and his two apprentices spiralled the blocks around the circumference, the arch curving ever inward. They bevelled every chunk, fitting them perfectly, giving strength to the vault against the wind. Taktut stroked every seam with his fingers, deciding if they were sound, then moved on to the next. He spoke reassuringly to his young Inuit, who carried out his orders, which were not orders but teachings. Lessons in every block, every slice of their pana, the snow becoming more than crystals, something sacred. When they reached the top, he disappeared, his hand the last remnant of him poking through the oculus.

He instructed his apprentices to cut a block of the clearest ice the width of his outstretched arms. When they returned with it, he positioned it in a vacant space directly above the platforms.

Outside I chinked the cracks with snow. I watched my hands packing powder as if they belonged to another being; the air electric and my lungs breathing—what? Murmurs. Aanaq and Anun, rustling around me, summoning every ancestral spirit, collecting them on the glacier's edge. A thousand pair of hands fashioned this temple of snow, all working in unison, striving for a common purpose working through me.

Ove observed me. "The old man," he said. "He's extraordinary."

"Yes."

"Something's shifting."

"Shifting is an understatement."

He placed his arm around my shoulder, and at that exact moment, the ice quaked.

The tremor rattled my memory. I transported back to one of my trips with Anun to Mount Odin. We were cruising the fiord to base camp when we confronted a massive living obstruction.

"Look!" but he was already aware of their presence. Arctic terns. Millions of them.

Anun lowered our speed to a troll, moving toward the undulation, their heads bobbing with the swells of the sea. The low hum of the motor stirred a squadron directly in front into flight, their wings stirring a breeze in the stillness. At first, our approach caused them to shift away from the bow, but as the birds became accustomed, they did not fly. The boat parted them, leaving a thin ribbon of sea behind that dissected the living throng.

Then he was with me, peering over the precipice at the ziggurat below. Anun, reaching out, touching my shoulder and I felt the breath of life in him.

"Remember that day?" His eyes fixed on his own imaginary horizon.

(Yes)

"The terns. The power."

(Anun, I...)

"You were born for this," he said. "Fly."

He vanished. The sound of the men bantering, the igloo solid before me. And Ove.

A million terns took flight, fixing in the heavens, holding their breath, balanced on the precipice, waiting in anticipation.

Taktut poked his head from the entrance. "We're ready."

I crawled through the tunnel into the chamber. Partially concealed behind a caribou curtain suspended from a bone rod, were the platforms Ove had built. Two quilliq illuminated the interior, casting a yellow blush.

The flame from a quilliq reflected in Taktut's eyes.

(What do you see?)

The flames never wavered in the turbulent air, an invisible shield protected their light. The igloo exuded safety, a protective bubble. I was uncertain if it was emanating from our proximity to the ziggurat or the old man himself.

Before the others entered, he said softly, "Today we answer the call of spirit. I will show you how. Today we fly."

He took my hand, leading me to an ice dais, and instructed me to wait while the three others clambered into the igloo, Ove being last, blocking the entrance with a sizeable chunk of snow. They brought blankets to cover both platforms, Taktut sitting on the adjacent ice altar.

"They will prepare me first," he said.

He removed his boots and socks, his parka and heavy trousers. Clad only in his undergarments, he shifted his legs on to the platform and leaned forward, his nose pressing his knees. The two young Inuit secured his ankles and bound his wrists behind his back, tying a thick leather strap around his back and upper thighs, holding him in place. Threading one final strap under his knees, they secured it around the nape of his neck, a large loop jutting out like an eye for a hook.

"Your tuurngaq will pull you skyward," Taktut said, and with that, he began a low indistinguishable chant.

The men turned to me, and I began removing my boots and outer clothing. I positioned myself on the dais and the moment the leather tightened on my skin, a sheath of refuge engulfed me, allowing me to see Aanaq, Anun, the sound of the men breathing, even the quilliq, its yellow tongue flickering with a voice of its own. Then, I was lying in a field at the foot of Mount Odin on a bed of Arctic heather.

Bring who you need.

I called—Chulyin—and Raven appeared.

I saw everything; Ove beyond the curtain, Mount Odin, Anun, the ziggurat and its city of enraptured souls.

I felt the sinews of the caribou hide on my wrists, my ankles, the strength of Raven surging into my body. As they tightened the straps, I felt Chulyin squeezing out, making way for Raven.

She rested on the dais, and I took flight.

My wings stretched, catching the currents, the updraft lifting me high over the face of the glacier. Exhilaration, pure joy, ascending into the heavens. I spiralled up and out past the planet to an orange glow. The pouch of stones Aanaq had left me on her deathbed, the pouch from the igloo. Untying the leather sack, I released the stones into the void. They circled the orange star orbiting it, closer and closer, until they fused, bursting into a flare where I saw everything below in minute detail. Olivia the maestro, Atticus in frantic conversation with a uniformed official, Isahah silent, brooding off to the side.

But he wasn't brooding.

(He's watching, waiting for me.)

Fear swelled inside me.

(He's going to destroy me.)

"No. He cannot see you." Taktut's voice purled in my ears.

The fear projected from my physical body on the dais. I banked clear of confrontation and swooped toward the metal menagerie of the industrial complex.

At the dock, a massive crane offloaded a large container from a cargo freighter. The boom hovering above the deck, slowly lifting and settling the steel box on a massive makeshift sled. Two metal-treaded tractors used for clearing snow from the helipad harnessed the sled, while uniformed personnel secured the cargo. Another platoon loaded snowmobiles, attaching trailers laden with bulky wooden crates.

I landed on the roof of a tractor and watched as they open the containers. The first piece was large and bulky, a metal chassis positioned on a rotunda of rails that allowed the device to swivel 360°. From another crate, they removed a solid glass barrel that funnelled to a flat circular tip perhaps half a metre in diameter. Fused to its opposite end were a series of metal flanges which the soldiers prepared to bolt on to the fuselage resting on the chassis. No wires or electronic mechanisms attached to the device. Once they secured the barrel, the tractors roared to life and began creeping forward.

I felt a thud, the sound of thunder. I watched her; Chulyin floating above the platform, the men outside the igloo startled with the sudden quake rocking the structure. Only Taktut remained placid, undisturbed on the dais beside me. I launched from the tractor, flying low into the base of the glacier, trusting the updraft would lift me faster back to the igloo. I hit the air stream and catapulted straight up, twisting high above the camp. The speed flipped me momentarily, but when I stabilized, I saw it.

A nanurluk.

Isahah's tuurngaq. A colossal polar bear larger than the ship in the harbour. It emerged from a massive hole in the ice, a giant bubbling cauldron of frothing sea. Its fur was blood-stained and dripping seawater, which it shook with a fury, sending a shower of boulder-sized projectiles, frozen shrapnel that sprayed half a kilometre around it. The nanurluk raised its head and loosed a deafening roar, shifting the stars, rattling the ground, a massive fissure zig-zagging across the glacier, the igloo perched on the edge of the abyss.

The bear raised its snout, sniffing for prey. I banked toward the igloo as men scrambled on the ice. The nanurluk spotted them, breaking into a gallop, trampling the ground with yawning footprints, cracks radiating from the sheer weight of the creature. It stormed the igloo, rising on its hind legs, then slammed both paws straddling the structure. The sheer force of the bear's pounce sent blocks flying, and the igloo disintegrated. I saw myself exposed, floating, bound by the leather straps and the loop behind my neck, an umbilical cord of silver light twisting, penetrating my wings.

(Power)

The others scattered, except Taktut, who floated next to me.

The nanurluk glanced at the fleeing figures, snarled, then turned its attention back to us. Lowering its snout a metre from us, I could smell it, the devoured blood of fish and the entrails of seal and walrus. It snorted and the spray from its nostrils showered us. The nanurluk chose Taktut, and just when I thought the creature would devour him, it reeled. An energy pulse from the old man spurned it with seismic force, and the beast roared in indignation, outraged by the power of the tiny creature.

The giant bear turned its attention to the others and bore down on them with ferocity. They jostled, frantic, harnessing the dogs to the sleds.

Ove, undetected by the beast, raised his rifle then—crack, crack, crack—the bullets useless, lost in its thick, vacillating fur. He scampered to his sled and was off. The other two, along with the dogs tangled in the reins, felt the creature's wrath. The nanurluk lurched, clamping the entire sled in its mouth, then threw it, dogs and men, into the air like toys.

Taktut was standing now, swirls of white filaments encircling him, gathering velocity, whistling in my ears.

"Pierce his eyes." The winds spoke, and I knew it was Taktut.

I flew straight at the nanurluk. Taktut simultaneously unleashed the filaments, tangling its legs, wrapping its body in an energy cocoon. I tucked my wings against my body and, with harpoon force, plunged straight into the eye of the nanurluk. The beast roared in anguish, and I reversed, driving back into its other eye. By this time, Taktut had completely tangled its legs, causing it to stumble and slam into the ice. Life ebbed from the creature until it dissolved; the tuurngaq leaving a perfect impression in the snow.

I tilted left and arced back toward the annihilated igloo. Chulyin floated above the dais, and Taktut had collapsed, Ove running toward him. The two young Inuit along with their dog team were in disarray but seemingly unharmed.

Diving straight toward my body, a salvo of convulsions overtook me. We crashed hard, and I realized the cold. The leather straps bound me and I gulped for air, then an exodus of energy, my cells, my heart and my lungs surged into my esophagus, vomiting. I had enough sense to turn myself sideways so I wouldn't choke. The violence of the ejection hurled the contents of my stomach into the snow, along with a lump of grey matter that spewed into the blackness. It hovered above me for a split second, then cracked like a lightning bolt, vanishing into the night.

"Untie her." I heard Ove's command. Hands at my neck and wrists, my body splayed like a gutted seal, limp and exposed.

"Wrap her up. She's freezing." Ove again, and I felt the softness of the blanket I'd been lying on before my journey.

"Get her on the sled. Let's get the hell out of here."

"No, no," I protested weakly. "The ziggurat. I have to go."

"To hell you say. We're moving out. Get that team organized," he barked at the two who had released my binds.

I grabbed his arm with a strength that caught his attention. "Ove. No. I have to go." I struggled to my knees. "Get my clothes. My coat," then fell into the snow.

"Impossible. There's no way."

"Yes. There is." I pointed without looking up. "The crack in the ice. My boots. I need my clothes. Taktut. Where is he?"

"He's in shock."

"I'd be dead if it wasn't for him," I said. "We have to get down there. They're going to destroy it. I saw them bringing some kind of weapon from the ship. They're pulling it up right now."

"What?"

"The nanurluk. It was Isahah."

He stared blankly.

One of the young Inuit interrupted. "We're ready to go, Mr. Hoj."

"Take him back. Fast as you can," Ove instructed. "I'll radio ahead to the medic. Move it."

They scampered off, driving the dogs with their precious cargo back to Qaanaaq.

The shortwave crackled, then Siti's voice. "What the hell's going on? Is everyone okay?"

I grabbed the microphone. "No. We've got to stop them."

"I'm locked in the lab," she returned.

"They're going to destroy the site. It's a weapon. They're moving it right now."

"Chulyin. They just brought Isahah back here a few minutes ago. I saw them transporting him to the infirmary. He was a bloody mess."

"He's on to us," I continued. "To me. I never saw it coming. He's a shaman."

"Listen," her voice controlled. "For ten full seconds, energy surged from the dome. Exposing a perfect bar of," she hesitated, "light. The manometer went crazy. I'm still trying to contact Dr. Kai to find out what's going on outside this bubble."

"It's a springboard." There was no science or data to my statement. I simply knew. "They're opening a passage to leave."

Fully dressed, I dropped the microphone and sprinted to the chasm, Ove close behind. At the mouth of the gorge, a narrow ridge appeared jutting from the vertical ice wall, descending into the flat. I started toward it when Ove's grip stalled me.

"Hold on. Let's get down there in one piece. Wait here."

He ran back to the sled and returned with two sets of traction cleats, ropes, and harnesses.

"Put this on." He snapped the harness around my shoulders and between my legs. He tied the rope to a metal ring and tugged hard, securing it, then wrapped the rope around his waist, tethering us like chain gang convicts.

Ove yanked the rope, satisfied it was tight. "If we go, we go together," and we began our descent into the crevasse.

At first, the path was narrow and treacherous, at one point barely wide enough to house the ball of my foot. Ove guided me along with the surety of a mountain goat. At one point, the ledge completely disappeared, but with a little coaxing, I made the leap to the other side.

The ledge widened as we descended until we could walk comfortably single file. We approached a sharp turn, and rounding it, the entire site erupting into view. We were twenty metres above the flat and I could see Olivia's team, which had doubled in size. Two hundred metres from them, the monstrosity offloaded from the freighter slithered forward. The tractor moan was surreal; the sound bouncing off the ice inside the crevasse, muffled and toylike as if it was part of a child's game. A tide of anticipation rolled from my gut and for a split second I felt the entire place hold its breath.

Then darkness, swallowing us in the Arctic night, tractors droning in the distance.

17. EXILED

Our boots had hardly touched the ice flat when the darkness spoke. "Welcome back," it said. "You're just in time, Dr. Nakasuk."

Eight silhouettes confronted us, red tracers from their rifles scribbling on our chests.

"Really? Time for what?"

Olivia, third shadow from the left, spoke. "To fly you out. For good."

"The guns. A bit of overkill, wouldn't you say?"

"I think not. You and Mr. Hoj have a hard time following instruction."

"The Ministry might object," Ove said.

"Oh, I've already spoken to your Ministry, Mr Hoj. They'll be waiting for you with open arms when you return to Nuuk."

"And your little collaborator, Dr. Okilo," Olivia addressed me. "We're going to fix her, too. Seems she's playing with the lights. Escort them to the helipad."

The lieutenants marched us to the perimeter of extinguished lights. For a place that was on lockdown, the area buzzed with activity. Not the Aquifor personnel from the complex, but a corps of mercenaries that arrived with the frigate.

Atticus barked orders at a team erecting a five-metre-high concrete barricade. "Anchor those deeper, goddamit." The bulwark bulged like a massive block boomerang, the forward section angled directly at the ziggurat. A vertical aperture, cut like the arrow slit of a medieval castle, split the façade. Another crew laboured installing a rail track that dead-ended just short of the opening.

"Wait," Olivia ordered our guards. She strolled over, then leaned in close. "Your replacement." She moved aside and pointed at a group congregating around a pack of snowmobiles. "You might know him. A countryman of mine."

Ten metres away, Ricardo Garcia Chavez. I'd met Chavez briefly at a symposium in Mexico City years earlier. He had written a paper on Aztec ideography, a brilliant piece, but not as brilliant as he suspected himself to be. The never-worn Canada Goose parka made him look like a tourist, and I wondered if he'd ever experienced a snowflake, never mind the -30°C chill. His charcoal moustache ossified white under the vapour of frozen breath, and when our eyes met, he turned away, pretending not to see me. "You two will get along fine," I said.

"Whatever was in your apartment is on the aircraft in Qaanaaq. The pilot will take you to Nuuk. After that? I don't care. You can fly anywhere you like. One way."

"How's Isahah?"

Her stride broke rhythm, and she called over her shoulder, "Good bye Dr. Nakasuk."

As soon as we touched down in Qaanaaq, they hustled us to the Aquifor jet, transporting us to Nuuk. On the way, I said, "I'm worried about Taktut."

"The old man is crafty," Ove returned. "It'll take more than a nanurluk to keep him down."

A zealous Aquifor rep bounced across the tarmac, greeting me at the foot of the airstairs in Nuuk Airport, while a Ministry vehicle whisked Ove away. I climbed into the back of a cab with Alicia, my public relations debutante. Alicia loved everything north of the Arctic circle; the ice, the perpetual darkness, but especially the indigenous attitudes and the native's accommodating demeanour. We rolled up to the Hans Egede hotel and Alicia insisted on seeing me to my room. I declined, ensuring her I could make the trip myself, leaving her wounded in the lobby, and rode the elevator to the fourth-floor suite.

Inside, hotel porters had neatly piled my gear and a box containing my computer and phone. I had completely forgotten about the phone. It was next to useless in Qaanaaq, between the weather and spotty reception. It showed twenty-six text messages, voicemails, and emails too many to count.

I opened my text messages first. Three were from Charles, four from Siti and nineteen from Asmed. Asmed's texts were consistent. Call Me. Urgent.

All the voicemails from Charles were about Asmed. "The young man seemed quite distraught. I hope you don't mind. I've forwarded your number and shared your whereabouts."

I dialled Asmed's number, and he answered immediately.

"Chulyin. Are you alright?"

"Other than my wounded ego, I'm fine."

"Chu, I have to speak with you."

"Go ahead."

"No. In person."

"I'm in Greenland."

"I know. Qaanaaq."

"No, I'm in Nuuk. Aquifor booted me out of Qaanaaq about six hours ago."

"Even better. I'm booking a flight to Nuuk. I'm hoping for Saturday evening."

"Where are you?"

"St. John's. Newfoundland. I can't talk about this over the phone, Chu. I'll be there in two days."

"It's good to hear your voice."

"You too. I wish it were different circumstances."

I hung up the phone. The sky bloomed pastel pink, and a blush rose in me, too. His voice, his concern. I really had been unfair to him, but he was no innocent bystander. Sulky and cantankerous when he didn't get his way. Maybe that's why I liked him. Still, what would motivate him to come to Nuuk? Forget it. Stop thinking. I plunked myself on a chair, staring out the window at the shifting scene.

Off to the west, Suvulliik, dipping toward the horizon. I closed my eyes, remembering. Aanaq, sending me outside to report on how our guideposts sat in the heavens, our morning stars hanging like diamonds on invisible threads. Asmed taught me their European names when we were at Rekeiz Lemgasem. Arcturus, larger, brighter, pulsing orange. And the other, Muphrid, dimmer, what he called the little orphan.

(The little orphan)

That's me. I never said a thing that day about how those words affected me. He described celestial objects, and I construed my life, a little orphan, slipping into the mindlessness of another day. In the desert, Arcturus was matter and gas, but at the top of the world, outside our door, it was Suvulliik, an eternal dancer, exquisite and profound.

When I returned to the house, Aanaq would ask, "Is Suvulliik hanging its head?" And I would say "yes, the big one falls behind the mountain." She would say, "their light shines in our eyes now," and would fill the kettle for her morning tea.

But today, no tea. No Aanaq.

I had been running on pure adrenaline from the moment we arrived at the rim of the glacier, my arms bruised, purple contusions swelling my legs from my clash with Isaiah and his tuurngaq. The tips of my fingers were raw, like I had scraped the skin with sandpaper, recalling the day I had tried to claw my way out of the igloo. Pain began acknowledging itself and there were no distractions keeping me from it. Worse was my inner depletion, a residue settling into every cell of my body. I heard a qallunaaq fable once about Humpty Dumpty, how he crashed to the ground and broke into a hundred pieces. That was me: Humpty Dumpty, pieces strewn about, wondering if something might ever put me back together again. I lifted from the chair.

(Take an inventory, girl.)

An inventory of what?

(Get to the ziggurat. At any cost.)

Think, think, think. I slammed my fist on the wall.

Stop.

(Stop? Stop what?)

Be still.

(Be still? Are you crazy?)

Do you forget so soon?

"Shut up!" I hollered at the walls, pulling my hair, wanting something real, something concrete.

"Chulyin?"

A muffled staccato and again, "Chulyin?"

A voice in the hallway. I rummaged through my pack and, at the bottom, a two-way radio. I picked it up, and it spoke again. "Chulyin. Do you read me?"

Siti.

"Yes. I'm here."

"I watched them load you into the helicopter. Where are you?"

"Nuuk. You?"

"Still at the Aquifor facility. They've got me under lock and key. Or so they think."

"We need to get you out of there."

"No. Chulyin. I'm exactly where I belong. We're going to work this together. Keep that radio close. I need to—have to go. The witch is at the door," and the radio went dead.

I fell on the couch and closed my eyes.

* * *

Sleep.

The open tundra outside Pang, the afternoon I buried Ms. Stevenson's letter. She stood in the heather, pointing to the stone, encouraging me to lift the rock, to see. Rolling it aside, the envelope was there, torn and soiled. I fumbled with it, feeling the amulet inside, dumping the contents into my palm. But there was no letter, no amulet, only a single Arctic springtail* beetle, shrivelled and dehydrated. Collecting a pinch of heather stiff with ice crystals, I squeezed, releasing a drop, soaking the springtail, its body absorbing the moisture. Another drop, and the tiny creature puffed to life, its carapace shifting from brown to green, like a crumpled leaf finding spring again.

It sat erect, then catapulted from my hand, ricocheting into a small patch of heather. My palm itched, and another springtail appeared, and another, all vaulting, arcing into the tundra, then streams of them, whistling like steam through a pressure cooker, bursting around me. Ms. Stevenson was there with Aanaq, Anun; the springtails exploded, blocking the sun.

Stillness.

Then Taktut stood before me, swarmed in springtails, orbiting, caressing him. Our eyes met, and I saw within his blindness what was impossible for

---

* Arctic springtails are arthropods that exsiccate during the long winter months to protect their bodies from freezing. Although the bug is shrivelled and appears dead, when spring arrives, they absorb moisture, revitalized from their winter stasis.

me to discern with my sighted eyes. In a blink, the springtails vanished, a vacuum sucking them from my dream.

Startled, I shot up from the couch. I could still feel the surrounding dream in me, and the smell of Arctic heather, crushed and pungent. On the table a springtail, its tiny antennae probing.

"Taktut?" I called, and the creature scampered over the table's edge, bouncing to the door, vanishing underneath it.

A crackle from the radio. "They're taking me to the site," Siti said in a hurried whisper. "I'll call when I return."

* * *

Next morning Ove was at my door.

"Have you been watching the news?" he said.

"No. I fell asleep."

He manoeuvred past me. "Where is the remote?"

I pointed to it and he activated the TV. "Hasn't hit CNN yet, but this is big news on KNR."

"KNR?"

"Our official public broadcasting station. Listen."

An interview was in progress, but in Kalaallisut, the native language of Greenland.

"What am I hearing?" I asked.

"They'll repeat it in English."

Less than a minute later, the anchor signed off with her interviewee and faced the camera.

"That was Andreas Domgaard, professor of seismic studies at the University of Copenhagen. At approximately 2:35 p.m. today a tectonic event occurred near Qaanaaq on Greenland's west coast registering 6.4 on the Richter scale. It's unconfirmed whether this was a natural or man-made event. Qaanaaq houses a water reclamation facility operated by global conglomerate Aquifor, harvesting ice to supply water for its food production facilities around the globe. The seismic Institute of Greenland has confirmed the severity of the tremor. A team from KNR is currently en route to Qaanaaq."

"An earthquake?" I asked.

"Doubtful. This is a localized event."

"The ziggurat. They've blown it up."

"I'm waiting for information from NASA. They're passing over Qaanaaq around the time KNR arrives. I'm trying to arrange a flight, but everything's on lockdown. Only emergency service in and out of Qaanaaq."

I remembered the radio. "Siti put this in my luggage. I was talking to her last night. She said they were taking her to the site."

"And nothing since?"

"No."

"Jesus. We have to wait. I got to go back to the office."

"They haven't fired you?"

"Hardly. A slap on the wrist. Aquifor has their claws deep in this government, but I have friends in higher places, too."

Asmed flooded into my mind. "Is Nuuk taking international flights?"

"As far as I know. Are you leaving us?"

"I got a call from an acquaintance last night. He's on his way here."

"That's some acquaintance." Ove looked at his watch. "Jesus. I have to get back. I've got a meeting with the premier. Aquifor is making waves." He rose from the table. "What time does your friend arrive?"

"Tomorrow afternoon."

He pointed at the TV. "I'll keep you up to date on unofficial business. Let me know when you contact Siti."

"I will," and he disappeared through the door.

Thirty minutes later, the KNR anchor announced the reporters were about to broadcast live from the airport in Qaanaaq. The cameraman scanned the runway and terminal building and as he panned farther out, I noticed two of the three Aquifor helicopters on the corner of the runway.

The reporter spoke Kalaallisut, strolling to the edge of the tarmac toward the ice shelf in the harbour. He gathered a scoop of snow and brought it forward to the camera. It was grey, looking more like volcanic ash.

The sound of snowmobiles fired behind them, and the feed cut to the studio. The anchor spoke in English - the crew was heading to Aquifor's industrial complex on the other side of the isthmus to investigate what appeared to be a massive explosion.

18. ASMED RETURNS

When I was thirteen, Anun took me to Halifax. He was organizing a small office there as a hub for adventurers booking flights to Pang. I had watched him so many times fly off our tiny airstrip, wishing I was going with him. It was the first time I'd been on a plane.

Halifax was like being transported to another universe. The hustle and bustle of the city, the people, so many people going in every direction. My mind was electric. One day, we ended up at the Halifax harbour train terminal. Anun was busy arranging a container of supplies for Qikiqtani Quests, while I scouted along the rail lines.

I had never seen a train before and marvelled at their size and power. Plodding in the yard, cars shunting, the screech of steel on steel, while the locomotives belched diesel, inching forward and back, and the domino cascade of couplings clanking in their unrelenting grip.

The trains, the material, the cargo, all this abundance in box cars, containers, racks of vehicles, thousands of them going—where? Suddenly I felt the vastness of the world. The possibilities. I saw myself chugging down my own track, going to places so far from Pang that I couldn't even imagine where or if they existed.

The train, the cars, the track I travelled since then flooded through me. And Asmed. He was a railcar coupled to me, precious cargo I'd picked up along the way. I missed him. Or maybe I was allowing myself the luxury of missing him in this memory because he was about to appear in my life again.

I'd picked up so many cars along the way, dropped so many off. Shunted back and forth with people in my life, people who served my purpose and those who didn't. The ones who could even remotely hurt me, or penetrate my defensive wall, I would unhook and leave in the yard, where they sat rusting, and I could move along my track. One of those cars was pulling back into my station. I felt a mixture of joy and apprehension at his arrival. But there was one thing about which there was no confusion; Asmed Akbari was my friend.

Asmed's plane arrived Saturday afternoon, the sole flight coming in that day, and I was there to meet him like he had done for me on that day so long ago in Algiers. He sauntered through the gate, lugging a large crate of camera equipment, not seeing me at first, but when he did, he lit up. He was wearing a thin overcoat, a Manchester United scarf knotted around his neck.

We embraced, then I held him at arm's length, looking him up and down. "Where's your coat?"

"I'm wearing it."

"This ain't the Sahara."

"We have to talk, Chulyin."

"Not before we get you a proper coat. It's hard talking when your teeth are chattering."

We loaded the cab, and I instructed the cabbie to drop his luggage off at our hotel after taking us to Grover's clothing store. Asmed was grateful we made Grover's our first stop. "Just take me someplace warm," he said after leaving the outlet.

We braved the cold, marching to the hotel where I scouted the lobby for Alicia. She'd been trolling for me earlier, and the last thing I needed was a barrage of forty questions about Asmed. In my suite, I dropped a Lipton's tea bag in a mug of water and nuked it in the microwave. "Sorry," I said. "No fancy ritual," plunking it in front of him.

"It's hot. That's all that counts."

"Okay. I can't stand it. What's this all about?"

"You. Aquifor."

"Should I be flattered or frightened?"

"A bit of both. These are ruthless people, Chu. And Olivia Pereira, she's a bloody assassin. Literally. Seventeen people are dead because of her. I have it documented."

He pulled his laptop from his bag. "Six months ago, Aquifor commissioned me to document an event between the Polisario and the Moroccans in Layounne. A peace negotiation. Aquifor billed it 'Growing Peace in the Sahara'. Everything was going great until day three, when all hell broke loose.

"My room was down the hall from the conference area. I'd forgotten a tripod and went back to fetch it. Praise Allah. Thirty seconds later, a war erupted outside my door. Never lasted long, three, maybe four minutes, but it felt like a bloody eternity.

"When it settled, I peeked out the door. All I had was my phone, and I took this video."

Smoke. Bullet holes in the walls, shattered glass. I could hear Asmed's breathing, laboured and shallow, the image bouncing as he crept through the corridor. Dropping to floor level, the phone recorded pandemonium down an intersecting hallway, a wounded hotel employee bleeding profusely on the floor. Hovering above him, five figures, two uniformed Aquifor personnel and three, what appeared to be terrorists. After a brief consultation, the Aquifor officer pushed his rifle into the man's chest and shot. He spoke in Arabic, his tone stilled, then the three terrorists ambled down the hallway out of sight.

Asmed translated. "He says 'go to the south exit. The way is clear for you'."

"Murderers."

"I'll say. Everybody's pointing fingers, except at the obvious. Aquifor planned the whole thing. They're not interested in peace. Or cooperation. They're setting up the Polisario to take the fall, and my bloody uncle is helping them do it. He was on the news accusing a Sahrawi splinter group of orchestrating the attack."

"Have you shown this to anyone?"

"No."

"Why not?"

"Because they think I'm dead. They firebombed the hotel after shooting everyone. Anyone inside that building burned beyond recognition. I was in the parking lot when the front of the hotel collapsed. And get this— Pereira was across town at another hotel.

"The night before the chaos, I got to talking with a Brazilian journalist. Seems Olivia had a twin brother who died mysteriously when they were kids. One newspaper reported the sister was being questioned. The journalist investigating the boy's death got a little too close. Authorities found his remains in a burned-out car two days later."

"Two workers died at Aquifor's facility while I was there. She called it an accident," I said.

"Not likely. Aquifor is backing her all the way. She fit right in with their plan, especially in Layounne. It's easier to get away with things where chaos has reigned for fifty years. Nobody's looking. Nobody cares. Aquifor can hide what they're doing under the insanity of our own craziness."

"I need to stop," I said. "My head is swimming. Let's get some fresh air."

Ice pellets pummelled us as we exited the hotel. A westerly blast was gathering force and although Asmed never complained, I could feel his discomfort. I steered him to a small café where we could watch the assault from the warmer side of a plate-glass window.

Settling in, I began. "I'm sorry I treated you so badly in Tifariti."

"We were under a lot of pressure."

"No. I was a jerk."

"Insensitive maybe."

"It was all about me. Getting what I wanted."

"Did you get it? Get what you wanted?"

"If getting ostracized from my last two digs makes up getting what I want, then I got plenty."

"I know how you feel. Getting ostracized. Can I ask you something, Chu? Something personal?"

"Could I stop you?"

He shifted forward on the table. "Have you ever been in love?"

"I'm in love with my work."

"Do you remember when we met outside Robarts library?"

"Mm hmm. You were pushy and loud."

"Do you think it was an accident I was there that day? I watched you for weeks. You went there after that class without fail."

"You were stalking me?"

"I had feelings for you. I've always wanted more than just friendship. I need you to know that."

Pushing back from the table, the feet of my chair scraped the terrazzo tile, and I laughed nervously. "That's interesting news. What is it you think I should say to that?"

"How about what's in your heart."

"I don't have time for what's in my heart. My head is ready to explode."

"You're still blind."

"You can see my life better than me?"

"No. I just see—"

"What?"

"A bruised little girl. You remember the last days in Rekeiz? When you called me on my shit? I was hurt, Chu. All I wanted was an ear. You wanted to fix me. Fix me the way you fix yourself with work. Work wasn't what I needed. I needed you to listen."

"I never tried to fix you. You were angry."

"Yes. Yes, I was angry. But whatever you did in Tifariti, I understand now you were being true to yourself. To your work. You told me to finish my film when I wanted to quit, and you were right. I was so caught up in my own bullshit. I'm not here to fix you either, Chu. I just want you to know you're not alone."

"That's hard for me."

He sipped his tea, staring at the white blanket blowing in from the harbour. "How did you feel when you stepped on the site at Rekeiz?"

"It was a fairy tale."

"And this? How do you feel about this?"

"More like a nightmare."

"I get that."

"How does feeling anything help? Feelings solve nothing." The last words came too loud, causing an elderly couple to scowl.

"Stuffing them into your guts makes it worse."

"I just don't want this to happen."

"What? What don't you want to happen?"

"This insanity," I blurted back. "I want it to stop. The destruction of that site. This is the most significant find since Olduvai Gorge. And they couldn't care less." I sucked in a deep breath. "This thing is alive."

"Alive?"

"Yes. These aren't artifacts like Rekeiz. They're bloody entities."

His eyes widened.

"Life caught in the rocks," I continued. "In the runes. Asmed, this thing is waking up, like a seed cracking through its shell, reaching for sunlight."

"Why does Pereira want to destroy it?"

"Because it's in her way. It's an obstruction."

"I had my film, Chu. This is your film, your contribution. Whatever called you to Qaanaaq, you need to finish."

"I wasn't called. They inflicted it."

"Do you believe that?"

"—No."

He reached across the table and squeezed my hands. "What do we do to expose these bastards?"

I spent the next hour bringing Asmed up to speed. All the players and, most notably, Siti. I told him about the visions at the ziggurat, how I connected with the PNs, my shamanic flight and my confrontation with Isaiah's tuurngaq. He believed it even more than me, my words sounding outrageous, concocted in my own ears, yet it was my voice telling the story. I felt like one of those trains I'd seen in Halifax, powering down the track, unstoppable in my momentum. It was the freest I'd felt since leaving for the U of T over a decade ago.

We returned to the hotel and planned to meet later for dinner. As he walked down the hall, I called, "Asmed."

He faced me.

"I'm glad you came."

* * *

As soon as the door clicked shut, Siti's voice was calling from the radio.

"What's going on up there?" I asked.

"They're keeping me isolated in the lab," she said. "There's been a huge influx of military personnel. Aquifor mercenaries, I'm guessing. No uniforms. I overheard them discussing Qaanaaq, about sending a force to secure the area. And that explosion. Rattled this place to the bones."

"Why would Aquifor want to secure Qaanaaq?"

"Restrict information."

"There's a news crew in Qaanaaq right now."

"Not sure what they can do. But I have been conducting my investigation. Ms. Pereira's optical clearance is extremely helpful. I've accessed her classified documentation."

"You hacked into the database?"

"Hacked? Such an uncivilized term." I could see her face in my mind's eye squinching in repugnance. "I prefer to call it covert browsing. Regardless, I've come up with some interesting findings. Aquifor is investigating the ziggurat as the source of tritium. But there's something else altering the atomic structure of the water that's tied directly to the energy disruption. As usual, their thinking is two-dimensional. There's no consideration for a biological component, which we've stressed from day one. It's leaving them with dead ends; every time they think they've come up with a solution, the physical material shifts and blocks their passage. A game of quantum chess, you might call it.

"In effect, the ziggurat is strategizing. Aquifor is being outmanoeuvred. The ziggurat—the beings composed within it—are pure mind. Thought without form. They shouldn't exist. Or we shouldn't be aware of them. The only comparison I can come up with is emotion. We feel our emotions and they drive our actions. They're as real as trees or rocks, but no one has ever discovered how to measure them. You can't put emotion in a container."

I drew in a large gulp of air. "What about the ziggurat?"

"The energy field is emanating farther out from the focal point of the dome and Dr. Kai has advised me there's been massive power fluctuations. Are you feeling anything, Chulyin? Any changes?"

"I'm not sure what I'm feeling anymore."

"Are you having visions? Is Raven—appearing?"

"Yes."

When I thought the radio had gone dead, she responded, "I can feel them too."

* * *

Ove joined Asmed and me for dinner later in the hotel's dining lounge. The two men took an immediate liking to each other, which relieved me.

I felt unstable as Arctic ice in June, and the tension between these two would have been another crack in my already wavering spirit.

"The cold is one thing, it's the lack of light," Asmed said.

"Next time come in summer," Ove returned. "But bring a shotgun. Mosquitoes are as big as vultures."

"Sounds delightful."

We ordered hors d'oeuvres and Ove dug into the shrimp and his conversation. "I'm getting reports Aquifor security has completely swamped Qaanaaq. And that detonation had a charge equivalent to a small nuclear device." He opened his phone and passed it to me. "One of the NASA satellites took this footage. That device they're setting up. It's a laser. Watch."

On the screen, the ziggurat, and the newly constructed concrete wall off to the left. Nothing—then a narrow shaft of light shot from the laser, sparks splattering from the surface of the dome. At first there was only an impressive light show, then the ziggurat began wobbling. Seconds later, a pulse walloped, reversing along the beam, sending a shock wave that rendered the laser useless, smouldering in a cloud of smoke and steam.

"If I was a betting man, I'd say that thing was defending itself. But get a load of this," and he took the phone from me, zooming in on the location of the laser. "Absolutely no effect on the soldiers. Or anything living. Seems the wave, or whatever it was, was selective in what it targeted."

"Selective?"

"Yes. Bypassed anything biological. But it disabled the entire electrical grid along with their little weapon. Except one thing. There's a single radio signal still transmitting from the complex."

"Siti," I said.

19. THE SOUND OF DRUMS

"It's breathing."

Siti's voice inflected excitement, an aberration from her typical matter-of-fact monotone when she explained the unexplainable of scientific phenomenon. Asmed and I crowded the radio, which I placed flat on the table.

"The ziggurat is oscillating. Short, powerful gulps like a diver coming up for air. And the energy itself, I can't even define it as a wave or a particle. We thought they were muons, but now? We just don't know. It's mutating at an incredible pace."

"Mutating into what?" Asmed asked.

"Indeterminate," she returned. "It's beyond my experience. Outside the realm of conventional science."

I changed gears. "The ziggurat. They tried to vaporize it."

"I knew something was up. I felt the ground shake. They came storming back in here like gazelles fleeing a pack of lions."

A loud knock, and Ove barged in, tossing a manila folder on the table.

"The water analysis. I just received it from Copenhagen. You won't believe it."

"At this stage of the game, I'd believe anything," I said.

He leaned forward, pressing on the table. "They thought it was amniotic fluid. Same chemical composition. Complete with all the proteins and gene signatures."

"What?" Siti chirped from the radio.

"There's more," he continued. "At first, they thought it was a mistake. That they crossed the samples with a paternity specimen. The technician called and asked where I collected the sample, and I told him, the glacier in Qaanaaq. He couldn't believe it. It seems our water sample is full of human DNA."

Ove continued: "The genetic analysis detected an anomaly in one chromosome. An anomaly that relates directly to brain function, driven from the amygdala. The term he used was 'hiding' when he described it— that a curtain of thymine DNA obscured an aberrant gene. And the gene, apparently, is producing viable amounts of an unidentified hormone."

"Fascinating," Siti said. "We've been recording biological data from our PNs since we began our investigation. Recently we detected an increase of transposons—genes that can jump from one location on a genome to another. We never made the correlation until a few days ago; the upsurge in transposon transference corresponds exactly with the date the ziggurat began emitting energy. Coupled with that, there was an exponential spike in our subjects' abilities to communicate telepathically."

"This thing is human? And you can communicate with it?" Asmed asked, perplexed.

"The jury's out on question one and we're working on question two," I returned. "We're trying to establish a link between the energy being emitted and the runes. If they are trying to talk to us, which I believe they are, it's in unfamiliar symbols and impressions. We just don't understand the language. One thing is for sure, these are beings beyond our reckoning of intelligence. There's a collective design going on, like bees in a hive, all working toward a common purpose."

"And we're part of the hive," Siti said.

"What on earth would their purpose be?" Asmed asked.

"To leave," Ove said. "Taktut said it. They are preparing to leave."

"Who's Taktut? Now they're leaving? To go where? And where did they come from in the first place?" Asmed pressed his hands against his head. "You're all giving me a headache."

"Taktut. He's right," I said. "He's known it all along. These are our genetic and biological ancestors. Not just mine, but everyone's. This is the common thread that binds us all."

A light flashed across Asmed's face. "After you left Rekeiz Lemgasem, my grandmother said something strange. She told me you would set them free. I asked her what she meant, and she drew this in the dirt."

He scrolled through his phone, then passed it to me. Scrawled in the dirt a crude Raven, wings fully spread, a stone in its beak, two smaller stones hovering above it.

"Then she pointed at the image and said 'when the bird flies, no more learning' and she scrubbed it away with the stick."

I glanced up and their faces were puppets in a black void.

(Can they see me like I see them? Is any of this real, or am I a stranger wandering a strange path inside someone else's dream?)

"Chulyin. Are you okay?" Asmed's voice tethered me back to the room.

"I'm—fine. Tired."

"You look like you saw a ghost."

"No. Just tired," I said. "Taktut. I need to find him."

They talked for another fifteen minutes, then left. I never asked them to leave, but maybe they read the glaze in my eyes, or my absence from their conversation. I kept asking them to repeat what they'd said. My ears detected their sounds, but I could not interpret their words, my comprehension frozen like the sea beyond my window. Maybe they saw that. Maybe.

I was about to implode. So much, all at once. My logical mind reeled. The circuits I had installed to protect me from my inner world of reckoning, frazzled. I had this design: me—the perfect woman, the famous archaeologist, the girl who made it from Pang, the entire hamlet chattering my name. I saw pictures of myself hanging on walls, collecting awards, unearthing incalculable treasures from hidden tombs. I'd be a liar if I said I never wanted to return to Pang victorious. Having made a name for myself, a genuine power of example.

Then this. This disruption. This left turn that spun me off in the very direction I was trying to avoid. No, I wasn't doing a thing for Pang, for my people, for my culture. All the work, all my effort, was for me. To make me feel—am I going to say this—superior? I wanted to feel a grade above them all. Inuit and qallunaat alike. I was better than all of them put together and I could prove that through my new label—archaeologist. Now it was the archaeologist who brought me to the very place of that left turn.

I needed to be alone. To shut the world off for a day, an hour, an instant. But I couldn't. I was like an Arctic char who didn't like being wet, that didn't want to swim anymore, knowing that not to swim meant certain death. And death? So what? What the hell did this life bring me, anyway? Misery, abandonment and a giant chip on my shoulder. Isahah was right. I was a fake. Not just a fake to the blood that pulsed through my veins, but a fake to the spirit that hid or called or wished for some kind of acknowledgement. But that acknowledgement was a dangerous thing. It would shatter this image I created for myself. Chulyin the untouchable, Chulyin the prized one, Chulyin the one who rose above every challenge, met every adversity, manifested every dream. Except one. The quiet voice of doubt that lay dehydrated under the stone of my icy heart like a shrivelled springtail.

My ears were discordant when I left Pang. Aanaq's voice, serene, her words telling me she loved me, sharing the spirit of our ancestors and the roots of all who came before us. They were irritations that deflected me from my own inventions, my own thoughts, to escape the very things she was trying to impress on me. Raven. Tuurngaq. Shaman. Me. No, no, no! I clonked my feet and told her I'd have no part of it. I rejected it all.

Now her words returned, beating down my defiance through the process of my pain. Someone said it to me once, that pain builds character. Sure. Sure, it does. Maybe your pain, but not mine. I wanted nothing to do with it.

(Pain builds character.)

There's stillness in it. If I could only believe it. Could I possibly accept this defeat, the defeat of my defiance of who, what, and where I came from? That I am Raven? Shaman? That I am the chosen one?

(The chosen one.)

Sleep. I needed to sleep, to forget, wake up and all this was just a crazy dream, nothing more than incongruous shapes, like smoke sifting through my fingers.

But sleep wouldn't come.

I laced my boots and decided a walk to the harbour would clear my head. I took the elevator and cased the lobby for Alicia. The last thing I needed was her nail-on-the-chalkboard voice and bouncy disposition. All clear. The desk clerk was busy with a guest, and I made it through the front doors to the street. It was cloudless, the wind crisp, scampering off somewhere north, north of Nuuk, north of my sleeplessness and my desire to be alone.

The sound of drums. I started walking toward them, and a nukaq darted past, heading in the same direction.

"Hey," I called out. "What's going on?"

"They're drumming in the park," she hollered over her shoulder.

"What for?"

She stopped and faced me, flabbergasted. "Are you crazy? To celebrate."

"To celebrate what?"

"The new sun."

"Where are they?"

"In the stadium. Follow the drums." And she sprinted up the street, out of sight.

The beat drew me like a magnet, a rhythmic throb that seduced me to a feast I could not see yet knew would satiate the hollowness in my belly. Above, the moon shone silver, a haloed crescent, dimpling the blankness like a single hammer stroke punched against the pewter of night.

I walked into Nuuk Stadium; the space cleared of snow and a tight circle of bodies closing the drummers from sight. They stomped and swayed to the rhythm; their limbs unified in a choreography that escalated the lure as I moved toward them.

The nukaq had squeezed her way into the outer ring. She glanced back, spotting me, then broke from holding hands and extended hers to me. I complied and linked with the circle. The inner sanctum, composed of twenty drummers, formed a tight circle around a snow stage. On it, two throat singers chirped, warbling in perfect singularity, their feet clumping the ground, hands rising, inviting the black sky to join the celebration. Their sound wove a fabric around the beat of the drums, notes drawn in shades, and scents that drifted like a mellifluous cacophony only the darkness understood.

Suddenly, a solitary figure leapt on the stage. Everything stopped, the earth absorbing the vibrations like a sponge, consuming the thud of feet and pounding drums. The retinue held its breath.

His back was to me and he crouched low, one hand pressed against the flat of the stage. I say 'he' based only on my intuitive assumption the figure was male. Feathers covered him, black, except for his boots, which were Raven's feet, three tines splayed forward and one protruding from the heel, all tipped with pronged hooks. At first, I couldn't see his head tucked deep into his chest, the feathers shrouding him from view. Then slowly he rose, extending his arms, his wings, reaching for the sky.

A bloodcurdling shriek shattered the silence, followed by a staccato of caws that impelled the drums into a frenzy. The ground quaked with a simultaneous pounding of feet, and when I looked down, my feet, too, had joined the foray.

Raven vaulted from the platform, bounding to the opposite side of the circle. He stood before every witness, flashing his wings, then moving on to the next.

"The shaman sets our spirit free," the nukaq said, ecstatic.

A break in the circle, then a ribbon of sycophants holding quilliqs filed in, placing them around the edge of the stage. Each quilliq touched the next until the entire circumference was lit. That done, they joined the circle, and Raven moved back to the centre. One by one he extinguished the lamps, and on the final quilliq, the drums and crowd hushed again.

Raven spoke: "Today a new light begins."

He spread his wings and pulled a single quilliq from his feathers.

"Who lights this flame?" he said, slowly rotating, scanning the crowd.

When he came to me, he stopped. The moment yawned in eternity and all else fell away, just the two of us, and somewhere the pulse of drums.

He advanced, and for the first time, I beheld his mask. It was bone, fashioned from the skeletons of every creature known to me, ossified in the skull of Raven. Nothing inhabited the sockets of its eyes; and when I say nothing, they were vacuums, gathering whatever passed too close or peered directly at them. I looked away but could still feel their charge, yet somehow I was unafraid. A beak of disproportionate size projected from the skull that was neither bone, nor wood, nor any substance known to me. It was alive in movement and fibres, reticulating cilia that possessed their own capacity to see and a propensity to reach out and share with me. I heard them; vacillating, whispering in languageless notes, and I knew instinctively their benevolence and desire to set me at ease.

The shaman raised his wings and removed the mask, placing it on my head. Drums walloped the air, feet cracking the earth, and I was—alone.

A tsunami of fear and thundering darkness crushed all knowable light. (This is blindness.)

See through the gateway of Raven.

I erupted from the darkness to my front yard in Pang. The gate I smashed after Anun's death lay splintered on the walkway, screws torn from their moorings, hinges twisted from the force of my rage. On top of the post that anchored the gate, Raven. Her back was to me and she chanted a low guttural croak, buk-luk-bwee-bwee, buk-luk-bwee-bwee, bobbing her head after each chirp. Then she took flight, out of sight over the harbour.

Pass through the gate.

My feet delivered me between the battered posts, ushering me to the ice, the day Aanaq brought me there. But this was not a memory; this was experience, time about-faced, backpedalling, the sound of the snowmobile swallowed in the night. Beside me, the nukaq from the park.

"Look!" she called, pointing to a figure crawling from an igloo. "Aanaq! It's not too late! You can still change what needs to be done."

(I don't know what needs to be done.)

"Yes, yes, you do. Look inside. She'll show you."

(Inside what? I can't see.)

The nukaq held my hand, staring forward, blissful. There was something peculiarly familiar, her hands rough and callused, thick with her own memories and sorrows. On the plain below, a figure laboured back to the other igloo, disappearing inside.

(Aanaq.)

We stood, hand in hand, then Aanaq's voice: "Do you think I've deserted you, my child? No. Your blindness comes in the same self-will that has always inflamed your defiance. You were never easy, and that is why I loved you so. But now there is an urgency in what needs to be done. It is not my patience that wears thin with your apprehension, but the constraints of time that call to you for action. The pieces are in motion, and you are the key that binds us to the next revelation. Time dictates these things. No more asking. No more learning."

(No more learning.)

Alone, I shifted to the tupiq behind our house in Pang. A lazy fire sent wisps of smoke into an oculus of blue, swallowing its grayness.

On the top shelf with the bones was the mask of the shaman. I jostled with a chair to stand on that I might retrieve it, and stretched my toes, extending on the balls of my feet like pivots on the jiggling chair, my calves burning knots.

(Just… a… little… more.)

It tickled my fingertips, then moved into my grasp, sending shivers up my arms. My flesh quivered and the skin on my fingers pixilated, then disappeared. I knew it was still there, the substance of my flesh; I could feel it, and I cognized the tiny gap between the surface of the mask and the bones holding it. Skin, muscle and sinew fell away like a wave receding into the immensity of the sea, exposing the sand and the foundation of bone which was seconds earlier, unseen.

This is the truth of who you are.

I placed the mask on my head. The skeletons of Aanaq's collection roused, revitalized in their familiar shapes and forms; coats of fur, scales of fish and the cartilage that fashioned fins draped their boney frames, all things dead brought back to life.

At my feet, a pool of liquid translucence, I surmised to be the remnants of my dripping flesh. It dribbled from the bones of my elbows like beads from an icicle in a spring thaw, revealing the scissored pincers of my ulna, my radius, joining my elbow to my hand. Along them, tiny impressions that clarified from blurred smudges to the detailed etchings Aanaq had carved into the bones. Projecting from the carpal bones of both hands, the rune Roscoe had shown me the day we visited the site, glittering sapphire.

See through us.

I pressed my palms against the sockets that had once housed my eyes. Drums erupted, and the shaman appeared on the other side of the circle, performing his rituals, calling in the sun.

"What did he give you?" the nukaq asked.

I opened my fist and, in my palm, a single springtail.

"Taktut."

"Who's Taktut?"

"A friend," I said. "The bringer of light."

20. TAKTUT

We are the collection, and they are the container. There is no commission until choice occurs; this knowledge is crucial. The one called Chulyin is the catalyst to this understanding, and her choice channels the release of the collection. Calibrating each component to the specified resonance is imperative before discharge of our collection becomes possible.

The container must be sound that we can reach critical mass. Once achieved, the collection becomes self-sustaining and we actuate to our next destination.

There is no expectation or predestined result. Ours is pure creation. A process understood by the container as magic; when a collection appears seemingly out of nowhere. We can tell you this: nowhere does not exist. Space contains all collections, and the power of choice ensures their manifestation. We do not presuppose your understanding will be complete, and that is the process of creation. We are The Foundlings, and this is how it has always been.

When the unit Chulyin ignites the spark, we fly, but we are never absent because we leave our footprint. The forms that inhabit the container adapt, and this adaptation is consistent with the cooperative spirit of units that comprise the container. How it develops we do not know. We cannot force an action on the container in any direction. The growth potential belongs to how the space receives it. It is space that is the creator, not the collection nor the container. When Chulyin realizes this with the others, her choice will set us free...

My fist cradled the springtail as I entered the hotel lobby. Beside the reception desk, Alicia had pinned Asmed against a pillar in a one-way conversation. He scanned above her, around her, searching for a polite escape, and when he noticed me, he waved elatedly.

I put the tiny creature in my pocket and strolled toward them.

"You two know each other?" Alicia asked, hungry to consume us in a smorgasbord of her self-directed conversation.

"Yes," I said. "We went to U of T a long time ago."

"Imagine that? Then meeting out here at the top of the world."

"Quite a coincidence."

"Oh, I don't believe in coincidences. Nothing happens by chance. Do you believe that, Dr. Nakasuk? That nothing happens by chance?"

Asmed rescued me. "Well, Alicia—it is Alicia, isn't it?—I'm not sure if it's the stars or fate or just darn good luck that brought me here, but I'm glad for it. We haven't talked in years. And we'd like to catch up. If you'll excuse us."

He grabbed the arm of my coat and tugged me toward the café. Her wounded face returned, the same one she had when I shooed her off the day we met.

"I have some flight options for you," she called as we walked away. "Whenever you have a minute."

"I felt like a cornered rat," Asmed said as we sat at the bistro table. "I'm glad you showed up before I had to bite her."

"She's Aquifor," I said. "My babysitter. I'm putting her off. They want me out of Greenland."

Just then, Ove walked in and plunked himself beside us.

"That Aquifor princess is relentless. She sticks like bear droppings to a blanket. You can't shake her."

We laughed, which anchored me to the room and the men and the sound of their voices. My skull still vibrated from the Raven mask, and I touched my hair to verify the mask was not still crowning my head.

"Qaanaaq is on forty-eight-hour lockdown," Ove said. "Aquifor petitioned the government, citing unstable conditions at the plant."

"That's a problem," I said. "We're going to have to connect from here."

"What do you mean, connect?" Asmed asked.

My sense of being grounded was short-lived. "Ilimmaqturniq," I said. "Shamanic flight. I have to join with the ziggurat through Raven.

Whatever is going on revolves around the winter equinox. And that's only two days away."

"What do you need from us, Chu?"

"Support. Ove, you've seen the preparation for this. We'll set it up in my room and go from there." I pulled the springtail from my pocket. "A shaman gave this to me earlier. I need to see what it means."

* * *

Ove left to collect material for my ilimmaqturniq, and Asmed retired for some much-needed rest. In my room, I plunked myself into a chair and peered out through the glass wall at Nuuk. The wind had vanished, and the clouds dispersed, the moon dipping west into the ice of the harbour.

That's when Taktut arrived.

I didn't see him right away; the light was dim. From the balcony above, an icicle hung like a crystal stalactite, refracting a thin ray on to the table. In the centre of the beam, the springtail, his antennae twitching batons, a maestro conducting a silent symphony for the audience of me. I watched curiously, intrigued, as the insect leapt to the arm of my chair, then crawled onto the back of my hand. My tactual input reverberated, and I could differentiate each of its six appendages pussyfooting on my skin.

I closed my eyes. Nothing. And when I say nothing, I do not mean a void or an unconsciousness like sleep. It was the nothingness of anticipation, the wonder of openness for what might come next.

From the darkness, movement. Wings, then the sensation of flight, Raven rising and looking down at a body, Chulyin's, there by the window, while the moon sank lower into the harbour ice. This mitosis differed from the flight over the glacier and the conflict with Isahah's nanurluk. The decibels of fear softened, and my apprehension, although still present, dwindled in volume.

The springtail reared on Taktut's hand, leaning back on its haunches like a stallion ready to bolt into a gallop.

"Welcome, my dear. So glad you came."

(I was worried. I thought you…)

"Died?"

(Yes.)

His eyes blazed. "It would take more than a nanurluk to squash this bug. In two days, the sun breaks free and returns to us. We have one last task to perform."

(What is it we need to do?)

"Make a hole in the sky."

(I don't understand.)

"It's time to tear the fabric of darkness for light to enter."

(How? How can I tear the sky?)

"Raven has this power."

(I'm not ready.)

"This is the voice of your flesh. You lack strength not in your ability, but in your capacity to believe you can make it so."

(My belief is weak.)

"No. Soolutvaluk is weak. She does not possess the power that Raven does. You arrived as Soolutvaluk and now your wings are restored. What you have chosen marks the progress of your healing and returns your capacity for flight. Soolutvaluk is no more. You are Raven, deliverer of light."

In that moment, every modicum of grief and anger, sorrow and loss appeared before me. My mother floating on the water; my anguish the day I found Anun at the foot of Odin; Aanaq's hands braiding my hair, her fingers brushing softly on the nape of my neck. There was no crash in the realization, only a serene flatness. A calm that tethered me to their lives, and to those who beget them, our ancestors, reversing time to every face, every spirit from which I'd sprung, culminating in the runes that populated the ziggurat.

There is no death, only transformation.

Raven looked down at Chulyin in the chair, and their eyes met.

"Do you see what you become?"

What were two entities melded into one, their amalgamation sending shreds of us into a vacuum that devoured everything except our wills to survive. Our memories dispelled like fleeing phantoms, leaving bare the full power of unrestricted choice. There was nothing left to gather or collect. Absolute. We were all and everything we needed.

(Yes.)

Delight shimmered on Taktut's face. "This is beautiful and perfect. When you release the desire to know, your openness ignites. That openness eliminates doubt, making way for boldness that spans the gap to ensure safe passage for The Foundlings' journey."

(How could I not have seen this before?)

"You were incomplete. This is not a fault or judgement. It is the natural order and the process of your healing."

The old man was ebbing, and he spread his arms toward Chulyin. "See through her eyes one last time. See the fear, the contempt in her heart. This holds her from exposure to the light. Her despair lives not in the darkness, but in the fear of it. Behold what lies within!"

My mother's corpse bobbed in the sea, a school of fish consuming her, biting her hands, her flesh. Her head, face down, searched the deep below, convulsing in the water with their feeding frenzy.

A herd of seals joined the foray, but not for the flesh of my mother. They were hungry for the fish. Their attack was swift, dispersing the school, but not before a boisterous pup devoured a minnow that was nibbling on my mother's thumb. In the turmoil, her body flipped, and all that remained were the eyeless cavities of her skull.

The seals frolicked through the waves to a rocky outcrop, a place to bask after their meal. The pup did not see her stalking; the polar bear approached with great stealth. She had three cubs to feed, and they were starving. She pounced and caught her prey, the pup that ate the minnow, the minnow that feasted on my mother's thumb.

This bear was aging—it was her last litter, and she could swim and walk no more. The aged mother bear nestled on the earth in a patch of soft moss where she died.

It wasn't long before scavengers sniffed a meal. Wolf, fox, gull, and the great snowy owl approached, eager to devour her, but not before Raven. Raven was first to arrive.

Cautious, Raven cackled and hopped beside bear, aware the others scented a feast, that they were on their way.

"What are you waiting for? Are you going to eat me?" the bear's spirit asked.

"I'm going to set you free," Raven replied. "I'm going to take your fear so you might be in peace."

"I'm not afraid, Raven."

"What about them?" Raven squawked. "Wolf is swift and smells your blood. He is not merciful."

"You are a liar. A trickster. There's no hope for me."

"I am your hope. Give me your eyes and I will take your light before it's too late."

Raven hopped closer.

"Stay away! I will tear you to shreds." Bear's words echoed off into the tundra, and the shine was dulling in her eyes.

"Suit yourself. But they are near."

Fifty metres away, the wolves charged, ears pinned back in swiftness, tongues salivating for an easy meal.

"Your gift is precious and so is mine. Your eyes will see farther, and your ears tune to the heartbeat of your prey. You will be the greatest of all hunting bears and never know hunger again."

"Raven, take my light. Be quick."

With that, Raven hopped on the great bear's head and took her eyes.

I was Chulyin, back in my bedroom in Pang, Raven perched on my bedpost. In the kitchen Anun, Aanaq, whispered, but my concentration turned to Raven. I did not look away as I did when I was a child, and curiosity replaced my fear. "Did you keep your promise to bear?"

"She did not suffer the ravages of the wolves."

"What did you do? What did you do with her light?"

"I brought it here for you."

My mother appeared on the edge of my bed as glinting moonlight on a rippled ocean. But she did not enter through my eyes; she plunged through a crevice in my heart and the ears of my soul, bursting through the surface of my consciousness like a breeching whale. The celerity of her arrival momentarily disoriented me, and then came the flood of my grief.

"Why did you leave me?" Tears welled in my eyes.

"I was wrong. I did not know the pain I would cause. I'm sorry, I'm so sorry I left you the way I did."

"You didn't care. You didn't give a damn."

She hung her head. "That is the appearance, but it is not the truth. I could not see past my suffering. It was a selfish act. Can you forgive me?"

"You abandoned me. Why?"

"You are right, my beautiful daughter. I left you because I was a coward. What I did was shameful. I make no excuses." A tear sparkled down her cheek. "Could you ever believe how much I love you?"

"Love? Deserting me is your way of showing love? It's too late! Why are you coming to me now?"

"To thank you."

"For what?"

"For being everything I was afraid to be."

She stood, and they were one, my mother and Raven, fluctuating between their two forms. Reaching forward, she pressed her hands lightly over my eyes.

"Take this sight… and the wings of Raven."

Her voice, waves crashing over me, throat singing on the beach, the day we danced. I brimmed, then spilled, a low murmur stirring, and the voice that shot from me penetrated inward to every cell of my body. I placed my fingers on my throat and opened my mouth, her vibration swelling ripe, and there was nothing I could do to stop it. The air and my lungs belonged to her.

My breath exhaled in an unending gust so intense I thought for sure it was my last. At the bottom of my lungs, I searched for the inhale, for eternity, then gulping, my throat opened, electrifying the cavity of my chest with magnificent air.

(I am an orphan no more.)

I sat in my breath, in the darkness, slowing the rhythm, welcoming every molecule of oxygen crossing the threshold from the room into my zealous lungs. Pumping, pulsing, giving me clarity that I was Chulyin, Raven, that I was a daughter, Bunny's daughter. I was a chunk of her, ice calving off the face of her glacier, sliding independent, yet intricately connected, into the sea of my experience.

(Bunny, I forgive you. Us.)

It began snowing. Fat fluffy flakes drifting, settling on my balcony, piling in curved little ridges along the black rail. I watched them drop, silent, each with its own individual expression, needing no permission or purpose, simply falling. These were the pieces of my heart finding their way back to me, deliverance from my anger and my shame, giving shape to the sanctity of my forgotten soul.

On the table the springtail, still and desiccated, the way the shaman had given it to me during the drum ceremony. Beside it, a single Raven's feather so black it consumed light that chanced to get too near. Black except for a single deviation—a spray of brilliance on the tip that rivaled the snowflakes on the rail, transmuting down the hooklets and barbules, an osmosis of intention making the whole feather white.

21. INDRA'S WEB

The snow was still falling when Siti's voice jarred me from sleep. "Chulyin? Are you there?"

The radio was on the nightstand, and I fumbled, grabbing it

"I'm here."

"I know what they're up to."

"Who?"

"Aquifor. Pereira. It's the stone they want. The ziggurat. It's a mountain of tritium. A piece of that ziggurat the size of my fist has enough energy to power a nuclear fusion reactor for a hundred years. Or enough firepower to obliterate half the planet.

"I hit the jackpot. I found the entire file on the ziggurat. Aquifor knew it was there months before they hit it with the ice harvester. They've been conducting their own analysis long before the energy surge shut down production. At first, they thought it was just an inconvenient obstruction. But the closer they got, they noticed a change in the chemical composition of the water. Elevated levels of tritium. Heavy water.

"Tritium is rare in the natural world, and synthetic manufacture can't produce enough to make the fusion process economically workable. With this supply, Aquifor can call the shots.

"They plan to break the ziggurat down into chunks and remove it from Greenland over the next six months. Without the knowledge of the Greenlandic or Danish governments. Then sell it to the highest bidder."

"Break it down?"

"With another blast from the laser."

"They already tried that. It backfired."

"Because of a miscalculation. A miscalculation I provided that falsified the target point. They suspect I fudged the numbers, so they sent my computations to their eggheads in Brussels for a second opinion. But it will take them a month to decipher what I gave them."

I heard her take a deep breath.

"Chulyin. We've got to incorporate Dr. Kai into the equation. The ziggurat. It's a biological fusion reactor."

"Explain."

"A fusion reaction requires three basic elements to occur. Raw material or plasma. A vacuum vessel to contain the plasma, and a magnetic cage that can cool the plasma temperature.

"Think of it this way. The ziggurat is the vacuum vessel. The runes are the plasma. Individual units of life collecting into a single mass of power. And the PNs are the magnetic cage. The biological force that holds it all together. We're the gun barrel. Once that life energy attains fusion ignition state, it can fire into the cosmos until they collide with another stellar object.

"Chulyin, this contravenes all conventional scientific thought. The biological inclusion as a component of creation, as opposed to resulting from it, is the core of electrogenetics. It's not the answer to what came first that's important. It's the question. It's the question that sparks our process. To learn. To expand. To grow. It's less about where we came from and why, and more about where we choose to go. If there is a mathematical formula for it, I'm at a loss. This," her voice cracked, "gets stuck in my throat. It's so vast. Yet I feel like I could hold it between my fingers."

A long pause and I broke the silence. "Let's put our biology to work. That's our advantage. But we have to act fast. Whatever is happening, it is going to take place at the precise moment of the winter equinox."

"How do you know?"

"Let's just say a not-so-little bird told me so."

"I have a meeting with Pereira in twenty minutes. I'll update you later this evening."

Siti signed off. Outside, the snow intensified its assault on the window, shattering into white dust that swirled and collected on the balcony.

Anun's voice wriggled into my head. Listen to your gut. It's the best compass you'll ever have.

* * *

Later that afternoon, I met with Asmed in the hotel café, and was relating Siti's revelations when Ove burst in.

"Have you heard?" He didn't wait for a response. "Pereira. She's giving a news conference in Qaanaaq at 2 o'clock."

It was 1:54.

"Put on KNR," he hollered to the barista, then spoke to us. "Aquifor sent a press release this morning."

"An update of lies," I said, and gave him a condensed version of my conversation with Siti.

"Turn that up," Ove shouted again at the barista, and Olivia's face erupted on the screen. Flanking her was Atticus and a nervous-looking Roscoe Valdez.

"Ahem," Olivia tapped the microphone. "Am I on? Okay. Thank you, everyone for coming. First, I want to allay any concerns about the blast recorded at our facility last Friday morning. One of our main geothermal pipelines approximately three kilometres below the bedrock ruptured. The sudden temperature variation caused a rapid expansion, which resulted in a significant seismic tremor. I've heard there were concerns about radiation fallout, and any information regarding radiation is false. There is no nuclear-powered equipment at the site. Also, there were no injuries and two alternate geothermal systems continue to power our operations. Repairs are currently underway to bring the damaged system back online."

"Lie number one," I said.

Olivia continued. "You are all aware we experienced a power fluctuation that disrupted the harvest of ice from the Qaanaaq glacier. Two weeks ago, we assembled an elite scientific team to solve the energy disruption emanating from a massive boulder uncovered by our ice excavators. The team has been working tirelessly to get production back online, and it seems they've come up with a solution. On their recommendation, we will emit a controlled laser pulse at the structure to neutralize its debilitating effects. This will take place on December 21st at precisely 9 AM."

A reporter off-camera asked: "Maybe we could hear from the scientific team on their rationale? The government designated it an important cultural and archaeological site. Would your plan destroy any hope of its recovery?"

"Our scientific personnel are working around the clock to ensure complete safety, with the full intention of preserving all archaeological artifacts. Atticus Day, our plant manager, is in constant contact with our advisors and can give you more technical details. Mr. Day."

"Thank you, Ms. Pereira." Atticus moved too close to the microphone, and it squelched. "The rationale is simply to disable the disruptive energy coming from the structure. A regulated and precision laser pulse will accomplish this. Much like a surgical procedure. Our attempt a few days ago deflected off—what I'll call a force field—that is insulating the edifice. Dr. Siti Okilo, head of our scientific investigation team, has calculated the coordinates to ensure we hit the sweet spot and disable the interfering buffer surrounding the structure. She assures us this will negate the energy without—and I use her words here—a single chip being broken from the structure."

Another reporter shouted out: "What are we dealing with here? What is the energy and why is it emanating from the stone?"

"According to Dr. Okilo, it is a muon-based pulse that is characteristic of typical cosmic radiation," Atticus said. "She will provide a full report to you and the rest of the scientific community once the crisis is resolved."

"Is there any possibility this laser pulse could endanger the residents in Qaanaaq?" the first reporter asked. "Or that your, what you call a precision strike, will unleash harmful disruptions?"

"Dr. Okilo assures us there is no danger regarding the muon pulsations. She states," he picked up a notepad and read, "'cosmic radiation constantly barrages the earth with emissions and subatomic particles every second of every day. These radiations are harmless and pass through biological matter as light would pass through glass.'"

"This Dr. Okilo is full of assurances. Was she here when two of your personnel died at the site?" the reporter pressed.

"That incident was both unfortunate and unrelated to anything our scientific team is currently working on. Our investigation into the cause of the accident has been delayed by evacuation orders currently in effect. The instant we can resume that inquiry, we will."

"Why isn't she here to answer questions?"

A hint of irritation flushed Atticus' expression. "I'm sure you'd agree Dr. Okilo's efforts are better served on site than here. Ensuring safety for the residents of Qaanaaq is a priority. This accounts for every second of her time."

Olivia interrupted, "Thank you, everyone. If there is nothing else, we need to get back to and complete preparations. Mr. Day will issue bulletins on our progress every six hours." Olivia ignored a raucous protest from behind the camera. "Mr. Valdez, here, will coordinate instructions to you regarding further safety precautions. Thank you."

Olivia and Atticus filed out, leaving Roscoe to deal with the wave of disgruntled reporters.

* * *

Siti hadn't called back, and that was not good news. I knew reaching out to her might prove disastrous, so I contacted Miatzo Kai. As a precaution, Asmed suggested we connect through his computer in case mine was compromised. We made the call and on the third ring, Dr. Kai popped on the screen.

"I'm worried," Dr. Kai said after we identified ourselves. "I haven't heard from her in three days."

"I spoke with her this morning. She's walking a thin line." Then I related how Siti hacked into Aquifor's security system and the discoveries she made.

"She's resourceful." Dr. Kai said, her tone less convincing.

"Resourceful, yes. Indestructible, no. Pereira is commanding her own personal army in Qaanaaq."

"Are you still there? In Qaanaaq?"

"No. I'm in Nuuk."

"Really? Whereabouts? Specifically?"

"The Hans Egede Hotel," I said.

Take a peek at this, Dr. Kai replied. A world map appeared on our screen showing clusters of glowing red dots. "The illuminations are neural transmission points where the PNs are located. Most of the brighter spots are our lab locations, and the dimmer dots are new transmissions that have appeared since your contact with the structure a few days ago. Qaanaaq is the densest concentration of this biological neural activity—the ziggurat. Now watch," and she focussed on the west coast of Greenland. "That's Nuuk," and she zoomed down on a brilliant red splotch until the image narrowed to a single building. "The Hans Egede Hotel."

She flipped back to the image of herself. "Yours is second in strength only to the ziggurat in Qaanaaq, Dr. Nakasuk. You are generating more energy than all other PNs combined. And these new transmissions number now in the hundreds of thousands. Individual PNs who are most likely unaware of what is happening. They may experience heightened sensitivity and perhaps the appearance of strange visions in their heads."

"Are you PN?"

"Yes. Although I've been trying to separate myself from the experimentation. Someone has to monitor this equipment. But I'll tell you. It's damn near impossible. I feel like an iron filing walking beside an industrial strength electro magnet. It's everything I can do to detach myself from the event. Especially that last one. The pull was incredible."

"Is Dr. Okilo PN?"

"All our testing shows no. That being said, she has an uncanny talent for predicting events moments before they happen. In fact, it was Dr. Okilo who suggested the telepathic nature of the PNs. I was only looking at the physiological characteristics of the aberration. At her suggestion, we started conducting experiments between PNs in Pretoria to determine if they could transmit and receive visual information. They could. During those trials, we detected an unidentified derivative of melatonin secreting from the pearl node in every subject. At first, we thought it was only influencing the occipital region responsible for sight. But it soon became apparent it suffused into the temporal lobe and the four major centres responsible for language. The flow of the hormone increased their ability to communicate telepathically, not only visually but conceptually, through a language only they understood. I've never seen it in all my years of research. Our encephalograms displayed identical brain patterns in the PNs. It wasn't until you connected with the ziggurat that we recorded a corresponding affinity from multiple sites."

"They want us to make a web," I blurted out.

"A web of what?" Asmed asked.

"Neural energy." Dr. Kai said.

I tossed my arms into the air. "Brain patterns. Alpha, beta, gamma. It's the image that's branded in my mind, not the terminology. All those red smudges on the map? That's us. PN's." I interlaced my fingers. "We have to connect and make this crazy trampoline. Collect. Join. Meld. Piece together. Become a single functioning unit. Surround the ziggurat with…"

"What?" Asmed asked.

"A biological magnet. A cosmic web constructed by sentient beings. A shield that contains–no–directs their energy. Siti said it. We're the barrel of a gun. They're going to fire themselves through the hole we make for them."

"A torus," Dr. Kai postulated. "We create a biological torus by weaving a neural web around the ziggurat."

Asmed scratched his head. "What's a torus?"

"It's a three-dimensional geometric doughnut," Dr. Kai said.

Suddenly, the nukaq who steered me into the park flashed in my mind. (The new sun.)

"When's the winter equinox?"

Asmed consulted the calendar on his phone. "The twenty-first. Three days from now."

"What time?".

"Ah, 2:01 p.m."

"That's Nuuk time," Dr. Kai said. "Qaanaaq is an hour behind."

"That's when we do it. That's when we make the web. Dr. Kai, can you coordinate this?"

"Dr. Nakasuk, I feel you are better qualified to sound the call for action than me. You've already imprinted your psychic energy on the group.

They've seen what you've seen, experienced what you did when you joined with the ziggurat. Besides, I'll be busy monitoring equipment."

"No," I said. "You're PN and we're going to need every morsel of energy we can muster."

"Can you do this from Nuuk?"

"I have no choice."

I hung up the phone.

"Indra's web," Asmed said.

"What's that?"

"You just described Indra's web. I took a course in world religions at U of T. Indra is a Hindu god and Indra's web is this net that hangs over Hindu heaven. Mount Meru. The axis Mundi that connects everything, a fabric where all the threads of life intertwine. And where they intersect, there are these jewels. Pearls. And if you pluck one from the web, the essence of every other pearl reflects every other pearl within it. No beginning. No end. Just this labyrinth of perpetuity. Is that what you're doing here, Chulyin? Spinning Indra's web?"

There were tears in his eyes. "Thank you Asmed. Thank you for being here for me." I grabbed his hand. "Help me make that web."

22. 77° NORTH

My phone rang, and it was Ove.

"Chulyin. You need to get to my office. It's about Siti."

Asmed and I skirted through the lobby and out the main doors to a -41° chill. Ove's office was literally across the street from our hotel in one of Greenland's state government buildings.

A bored security guard glanced toward the elevators and instructed us to the third floor. Ove was waiting when the elevator doors opened, and we followed him through a labyrinth of short corridors that ended in a spacious suite, peering west over the frozen harbour.

"Roscoe Valdez sent this communication to my secure network about an hour ago," Ove began, activating a projector that levitated from a hatch in the centre of the conference table. Roscoe's face filled the screen.

"Mr. Hoj, I hope you get this message before it's too late. I'm concerned for Dr. Okilo's life."

Roscoe's hand moved toward the recording device, adjusting the camera.

"Where do I start? I overheard Pereira talking to Maxwell Hursche. I know I only got half of the conversation, but there was no mistaking what they were discussing.

"Pereira said 'the physicist has to go. She knows too much'. They're certain Dr. Okilo has breached the security system. But they're not sure what she's uncovered. They're nervous.

"Mr. Hoj, she said there would be an—accident. On the same day, they announced the laser pulse on the ziggurat. And Mr. Day is in their crosshairs too. Pereira said he was going to accompany the physicist. He knew too much. That he's expendable. Then she said, 'yes, we can eliminate them both in one shot.' One shot, Mr. Hoj. That's what she said.

"They have no intention of a controlled pulse. They're going to blow that thing up. And not at nine. At seven. They are going to send Dr. Okilo and Mr. Day out to inspect the site at seven a.m. Two hours before the scheduled strike. That's when they're going to kill them both.

"I'm trying to warn Dr. Okilo, but they're keeping her isolated. And forget Atticus. He's so far up Pereira's ass he'd never believe me.

"One more thing. Tell Dr. Nakasuk these runes are shifting. Three dominant patterns are forming. Figures. Walking stick figures, like they're off on a stroll somewhere. I've attached the images at the end of the video."

There was a loud bang, and Roscoe jumped. "Jesus. Signing off," and the screen went dead for a moment, then three figures appeared.

"Rekeiz Lemgasem," Asmed said.

I pressed my head in my hands. "I feel bloody useless."

"I can get us to Qaanaaq through a back door," Ove said. "I have a plane."

"I thought they shut down the airport."

"They have. In Qaanaaq. But I can get us to Pituffik. It's about a hundred kilometres south. My cousin flies a supply plane in there, and he's agreed to take us in. He's set to go tonight at 22:00 hours. I've also arranged a couple of snowmobiles. We can be in Qaanaaq in less than four hours."

"I'm coming," Asmed said. "I can document the whole thing."

Ove shook his head. "No. My cousin won't allow it. Weight restrictions."

"Then throw something off," I said. "Call in another favour. We need independent proof of what's going on."

"Okay," Ove conceded. "Chulyin, there's something else. I was studying footage of the press conference and found this."

He fiddled with the computer and brought up a video showing Olivia, Atticus and Roscoe rising from their seats. Then the camera panning to a reporter summarizing the conference, the crowd dispersing behind him.

Ove paused the video. "There. To the right. Over the reporter's shoulder."

Staring directly into the camera was Isahah. His eyes clear and menacing. A chill rolled up my spine. "He's going after Taktut."

"What do you mean?" Asmed said.

"He's going to hurt Taktut."

"How do you know?"

"I feel it. I feel it in my gut."

Ove was already on the phone with his cousin. "Let's go," he said, and we charged to the exit, making our way to Nuuk airport.

Ove's cousin, Oluf, looked like a character who'd fallen out of a Hollywood adventure movie. A half-chewed stogey dangled from the corner of his mouth, staining his lips espresso, the visor of his captain's cap threadbare and torn around the edges. His hair hung in dishevelled strands, wild beneath it.

"I thought there was only one." He eyeballed Ove and spoke as if we didn't exist.

"A change in plans."

He licked his lips and spat a glob of tobacco on to the hangar floor. "No worries," he said. "I've taken her up five hundred kilos overweight before."

We boarded an equally ragged craft brimming with crates and medical supplies.

"Grab on to anything that looks like it won't move," Oluf barked as he strapped himself into the cockpit. Bowing his head onto the yoke, he began mumbling, gently coaxing, encouraging the craft like a lover to lift us from the ground. Then he leaned back and fired the engines.

Pituffik housed the 821st Air Base Group, an American enclave established to peer over the top of the world. When we touched down, Ove handed us specialized travel permits, and we presented the documents to a corporal who verified them, then whisked us out of the tiny administration hut to a trio of idling snowmobiles. Within minutes, we were on our way to Qaanaaq.

* * *

The drone of the snowmobiles lulled me into deep contemplation. I couldn't get the image of the three figures from my mind. The runes.

I pressed the welts on my wrists, and a sense of intimacy, knowing what appeared on my skin was neither foreign nor malignant, welled up in me. Ancestors. My ancestors, speaking in impressions rather than memories, impressions that required no explanation, only acknowledgement.

Indra's web. Asmed's description tumbled in my mind. This conjured lattice of humanity, mirroring back upon itself, again and again, into shards of infinite and intimate human experience. The runes were the diamonds, the jewels. The PNs, every one of us, an entire universe contained within ourselves.

A stillness poured into me, except for the wind. It brought the voice of those diamonds, a vein of gems we'd uncovered at the ziggurat, a profoundness that aroused a greater recognition; that we were diamonds, too. Chips of precious gems. Pearls, circumnavigating the neck of earth, like sparkling leftovers waiting to be linked. We were water and fire, earth and air combined, the essence of life, and in that brief instant, a harmonic synthesis settled over my entire being.

Were the others experiencing this? I wasn't sure I wanted to believe they could, so I might hold it all for myself. But I knew the folly of that inclination. It was a gift, and a gift is for passing along. Hoarding my experience, or the power to create this web, whether in the privacy of my own thoughts or expressed through selfish actions, would only negate its essence.

Yes, the others felt it too. I saw it in Asmed before we left Nuuk, his eyes wide as moons, his jaw slack. That's what it was. The feeling. One of width rather than depth or length. The physical space expanding into peripheral infinity, a thin razor film that contained every piece of knowledge or understanding I ever wished to find. There was no reference point, but somehow, I knew exactly where I was. The web, the energy, the ziggurat. Yes, yes, yes, was the feeling. It was so obvious. All I had to do was remove the debris of my resistance to reveal the treasure hidden beneath. Like Aanaq's violets. Buds when I went to bed, and in the morning, blooms, waiting for my eyes to greet them.

Qaanaaq glowed on the horizon, and as we approached, a foreboding malevolence triggered a heightened awareness. Clamminess dappled my palms and Isahah's face flashed in my mind, his handshake as palpable as the day he showed up at my door in Pang.

(An Arctic char.)

We arrived in the hamlet, weaving through late-night walkers, and made our way to Taktut's house, killing the engines.

An imposing heaviness weighed on my body, my mind. "Isahah," I said. "He's here."

"Let me go in first." Asmed said, dismounting, moving toward the door.

"No. I need to do this alone."

There was no time to prepare like we did before we confronted the nanurluk. No igloo, no altar, no bindings. I dropped to the ground, jammed my knees into my chest, my arms squeezing them in ever closer.

(Ilimmaqturniq.)

The transformation was instantaneous—Raven's wings, and I was sky bound, soaring over Qaanaaq, diving toward Taktut's shack. I circled, probing for Isaiah's presence, hoping he could not detect me.

(Clear.)

I probed but could not feel him. Choosing stealth, I dropped silently just inside the front door.

Taktut sat in his chair.

(Is he dead?)

A presence, and my awareness magnified, but I could not pinpoint its whereabouts. Moonlight was leaking through the window, casting a pale radiance across Taktut's arm, his body, his head immersed in a cloud of shade dissecting diagonally across his neck.

My first instinct was to wake him, warn him of the danger. I hopped closer, and the darkness shimmered behind him.

It spoke. "You're too late."

A viscous opacity repelled the moonlight and wrapped Taktut's body in a twisting murk that defied shape or form. For a moment, I lost contact with the old man; obliterated, until I realized it was Isahah's tuurngaq, the very darkness itself. I struggled to gain composure, my shamanic balance, but Isaiah's intensity overpowered me. I fell back, stumbling, knowing I had to remain in the physical structure of the house or all would perish. Isahah slammed me against the wall and pressed with such violence it melded me there, between the timbers that groaned and cracked with the pressure. I fluctuated between skin and feathers, arms and wings, overwhelmed by Isahah and his unrelenting tuurngaq of darkness.

Then Aanaq appeared brilliant, her back to the darkness. She raised a seal hide, ripping it down the centre, hurling the two scraps to the floor.

"Tear the darkness!" she roared, then vanished in a crack of blinding light.

Invigorated, I pressed from the wall. My wings drank his darkness like nectar, and I forged my way forward into the room. It was his turn to feel my power, and he shifted his focus from Taktut to fend me off. I pushed harder, harder; his darkness resisting in kind. Deadlocked, the clash of our energies showered trails of celestial exhaust skyward, like comets butting heads in the arena of some never perceived expanse.

(He's there… keep… pressing.)

The gloom skittered. Then Isahah appeared, exposed from behind his cloak of darkness, his hands clutching Taktut's throat.

(I am the harbinger of light.)

I thrust forward, plunging with my beak. At first, nothing. He resisted fiercely, but I penetrated, like Aanaq's needle pushing through caribou hide. I doubled my effort, and he broke, relinquishing the death grip on Taktut so he might direct all his power toward me.

Taktut's eyes flashed open, and in his hand, the springtail. Before Isahah could react to the old man, the springtail leapt and clamped itself to the nape of his neck. Isahah howled, flailing at the tiny creature, but to no avail. The springtail devoured him, shredding, consuming his darkness, his tuurngaq, and he fell to the floor writhing, disintegrating into a beam of silver moonlight.

(Clear light.)

Outside, I unravelled from my foetal state. The moon bled pearl onto the road and on the expressions of the men who had witnessed only the contortions of my physical body.

Asmed said, "Are you with us?"

I heaved a cough and sucked in the silver essence. "Yes. I believe so."

He lifted me from the ground.

"He's dead," I said.

"Who?" they chimed simultaneously.

"Isahah."

I opened my fists and my palms were bloody from clenching, my nails breaking the skin, four crescents of red leering back from each hand.

"What about Taktut?" Ove asked.

I pointed to the door and Ove burst through.

Inside, Taktut sat in his chair. A gossamer of fine black particles floated, independent and unaffected by the frigid air blowing in from the open door. Charcoal powder was everywhere, and a perfect mound surrounded him, burying his feet. I coughed as I breathed the acrid dust. It coated my tongue and throat, stabbing my sinuses with the same metallic reek of engine-worn motor oil and fish guts I recalled from the harbour in Pang.

My knees buckled beneath me, and Asmed caught me before I hit the floor, setting me on the bed. My muscles burned, and my bones ached with a dull, omnipresent throb. Every sinew clung to every joint, straining for dear life, that if they dared let go, I would surely spatter to pieces on the walls.

Asmed and Ove continued speaking, my eardrums capturing a melody of garbled intonations, their words floating without meaning or attachment, mere projections issued from their mouths. I nestled somewhere behind the place from where their words sprang, the thoughts and emotions that preceded them. At first, it was a muffled din, white noise, but as I attuned to the cadence, a peculiar awareness filtered into my consciousness. I became curious, and as I did, Asmed and Ove floated beyond its outskirts, leaving me drifting in an ocean of indiscernible whispers.

I was back in the park, in Nuuk. The circle, the shaman. Raven, singing, chanting to the sky, and Suvulliik appeared, not in a cluster of stars, but runes. Runes, filling the sky and pulsing on my wrists like the pounding of drums, charging my vocal cords to call out, to sing, to gather these voices in a reverberating assembly of joy.

Outside of my body, Ove and Asmed were talking.

(They think I'm sleeping.)

The thought amused me.

(Who are these singers calling me to the sun?)

Anun, Aanaq, speaking softly from the kitchen. But that was just a memory. These voices did not speak from conscious recollection. They came from within, from around, from up, down, from every direction I identified as space, articulating in something beyond the constraints of language.

I remembered Father McMurtry preaching a sermon once on the Tower of Babel. Voices speaking, but no one could understand. I was veering through those voices, the sounds of language but a language foreign, all the while knowing what they uttered was just for me. There were so many, so tender, and there was excitement in their inflection, an appreciation on their part not to overpower or frightened me. A river of voices immersing me in a sound that caught me in their flow, carrying me to a sea of reciprocity. Then I realized I was not something in the river, I was the river. I was the flow, the gush, the voices themselves; the source.

(Am I dreaming? Am I sleeping? I cannot tell.)

From beneath my eyelids a sound for my ears, the voice of men and the click of a door. Air drifting in and out of my lungs, slowly, the cells of my body taking up the oxygen, gifting it to my brain.

Touch. Hands on hands and the sensation, distracting.

(I do not want to leave you.)

You must child. We have granted you the gift. It cannot be possessed. Now you must pass it along that others may do the same.

(Who are the others?)

We are the others. We are the Foundlings.

(What is this gift I present?)

The darkness. The void of creation.

I open my eyes and Asmed was beside the bed caressing my hand.

"Did you sleep?"

"I—I was listening."

"To what?"

"The runes. The Foundlings. They were speaking to me."

"What did they say?"

"That I had to pass along the gift."

Asmed shrugged.

"The gift. It's the darkness." I sat up on the edge of the bed. "They're calling us. The PNs. They want us to surround them in darkness. We're all part of it, Asmed. Everyone. We have to get to the ziggurat."

Across the room, Taktut sat grinning and alert. "Now we holders of darkness."

23. RELEASE

It was three hours to midnight on the eve of the winter equinox when we set out with two teams for the ziggurat. The dogs yelped, impatient, aroused by an instinctive precognition to get our journey underway. Ove led the charge with Asmed and his video equipment. I followed close behind, driving the team, while Taktut rocked and chanted, invoking his new tuurngaq of darkness.

We walked the last kilometre to the precipice, the top of the glacier littered with evidence of our encounter with the nanurluk. A deep impression outlined the grave of the fallen beast, drifting snow tailing from the northern edge of the indentation, and the creature's scattered paw prints obliterated by the ever-present wind. The great eraser. That's what the wind was, an exterminator of time and events, wiping them clean into the realm of dreams.

Asmed scouted the rim of the glacier for the best vantage point. He settled on an outcrop of ice jutting out south of the dome, giving a clear view of both the ziggurat and the Aquifor encampment. Unpacking his equipment, I noticed he'd parked himself precariously close to the edge.

"Don't sneeze," I said, craning my neck, peering into the abyss.

Ove was already driving a spike into the primal ice.

"Strap this on," and he tossed Asmed a harness, securing him with a rope to the anchor, tugging the chord, making sure the pin was secure. "That's a one-way trip," he said, pointing with his eyes into the abyss.

We made haste to the crevice that led down to the ziggurat. "Good luck," Asmed said, his voice thin, and his eyes plaintive, like the night at Rekeiz Lemgasem when we parted. Except now it was me turning my back on him. I opened my mouth to speak, but no words came out, and I swelled with the same hollowness I felt in the desert.

Walking in silence, Taktut led the pack. He seemed spry, youthful, as we approached the chasm leading to the ziggurat. Even Ove hustled to keep up. I couldn't decide if it was my muscles or my mind that produced the heaviness in my legs. Either way, I was aware of my resistance, that in another circumstance might have me turning back, turning away from the very thing I knew was propelling me forward.

"They cannot see us," Taktut said. "Come."

He leaped onto the first ledge and we began our descent. The moment my feet touched the ice sill, the shadow thickened. I felt gravity tugging my feet, the cold on my face, but the physical exposure of weight and temperature fluctuated in a blanket that projected from the old man. We were in a cocoon of shadow that enveloped us as we slipped lower toward the ice plain. I looked up, and blackness engulfed the stars too, except for one, orange and glowing.

(Suvulliik)

Above it, the stick figures from Rekeiz Lemgasem materialized, but now they billowed, like thunder clouds rolling toward a horizon only their eyes could comprehend.

"Can you see them?" Taktut called from the darkness.

"Yes," I said, but I was uncertain who I addressed. Taktut wavered in and out of my vision, a mirage flickering between darkness and the man I perceived projecting it. I thought for a moment I was in the common room at Aquifor, surrounded by holograms. Yet the glacier, the ledge, the plain below was authentic enough. But this? There was no reference point, no place where I might measure my experience to compare it against something solid, something known. Even Raven, when she showed, provided a modicum of familiarity. Here, I dissolved into the shadow like salt stirred into water. The darkness was not an entity imposed on me, but a presence I welcomed with simple curiosity, void of fear or conjecture. My skin tingled. I flexed my hand, verifying they were still flesh and bone and not feathers.

Suddenly, the idea of locking Raven away in a cage seemed absurd. The bars were my own creations. All these years I'd wedged her in a secret corner of my mind, alleging that if I wished long enough, she would vanish, liberating me. But liberated from what? To do what? Yes, Aanaq, you were right. Raven showed up exactly when I needed her. Denial of that fact fed my resistance, but now I realized how precious she was. Raven was a gift. Something to be cherished. Not a malicious, terrorizing phantom, but an integral piece of me I had refused to acknowledge.

Chulyin, come forward.

(Who calls me?)

We reached the flat, and the lights from the perimeter blared on the ziggurat.

(They can see us.)

Panic ballooned in my chest.

Ove's laughter pulled me from a tailspin. Ten metres away, Aquifor technicians hovered around the ziggurat, measuring and marking the structure with fluorescent paint.

"Hey assholes!" Ove hollered, then looked at me and roared again with laughter. "Wherever you are, old man, you need to teach me this trick." He kicked a clump of snow that disintegrated in a spray of white powder while the team worked, oblivious to our presence.

Taktut's mimicry of darkness created a perceptual conundrum. I knew they couldn't see me and assumed the veil that kept me undetected would somehow impede my ability to see them. But there was no ambiguity. The activity of the crew mulling around the ziggurat actually heightened my awareness, as if I could see what they were doing before they did it. And why. I felt them, heard their thoughts, not in an intrusive or disruptive way. The darkness granted me access to their consciousness, and I rode it like a leaf gliding down a bubbling stream.

"This is goddam ridiculous," one of them said. "We've done this ten times." Under his words, I sensed his nervousness and fear. A picture in his mind; a wife and a little boy playing on the floor with Lego blocks, and the wish, I want to go home.

"If they don't hit the right spot this time, they can go fuck themselves," a second man said. "I don't give a shit."

Siti flashed in my mind, and I smirked.

(Did you give them the right coordinates this time?)

With the darkness came a sugary essence I remembered smelling in Guatemala before a thunderstorm, a sweetness of what I learned later to be ozone. This scent was amicable, but there was an added freshness, one more of thought than olfactory stimulation. A newness that smelled like Odin and the anticipation I felt before Anun and I hiked to the mountain.

The grinding of steel on steel interrupted my recollection. The squeal of carriage wheels on the rails scratched the frigid Arctic air, and the nose of the laser cannon poked farther through the slit of the barricade, tilting slightly downward. I projected the beam in my mind to the bull's eye on the stone.

At that moment, a dog team emerged from behind the barrier and charged toward the ziggurat. Olivia and Atticus halted ten metres from us.

They crossed a newly constructed catwalk to the ziggurat, and we followed. As they approached the dome, and I moved closer that I might hear, aware of a tightness around me, and I knew it was Taktut wrapping me close, fending off their vision.

I could smell the perfumed soap Olivia used to wash that morning. From Atticus, an acrid whiff of what I could only describe as the expectation of imminent power. It leached from him like vapour from a simmering pot.

"All things change from this time forward," Atticus said.

Olivia stood silent; her hands folded in front.

"The sun in our hands," he continued, intoxicated by the prospect of his personal hegemony. "With this, we can reshape human destiny." Atticus inhaled deeply. "To be here at this precise moment. To be part of this discovery."

"You have been instrumental in our success from the beginning," Olivia said. "Aquifor is grateful—I am grateful—for your dedication. And loyalty. All of this is our reward. Your reward, Mr. Day. A reward about to be realized."

"The sheer power."

"For you? Or for Aquifor?"

"Aquifor, of course." His demeanour shifted. "This company is my life. I'm indebted to the opportunities afforded me. And now this."

"Yes, but there are a few more hurtles. And risks. Risks I know you will embrace. I'll leave you here to do a last check. I don't trust the physicist's

calculations. She's screwed us once. Make sure she doesn't do it again."
She looked back toward the concrete barrier where a gigantic clock ticked
its countdown. "Just over three hours. How long will it take you to verify
all the calculations?"

"Less than an hour."

"Good. I'll send transportation for you in sixty minutes." Olivia strolled
back to the bridge and halfway across she turned and said, "I hope you
enjoy the future about to unfold, Mr. Day."

"She's going to kill him," Ove said flatly.

Ove's observation floated into the ether. Instead, I heard—

Does Suvulliik hang its head?

It was time to begin.

I turned to face the ziggurat, which had slept silently for unmeasured
time, and was now about to wake. It seemed to shrink, not in size but in
my perceptual acuity. The space it occupied transmuted to translucence,
my mind following suit, a lucid channel opening between myself and a
vulnerability it projected. I felt its consciousness become clearer, like the
sun burning a fog from a hazy morning. The life inside the shell, the pod
that was preparing to erupt.

It's time.

I stood on an island of flickering glass, like the day Siti and I encountered
it for the first time. On the peak of the dome a white droplet emerged, two
orange threads snaking from its centre. They slithered outward, finding the
two lesser asteroids orbiting it, one stone exposed on the plain, the other
imbedded in the glacier. The moment they made contact, a gentle tremor
quivered. The ground beneath me, and the satellites shone orange, feeding
from the energy flowing from the droplet.

What I might have deemed preposterous now seemed so blatantly
obvious. I hesitate to call it ordinary—it wasn't—but in my recognition of
this new awareness, every cell in my body became a receptor. A receptor
assimilating sentience beyond the attainable spectrum of my physical
eyes, or the audible sensitivity of my ears. I heard every conversation.
Not jumbled as the din of chatter from a crowd, but each individual voice,
distinct of language and thought in unmistakable clarity. Atticus and his
crew beside me, Olivia barking orders to prepare the laser, even Asmed at

the top of the glacier, cursing the cold, fearful for what might happen on the plain below.

I heard every voice except one. Siti. A rush of panic flooded through me. (Where are you?)

Darkness flickering between the brilliance of the incandescent lights. Three metres away, Atticus, his mouth agape, startled like he had just seen a ghost.

"Where the hell did you come from?"

I lurched back, and he lunged, causing me to stumble. Atticus pounced, and the instant his hands contacted my parka, he recoiled like he'd grabbed a high voltage wire.

Taktut flashed, shrouding me behind his cloak once again. Atticus collected himself from the shock, exasperated. He stomped the spot where I had fallen, poking the ground like I had dropped into an invisible abyss.

"Did you see that?" He hollered to a worker close by.

"See what?"

"I thought I... Never mind. Get back to work."

Thirty minutes later, a dog team arrived and transported the crew to the encampment. Atticus nervously glanced back.

Their departure brought an imposing stillness. In it, I noticed my mind bending to the runes and the three figures that had positioned themselves around the orbs.

Here.

Across the causeway, the exposed satellite on the plain called to my attention. I floated toward it and as I approached, brilliant silver effusions sparked from its core, fuelling a fiery radiance that twirled in the darkness Taktut had prepared for us. I moved closer, and as I did, a profound awareness surged inside me, an expectancy of what I can only describe as joy. That feeling of returning home after a long and arduous trip.

I touched the orb.

Taktut spoke. "This is your final preparation."

I looked down at my chest, feeling his darkness stirring. It was as ancient as the old man, but he was just a symbol of the churning. This was a force wanting out, but less from its own desire to escape than mine to release it.

Then I saw it. The tuurngaq of darkness. It was not around me protecting me; it was in me. The crucible of every remembered and forgotten experience, every secret of every single ancestor since beginningless time. Raven. I basked in the knowledge of her, not as the bird, but the colours, the absorption of light in her feathers, consuming, devouring my resistance and then—

I was that little girl back on the ice, in the igloo, the quilliq flickering orange. Instead of the altar, the crest of the ziggurat stabbed through the igloo floor. Splayed across the top, soolutvaluk, lifeless, one wing torn from her torso.

"Why did she bring me here?" The nukaq who had guided me to the park sat beside me. She rubbed her hands, and I saw the tips of her fingers, raw. Her hair was blacker than night, long and straight, and the orange glow from the quilliq danced along each strand.

"To—" I stammered.

"To what? I'm cold. I want to go home," she huffed. "Who are you?"

"I'm Chulyin."

"I knew a girl with that name once. She was afraid. Afraid of everything."

"Are you afraid?"

"No. Except for that," and she pointed to soolutvaluk. "They think I know how to make her wing grow back."

"Do you?"

"No. And I don't care. I just want to go home. I'm scared."

"I'm scared too."

"That's silly. Grown-ups don't get scared." A flash of recognition lit her eyes. "Hey, I know you. You were at the drum ceremony. The shaman. He gave you his mask. I know. Why don't you fix its wing? Then we can go home."

"I'm not sure I know how."

"Then why are you here? What good are you if you can't make it fly?"

The flame in the quilliq flickered low.

"Hurry! There's no more oil! When it runs out, we'll never get out of here!"

"The bird is dead."

She stood, agitated. "You're so stupid! It's not dead. It just needs Raven's help to wake up."

It's only sleeping.

The nukaq edged toward the dome, to soolutvaluk, then gently grasped the bird, cupping it in her hands, bringing her lips close to its head. She whispered something inaudible, then brought the carcass to me. Soolutvaluk stirred and its eyes fluttered open.

"See? I told you. She was only sleeping."

The igloo disappeared, and we were on the ice in an open sea, a floating island that rolled in swells of indigo water. The two orange satellites revolved around the sun of the ziggurat, and I couldn't tell up from down. In fact, there was no up or down. Runes inside the orbs amplified, their appendages flexing nimbly, more animated. Our orbit spiralled closer to the apex of the ziggurat, spilling orange litter onto the plain and sky like lava, raining down on the structures of Aquifor's encampment.

"Can you fix her wing?"

The nukaq reached forward, and I took soolutvaluk. Reaching to the dome, I placed the bird down, pressing my hands to the stone.

The reaction—instantaneous. Voices; tens, hundreds, thousands resonating in a common space of incalculable intimacy. Life within the runes shivered into me; platinum silk raveled, arcing out, sending legions of strands bursting, forming a great circular fabric around the space that was once the ziggurat. A torus formed a matrix of pastel blue encircling the void, protecting the life within. At each intersecting point of fibres, they appeared. An army of PNs, collecting there with me to build a shield, an impenetrable torus of cerulean energy. We drew together like a cosmic cloak and I was the needle sewing it in place. Inside the torus, the egg of the ziggurat was cracking. Fractals radiated from the centre where it once stood, fault lines emitting great streams of blinding light boiling through the darkness and collecting at a single point somewhere beyond the level of my comprehension.

The thin orange strands that connected the three orbs had amassed into thick bundles of impenetrable cord, cables of light that now extended between the satellites.

Then three figures. First, like sticks, the paintings in the cave at Rekeiz Lemgasem. I looked down at my wrists and the runes pulsed, the same runes blazing on the chests of the three Foundlings.

Soolutvaluk clucked and jounced on the fiery dome. From the place where no wing existed, a new one was born, and as the wing grew, she stretched, lengthening the span with each gesture. Feathers tarred the light, filling her bones with black wholeness. All the while, the runes narrowed inside the torus, aggregating at the point where my hands melded with the ziggurat. As they did, they shrank in size but increased in luminescence, orange, yellow, then a brilliant blinding white that fizzled, spattering in the air like water sizzling on a skillet.

Soolutvaluk no more.

24. THE FOUNDLINGS

The shaman from the park stood on the apex of the ziggurat. Around us, the torus reticulated in lazy rotation, unconcerned about anything other than its existence. We were aloft in a gaseous array of outlandish constellations, scintillating the firmament, charging the shaman with a colourless brilliance that attracted me like an insect to a flame. My heart hammered, and from my vantage point, I saw a woman entwined with the torus, distant yet familiar, as my hands embraced the stone.

The shaman slowly raised his arms and removed the mask. The nukaq from the park, the child from inside the igloo, the woman pressing the ziggurat melded in a single shape, black and void as night.

Raven.

The nodes of light on the torus merged, amalgamating into a cohesiveness that manifested back as—Chulyin. I was there in all of them and they in me. One node gleamed brighter, twinkling and hanging her head, not in shame or submission, but in sheer awe, like Suvulliik calling the dawn. The PNs, the torus, the runes, the little girls on the ice. All of them. Everything was me and I opened to it.

Fear evaporated. My sense of grief at the death of Anun, Aanaq, my mother, all sat raw before me. The ice, the land, every soul in my hamlet of Pangnirtung infused my spirit, spilling my pain into the open blackness that loved it, healed it with the balm of acceptance.

Siti's voice crashed through the spectacle playing within me. A conversation she shared, but I'd never given credence to until now.

"The mathematics of love," she'd said. "Is there any equation for this? Einstein's E = MC2. Love equals—what? Is there a mathematical formula for a perfect heart beat? How can we express that as an equation? Mathematics is the only way of declaring impermanence in an equation. Quantified infinity. The shape and structure of the stars. The constellations of—what do you call it—Suvulliik? The talisman and the ziggurat. The impressions on the end of my grandfather's rungu.

"What is the geometry of love? And is it the true creative force? Can we quantify love? Or do we need to? If we choose not to classify mathematics as a science, then what is it? It's an exploration of the unknown. An adventure into both the shadow and the light. An exposition of balance, an opportunity to bring forth unquantifiable elements that exist only in our experience. Our feelings.

"There is a supreme purity in it. The mathematics of love gathers every piece of the universe and gives profound meaning to what our lives are, and to what they mean. The shape, the geometry, exists in every atom that comprises the cosmos. It's this simplicity that makes it so elusive, so unfathomable, that something of such profound meaning could be so uncomplicated. Love. Enigmatic. An equation that forms itself through it's ability to remain ambiguous.

"This new biological structure, this pearl node, is a gateway to recognizing love is not some strange anomaly apart from mathematics. It's an integral piece of it. An integer to our equation of living true to ourselves as a species.

"You, my dear, are the spearhead, the next phase of evolution. Darwin was right in some respects. That our ability to adapt to changing conditions will ensure our survival. This new adaptability comes in integrating love into our continuum. We've had scraps of it throughout history. Visionaries have speculated about utopia for millennia. Now it's time for science to catch up. It will be a Big Bang for a few of us. But for most, a gradual ebbing like a tide pulling us into a vast and loving cosmic ocean."

I lifted my hands from the ziggurat, and the welts of the runes had disappeared. Raising my head, Taktut now stood in the place where the shaman had been. The three figures clustered at a point on his chest, a pinprick of black, that I couldn't determine whether it was so large it engulfed everything around it or it was so small, I only imagined its existence.

Does this form please you?

(Taktut. Is that you?)

If you wish it to be.

(What does that mean?)

You know this form and we would speak with you through it.

(Does he still exist?)

Not in your current understanding. He would be in the place you call the moon. With others of his kind.

(He's dead?)

Transformed.

(Are you them?)

We are the Foundlings. We give you this name that you might grasp in the tool you call language. Rather, we are the in between beings. Things of no words or labels, the space that holds the shape of what you would have us be. Orphans like you, we understand the loneliness you bear and the shapelessness it projects.

Stars shivered.

Know this: you have never been alone nor ever will be. Loneliness is an illusion that fades with knowledge.

(What kind of knowledge does this?)

Knowledge that comes from a location you found at the foot of Odin. Anun, Aanaq, when she gave you the pouch with the three jewels. Taktut standing before you and beside you in the igloo's darkness. Can you not see them now?

(How can I see anything but death?)

With amenable eyes.

Taktut raised his arms to the heavens and gazed at the torus revolving, the cosmos fluctuating all around us.

This is your gift to us. Your gift of choice, and the incalculable choices made by every ancestor preceding you.

(What tuurngaq are you? Did you create this place?)

We are not creators but creations like yourself. We are pods that fell from the sky, children of choice and repositors of continuity. Our tuurngaq came to you as Raven, but now Taktut, to ensure choice remains the crucible of creation. We are only guides. Turn into yourself and see the power that you wield. Time steps beyond the fringe of your comfort and moves into the next stage of your development. This is not something we mete out to you. We are mere reflections, mirroring capabilities you already possess.

(How am I this gift to you?)

Look around. This torus arrives because you chose it. With it comes the release and perpetuation of what you classify as human. What you could not see was our broken wing, which heals with your existence. We knew it would take time for your seed to root and your pod to burst. We receive this gift. This gift of safety, where freedom is most vulnerable. Here lies the gap where we become Foundlings renewed, strewn into the stretches where we might plant ourselves again.

Embrace the gift you are. What you plant from here on in will bear the fruit of your choices. The great mother lies beneath your feet.

Raven appeared, absorbing the darkness, the pinpricks of stars and planets and suns, becoming brilliant sky. Suvulliik hung orange before her, and she snatched the orb in her beak. I reached out, and she placed the star in my palm.

This is yours to do with what you will. Our time concludes. Creation lies in your hands now.

(Can you stay longer?)

No. There is withering in the ice that foreshadows our demise.

(Where will you go?)

To the next place. We do not attach to the outcome of where our seeds lodge.

(Where do you come from?)

The orange star in your palm you call Suvulliik. A moon on a planet whose time had expired.

(Why was I chosen?)

Your seed is strongest. There is truth in what you label evolution, but that, too, has limitations. You are the beginning of a new understanding that transcends these constructs, called words and language, the things that separate and compartmentalize. You are the conduit. Your choices are your 'why'.

(How can I do these things?)

Knowledge builds from foundations already established. Power is in the connection which recognizes something greater than individuality. What defined once as chaos aligns in immaculate symmetry. Seeing roves past linear concepts; this sense supersedes all previous truths. There is no label for this, no words or tag to identify it. We do not expect your complete understanding of these words, because the words themselves are masks to the reality of what lies behind them. When words fall away, the irrefutable connection between individuals comes into clear view.

(I… do not understand.)

That is why we came as Raven. To be familiar, a label you could comprehend. Raven is the source of power planted in you by the collective spirits of your ancestors, who are the collective spirits of us, the Foundlings. We are Raven and all those who existed before and all those about to come.

Take Suvulliik and eat. This will cause the stars to become familiar. Know the power of regeneration exists within you.

I took the orb and placed it on my tongue.

There is no death. There is only this—continuity—a movement from one state, one existence to the next.

The ziggurat grew solid, and the runes ignited, glowing on the surface. A low hum ascended from somewhere beneath it, increasing in volume to a deafening bass that pounded my eardrums. I covered my ears to deflect the onslaught, and just when I thought they would burst, lightning flashed and the sound dissipated faster than my eyes could blink. Blackness rolled in again like fog from the sea, only there was a living presence in it that breathed a familiar sweetness; ozone from the thunderstorm in Guatemala. The tumult of life was about to pour into the void the torus provided.

I strained into the fog, detecting movement. Nothing at first, then a murder of Ravens. They birthed from the ziggurat, slowly, one by one, doubling, tripling, until an exponential explosion sucked the stone into their living forms. They became a single mass, spiralling into the sanctity of nothingness forged by the torus, their wings and feathers absorbing the darkness. It spewed virility—the energy and the void—an abstraction of order searching the chaos, propelling itself outward, inward. I could not tell. Time dissolved too, irrelevant against the moment, forgotten somewhere beyond the fringes of any sense I had previously known as common.

Then I saw them. Aanaq's hands, in another corner of my mind, sewing, tailoring the garments she had made for me when I was a little girl. The knowledge that ordained the movement of her fingers fabricating my safety from the cold, from the elements. And here I was, harnessing that same energy, the agility of her hands, and the hands of countless generations, on this ice plain, working through me to weave the shelter of the torus.

I opened my mouth, and Suvulliik drifted out, venting rays into the sheath of the torus. A giddiness overcame me, a curiosity that prompted my urge to pluck it from the air. Instead, I blew gently, causing it to tumble and cross into the cavity of space.

The torus quivered. The lacework of light dwindled, and the network of PNs loosened, dispersing into a sea of individuality, returning me to a state of solitude. A frigid Arctic breeze slapped across my cheeks. I looked up and Suvulliik had lowered its head. At my feet, Raven, bleached and white as snow, a tiny black pea clenched in her beak.

The ziggurat was barren. A million-year-old stone poked through the ice, fringed by the moat Aquifor had dug in their attempt to dislodge it. The ice harvesters, lifeless too, their jaws caked in rime and the stiff ineptitude of mechanical rigor mortis. I bent down and plucked the pebble from her beak.

A shrill pitch pierced the air and the clock on the barricade melted time: 1:51–1:50–1:49… They were charging the laser.

"We've got to get the hell out of here now," Ove yelled. "They're going to blow this thing."

He grabbed my sleeve and yanked me to the causeway. In seconds we were across, bolting for cover toward the cliff that the nanurluk had cleaved, jutting out from the wall of the glacier. The frequency climbed to a crescendo, and I stole one last glance at the clock–0:03–0:02–0:01. We were ten metres short when it struck, the shock wave propelling us like paper in a hurricane, slamming us into the alcove of ice.

In seconds, we were on our feet. The red beam arced, spewing globs of molten rock that sizzled as they plunged into the surrounding glacier.

The heat and vibration knocked loose an avalanche of ice boulders that rained into the moat, demolishing the metal causeway and ice harvesters. From our vantage point, we could not see the encampment; only the beam devouring the crest of the monolith like a voracious dragon. At the impact point, an image appeared in the plasma discharge. The rune that had embossed on my wrists dilated with an appetite of its own and discharged a tsunami, gorging the beam, reversing back upon the laser.

We scampered from our protective recess onto the flat. From the encampment, Aquifor personnel spurted in every direction, dashing for a cover that was nowhere to be found. The concrete barrier crumbled like a sandcastle consumed in a rushing tide, and the influx from the rune subjugated the laser's thin red beam. The cannon flushed, then ignited. Below, a massive breach in the primordial rock yawned, swallowing the weapon along with everything else above its fault line.

Baffin Bay deluged the hollow, slamming her bounty against rock that had never known water, geysering a hundred metres straight up. The sea hailed down in chunks of ice and stone, sheets of spray freezing along the edges of the newly formed shoreline the instant it hit the ground. A twenty-metre-wide trench now cleaved the production facility from the mainland, creating an island that hadn't existed only seconds before.

Where the ziggurat once stood, a massive crater now took its place. Perfectly round and smooth, and at the bottom, the crumpled ice harvesters, their twisted metal bodies lying on Greenland's bedrock, which was exposed for the first time in three million years.

I scanned the horizon. Twenty, perhaps thirty Aquifor workers found themselves isolated on our side of the chasm. Those who were uninjured tended to the moans and cries of those who were in the best way they could. Ove had dug a radio from his backpack and was barking instructions to get medics on the scene.

(Asmed.)

"We need to climb up," I said, frantic. "Asmed."

Ove stopped in mid-sentence. "Drop one of those choppers on the top of the glacier. We've got personnel up there needing attention." He stuffed the radio into the backpack. "Let's go."

We scaled the passage in record time. When we reached the summit, Asmed sat, visibly shaken, his arms clutching his knees into his chest.

"Are you hurt?" I asked, running toward him.

"No. Just a little rattled." He looked at Ove. "Thanks for the rope. I fell when that thing exploded. This place turned into a trampoline. Took me fifteen minutes to pull myself back up." He held up one of his cameras, grinning. "But I saved this. I recorded the whole thing. The other one. At the bottom somewhere."

Ove eased himself to the precipice. "I see it. We'll get that when the chopper lands."

"Some people will do anything to get the perfect selfie," I said, and we laughed.

In the distance, the whir of copter blades bit into the Arctic stillness.

25. WHERE IS SITI?

Two helicopters materialized with the Aquifor insignia emblazoned on the fuselage. One roared past to land on the flat below, while the other touched down a hundred metres from us. When Asmed attempted to get up, he toppled to his knees.

We hoisted him from the ground and helped him hobble to the copter. Behind the bubble of glass was Oluf, signalling us to get in.

"My camera," Asmed said. "We've got to get it."

Ove scrambled to the cockpit and had a brief conversation with Oluf. "Okay. One problem. Someone needs to work the winch. I'm the only one who knows how." Ove looked at me. "Looks like you're the lucky one to fetch it."

Ove strapped the harness around me, snapping the clevis hook through the metal eye on my belt, and handed me a pair of headphones. He tugged on the rope. "Don't worry. We'll let you down slow." He winked, then addressed Asmed. "Let's get you up front with Oluf. Show him where he needs to go."

Oluf goosed the power, and the blades churned a tornado of snow. We lifted gently above the tumult and moved snail-like to the jagged edge of the cliff.

Oluf positioned the craft, and his voice crackled over the headphones. "This is it. Drop her down."

I stepped from the helicopter, and Ove lowered me into the gorge. The wind picked up, twisting me like a corkscrew as I dropped into the maw, and just as I entered the cleft, a gust jigged the copter, slamming me into the ice cliff. Luckily, I'd seen it coming and cushioned the blow with my legs.

Inside the laceration of ice, the wind and sway died. I could see Asmed's camera wedged in a narrow gap below.

"I can't reach it," I said.

"How far away is it?"

"A metre and a half. Maybe two."

"Help is on the way," Ove said.

Another line descended with a gaff clipped to it. I unhooked the tool, probing into the crack, and snagged the strap of the camera.

The instant Ove pulled me through the door, Oluf catapulted us toward the facility. We steered toward the islet, and as we passed the first copter, I spotted Atticus strapped to a stretcher, two attendants loading him into the open door of the helicopter.

Below, a thin channel of coffee-coloured sea churned. Anything that could float, did—smashed wooden crates and a fleet of shattered Styrofoam waggled on the choppy water. The laser, the concrete embankment, the vehicles and every provision that existed only hours before, gobbled by the sea. Ahead, the production facility perched on the western edge of the newly formed islet. A metal chimney had collapsed and crushed an exclamation mark into a bed of crumpled pipe. The dock had completely disappeared. Cargo bays, along with the primary structure housing the labs, conference areas and living quarters, were all intact.

Oluf touched down. "I'm heading back to help on the other side," he said over the intercom. "I'll be back in less than an hour. Ove. Take this," and he offered him a semi-automatic revolver.

"No," Ove said. "I don't need it."

"Give it to me," I said and snatched the weapon from his hand.

"That's no gun for little girls," he said.

"When you see one, you can tell her that." I stuffed the revolver into my pocket.

"I'm coming," Asmed said.

"Your bloody ankle's broken," Ove said.

"Nope. Just sprained. I wrapped it up." He hauled himself from the co-pilot's chair, grimacing, biting deeper into his resolve. "Give me that spear," pointing to the gaff. "Let's go."

"One hour," Oluf said, lifting the copter the instant we hit the ground.

Our trio paraded across the helipad making our way into the warehouse bay, Asmed trailing, but not far behind. The electrical system was still functioning, and the doors swung open as we approached. Siti was our first concern, and we agreed the most likely place to find her was the lab. Navigating the empty corridors leading to the laboratory, I heard the autofocus on the security camera hum above the door.

"Somebody's watching," I said.

Inside, the lab was vacant and a complete disaster. A carpet of shattered glass crunched under our boots, equipment toppled on the floor.

"Let's check her apartment," I said, and we moved through the hallways into the living quarters. All the doors were unlatched, and when we came to hers, it was slightly ajar.

I nudged it open and felt for the revolver in my pocket.

"Siti?"

Quiet.

We prowled in. A mountain of paper covered the kitchen table, the pages congested with equations written out, then crossed off, arrows and notes scribbled haphazardly along the edges of any vacant space her pen could find. I called again. No response.

(Where are you, Dr. Okilo?)

Nausea churned my gut. "Conference room," I said, and we marched into the corridors again, leading to the common area, the seminar suites on its farther side.

The doors to the common area swished open, and the scene had completely changed. We stood on a dusty trail on a grassy plain. The sun hovered directly above in noonday brilliance, our shadows hidden beneath the soles of our boots. In the distance, a village surrounded by a scrub fence, thatched roofs rising above it in harvests of golden straw. It was hot but not stifling, and we removed our coats, tossing them in the dry grass.

We walked through a narrow gate in the thorny enclosure and into an inner courtyard. In the centre, a paddock with lowing cattle. Eight adobe huts pressed close to the edge of the prickly hedge, standing like loaves of baked bread risen from the oven of tawny earth. From one hut, a wisp of smoke drifted from a hole above its doorway.

"There," I pointed, and we stepped across the hoof-dappled ground to the abode.

A small fire was the only light, except for the day streaming in from the door behind us. There, sitting beside the fire, was Siti, a cloth of multicoloured beads spread before her. She set an ornate necklace onto the mat and looked up nonchalantly.

"What took you so long?" she said.

The three of us roared with laughter while she waited for a response.

"I should have known better than to worry about you," I said.

"Precisely." She looked at Asmed. "Who's this young man?"

"Asmed Akbari," he said, extending his hand.

Her hands remained on her lap. "No offense."

He dipped his head in a gracious bow.

"It's stuffy in here. Let's go outside where there's a breeze." Siti led us to a huge acacia tree.

"What the hell is all this?" I asked.

"It's a boma. A traditional Maasai village. You like?"

We nodded.

"I figured out how to alter the hologram. Quite simple, really. A few tweaks and here we are on the Serengeti."

"Impressive," Ove said. "What about Pereira?"

"In a pen. With the rest of the herd. She's not going anywhere soon. Did you accomplish your goal?" She directed this question to me.

"Yes."

"With Dr. Kai? Was she helpful?"

"She certainly was," I said.

"Excellent. There was quite a ruckus a while back. Perhaps you could update me?"

We relayed the events from the ziggurat.

"Why couldn't I connect with you?" I asked. "I thought you were dead."

"Hardly. I needed to focus. Disconnect from everything so I could concentrate solely on the task at hand. Fudging the numbers once was tricky. But twice? I needed to give Aquifor's think tank something impossible to refute. The team in Brussels is very bright.

"I was well aware Ms. Pereira knew I'd breached the security system. That was my bigger challenge. I created a phoney trail that spun her off in another direction, and while doing so, stumbled on her private journals buried in layers of security cryptograms. It seems Ms. Pereira had a twin brother. A brother she murdered when she was twelve."

"The journalist from Brazil was right," Asmed said.

"She strangled him," Siti continued. "Told the police her brother hit his head on the coping of the pool. But in her journal, she recounts how she knocked him out with a quartz ashtray before strangling him and tossing him in the water. Accidental drowning. That's how her brother's death was reported. But the official autopsy recorded ligature marks on his neck and no water in his lungs. Ms. Pereira had the audacity to attach the document to her journal. Daddy destroyed the original and had the coroner murdered. Even your tragedy in Layounne, Mr. Akbari. She gives a full detailed account."

"Where is she?" I asked.

"In her castle. Would you like to see?"

Before we left the common room, Siti ducked into her hut and retrieved her rungu. As we made our way through the corridors, she described how she lured the few remaining Aquifor personnel into the cafeteria, locking them in.

We arrived at a double-wide door, the entrance to Olivia's apartment. "Wood from the Ipê tree," she said. "An endangered species from the Amazon rain forest." She brought her eye to the optical scanner. "Daddy's company relentlessly cuts them down." She entered another code manually on a digital pad and the door opened. "Extra protection." We entered a foyer that was twice the size of my previous apartment. "This way," leading us into a spacious bedroom.

On the bed, Olivia was duct taped to one of the thick bedposts that rose three metres to the ceiling. Tape secured her wrists and ankles, her knees clasped tightly together, and her arms pinned to her torso with a wide grey bandage strapped around her chest. Another strip swathed her mouth, dishevelling her thick black hair. On the left side of her head, a goose egg hatched from her temple.

"I had to hit her with this," Siti said, tapping the knob of the rungu into her palm. "When I told her I knew about the tritium, she became quite agitated." To Olivia: "Isn't that right, dear?"

"How many rolls of tape did you use?" Ove asked, grinning.

"Enough. Enough to keep the lion tamed. Shall we fetch our coats and prepare for the helicopter?" Again to Olivia: "Mind waiting? We'll be back shortly to pick you up."

It was the second time we laughed from our bellies.

26. SUVULLIIK DISAPPEARS

We were waiting in the cargo bay when Oluf touched down on the helipad. Asmed's ankle was indeed broken and had ballooned to where we had to cut his boot from his foot. Siti released the remaining Aquifor personnel from their incarceration in the kitchen, apologizing profusely for her decision, which she stressed was in the interest of their safety.

Ove was on his phone barking Danish in a heated argument, which broke off abruptly. "Bloody idiot," he said, staring at his phone.

"Who?" I asked.

"The Chief Constable in Nuuk. I told him we had Pereira in custody."

"And?"

"He's insisting we release her. That if we don't, it's going to cause an international incident. Aquifor has contacted the powers in Copenhagen and they're pressing to get her off the island."

"They don't know we have her wrapped in duct tape?" Asmed asked.

"I forgot to mention that," Ove said.

Siti piped in. "Maybe when news gets out, they'll do an about face. I sent her journal to Dr. Kai twenty minutes ago. She's disseminating it to Interpol and three major global news agencies, including Denmark's Politiken."

"Genius," I said. "But what are we going to do with her in the meantime?"

Oluf was standing in the cargo bay listening to our conversation. "Maybe she could be my guest. I have accommodations in my hangar in Nuuk. Very private. And soundproof."

"We're going to kidnap a corporate executive?" Ove asked.

"Borrow," I said.

"Take these folks to Qaanaaq," Ove said to Oluf. "I'll stay behind and keep the princess company. Come back and get us when you're done."

Oluf spat a clump of tobacco onto the floor. "What about him?" He pointed at Asmed.

"He can stay with me," Ove said. "We'll get him to the hospital in Nuuk."

Asmed was beyond the point of protest.

"When will you be coming back to Qaanaaq?" I asked Oluf.

"Tomorrow."

"Perfect," I said. "I have something I need to do before I leave this place." Then to Siti, "Would you join me?"

"Of course."

We boarded the helicopter and were on our way to Qaanaaq in less than ten minutes.

As we approached, the airstrip was bustling with activity. Below, a crew unloaded skids of food and medical supplies. Skidoos with trailers raced back and forth between the terminal and town, the streets bustling with activity. Oluf dropped us on the runway and immediately lifted off to collect the others at the Aquifor facility. Siti and I headed into Qaanaaq.

"Taktut. I know he's gone," I said. "But there's something inside me that doesn't want to believe it."

"Denial is useful, sometimes," Siti returned. "But when it hides the truth, not so much."

"It's more than that. It's a memory. From when I was a little girl. There's a ritual where shamans meet their tuurngaq. It's like a job interview on the ethereal plane. Once a shaman accepts their tuurngaq, there's no turning back. They're bonded for life.

"A man was with Aanaq that day. My whole life, I wanted to believe it was my uncle Anun, but in my heart, I knew it wasn't. I remember that man telling Aanaq there was a pouch in the igloo with a quilliq and oil. It was Taktut."

"This is your truth shining through, like your lamp," Siti said.

251

"I put a feather in that pouch. I don't know why, I just did. And that pouch, I'd recognize it anywhere. I clung to it for three days in the dark. There was a Raven sewn on it. My fingers will never forget it."

We approached the door.

Emptiness saturated the threshold, a hollowness that resonated from every object, echoing into the fibre of shadow that was the room. A balm of blueberry tea tinctured the air. All about were signs of our struggle with Isahah. The old man's chair flipped, and the wall broken where I'd slammed against it. Every pane of glass cracked, injured but not shattered at what the light witnessed as it passed through them.

We didn't have to look too far. He'd left the pouch there in full view on the kitchen table. I took it up and stroked my thumbs across the Raven, then unravelled the sinew string, the smell of seal oil mingling with tea. Reaching in, the feather. And something else. A springback. I tapped the creature from the pouch into my palm, and the moment it touched my skin, it atomized into nothingness. A tear trickled down my cheek. "Thank you, my friend," I said to the darkness, then to Siti. "We can go. I'm done."

I placed the pouch back on the table, and we withdrew into the hectic streets of Qaanaaq.

* * *

Oluf was true to his word and the next day we were in Nuuk sitting in the lobby of the Hans Egede Hotel. Asmed was undergoing emergency surgery to reconstruct his ankle, and Olivia never made it to Oluf's special accommodations. Siti's information had hit the media, exploding in a frenzy of speculation and sensationalism that set Aquifor under the scrutiny of a global microscope. While we were in the air heading to Nuuk, a contingent of Greenlandic police had arrived in Qaanaaq to apprehend her.

On a large television suspended above the reception desk, a rumpled man with hair detonating from his head in a spray of curly grey smog, was being interviewed.

"I know him," I said. "He's a professor of astronomy at the University of Toronto." I called to the desk clerk. "Could you give us more volume, please?"

The anchor spoke: "For the past few days astronomers have been buzzing over a celestial event that has them baffled. Arcturus, the brightest star in the northern sky, has vanished. A team of student astronomers recorded the event, headed by Professor Wilfred Kimmers of the University of Toronto. The short video, filmed through their high-resolution telescope, captured the star at the exact moment of its disappearance. The team, stationed at Alert, the most northerly habitation on the planet, sits in the Canadian Arctic Archipelago on Ellesmere Island. We join professor Kimmers now by satellite. Welcome professor. How's the weather up there?"

"Hello Natasha," Kimmers returned. "I would call it chilly."

"Tell us. What happened to Arcturus?"

"A great question, Natasha. Point blank, we're not sure."

"Can you take us through what happened?"

"We came up initially to record the aurora borealis and how the Earth's magnetic field effects that phenomenon. The aurora wasn't cooperating last Thursday, so we trained our telescope on the sky. Arcturus specifically. We had just begun recording when this happened."

The image switched to the video of the constellations. At the bottom of the screen, a brilliant white blotch hazed in a silver halo. "That's Arcturus. Now look closely. The colour changes to orange then, don't blink," and it disappeared.

"We thought someone had knocked the tripod," Kimmers continued. "But Arcturus is a first magnitude star, which means it's visible to the naked eye."

The brief clip repeated, then cut back live to Kimmers.

"We checked our instrumentation. Everything was functioning perfectly. Then we found out observatories around the globe were reporting the same phenomenon. I understand NASA has captured the event from the James Webb telescope. We're waiting for their assessment so we might make a more calculated determination about what has happened."

"What you're telling me, Professor, is that no one knows the whereabouts of Arcturus?"

"That's right Natasha. Another mystery of science."

"Well thank you, Professor Kimmers. We'll stay in touch for further developments."

"You're welcome. As soon as we find it, we'll put it right back," he grinned.

The newscast blared back to more important things. Aquifor's stock price had plummeted to a new low.

Ove broke the silence. "We need to get out of here. Someplace warm."

"What did you have in mind?" I asked.

"Reykjavik. It's 5°C today."

"I'll pack my shorts," I said.

* * *

Three days later, we were guests at the University of Iceland. Ove and the Dean were on a first name basis, and the Dean set us up in a luxurious three level townhome in the upscale neighbourhood of Vesterbær.

Against the better judgement of the surgeon in Nuuk, Asmed was adamant about leaving with us. "Handcuff me to the bed," he told the doctor. "It's the only way I'm staying." They equipped him with an ankle brace and a bottle of Tramadol, which he expeditiously tossed into the trash bin on the way out the door.

I was pleased to hear Dr. Kai would join us. She arrived later that afternoon and it was the first time I had witnessed an expression of delight from Siti. Their hands told the story; they couldn't keep themselves from each other.

After dinner, we congregated in a colossal library with a cathedral ceiling that extended into the second level of the building.

"This is better than the common room at Aquifor," Siti observed.

"Because it's the real thing," I said, scanning a collection of musty books. "Some of these are first editions."

"We're all first editions," Siti said. "Imagine what it would be like without all these words," looking up toward the ceiling.

"I think I did," I said. "At the ziggurat. Only it wasn't my imagination." I address Dr. Kai. "What happened? What happened when they jumped? The connection just disappeared. I haven't been able to reestablish it since."

"Interesting you say that," she returned. "All the PNs reported the same thing. I've done preliminary tests on the pearl nodes, and the hormonal secretions have stopped. Gone into some kind of stasis. As if they had a job to do and now that it's done, they can go back to sleep."

Asmed asked, "These Foundlings. Do you think they've left anything behind to activate the energy again?"

"This is something only time will tell," Siti said. "I believe there is a cyclic structure to the universe. All matter shifts through the process of degradation and reconstruction."

"Spoken like a true physicist," Ove said, and we laughed.

"We are what they left behind," I said. "We're the artifacts, their artifacts. Every one of us is a vessel in the tiny space we're allotted. I can still see it. Feel it. That torus, that ring. It seemed so solid. It's up to us to find the pieces and put them back together again. We're all broken pots. Taking something from the past, something smashed, and reassembling it into a deeper understanding. When I was in that torus, we were all one. It was—the only word that comes to me is humbling."

"In Japan, we have an art form called kintsukuroi," Dr. Kai added. "When a dish or vase broke, an artisan would mend it with a lacquer mixed with powdered gold. Veins of gold held the shards together, and what might have been discarded as useless or ugly changed into something precious. Beauty from imperfection. Maybe that's what the Foundlings have left behind. Kintsukuroi to fix our broken selves." Her last thought drifted into the library and settled somewhere between the covers of our own books, leaving us silent.

It was getting late, and our party dwindled to Asmed and I.

"We met at the library in Toronto. Remember?"

"I do."

"You didn't like me much."

"I thought you were arrogant."

"I was. It was a coverup. What did you like about me, Chu?"

"Your humour. Your honesty. You gave it to me straight, even when I didn't want to hear it."

"What happened when you touched that thing?"

"It was like I tied into something bigger than myself. Not that I became insignificant. It was the opposite. I just knew—it, the thing I believed I needed to find, was right there with me all along. Like the nose on my face. I was it. The thing I was looking for. The Foundlings. They showed me."

"What about Raven?"

"She's with them."

"Where does that leave you?"

"Right here. The little girl from Pangnirtung, all grown up."

"Hmm," he shifted in his chair and reached for his crutches. "This leg is killing me. I'm heading to bed. See you in the morning."

I watched as he hobbled up the stairs, never glancing back.

* * *

At breakfast, Asmed disclosed he'd be flying to London later that afternoon. "Scotland Yard wants to inspect the footage I shot in Qaanaaq. More evidence against Aquifor."

His announcement hijacked my appetite. On our way back to our rooms, I caught his arm in the hallway. "Thanks for being there for me, Asmed."

"Worked out for me too," he said, looking away. "What are friends for?"

"I'm heading back to Pang in a couple more days."

"Home for me too. Tifariti. After London."

"Well, that's it," I smiled and released his arm. "Be safe."

"You too. Get over here," he said, dropping his crutches and pivoting on one foot. We hugged tight and released, and he took a couple of steps, then faced me. "Do you remember the old woman at the camel race? The one who gave you the silver ornament?"

I reached into my pocket and brought it out. "You mean this?"

He looked at me in amazement. "Yes. That old woman was my grandmother. She was a shaman. She told me you'd be going with the sky people and wouldn't be back."

"Yet here we are."

"So much for shamans."

* * *

His plane took off for London after seven.

Next morning, I'd just climbed out of the shower and answered my phone. Charles blared from the other end. "Why weren't you picking up? There's a thousand people here worried sick. And the press. They're voracious. What's going on? Where are you?"

"Reykjavik."

"Reykjavik? What the hell? When are you coming back to Toronto?"

"Soon."

"More specific."

"I have to go home first. After that."

"We need you here."

"Charles, please stop. Tell everyone I'm fine and I miss them. You know how to handle the press."

"Did you know they've charged Olivia Pereira with murder?"

"No. I'm in a news cleanse."

"Well then. I guess you don't know about the indictments against Aquifor, either. Six countries and counting are delving into their corporate activities. Political implications spilling over here, too. Canadian Intelligence is investigating our own Minister of the Environment. And that gratuity Hursche promised the university? Paid in full."

"Thanks for the update."

"I know Chulyin, I'm sorry. It's crazy here. When do you think we'll see you?"

"I'll let you know in a few days. Oh, and Charles. Thank you for your concern. I appreciate it."

"You're welcome. I'm glad you're safe."

I knew he meant it.

Two days later, I bid farewell to my companions. Ove was staying in Reykjavik for a glaciological summit on the projected diminishment of polar ice sheets. Siti and Miatzo were off exploring the island.

I glued my face to the window as the plane veered west, the north Atlantic swallowing the glitter of Reykjavik. Outside, aurora borealis flickered in tidal magnificence, forcing stars to lesser status.

27. RETURN TO ODIN

A frenzy of academic activity stole my attention when I returned to Toronto, along with an insatiable curiosity from staff and students who wanted a firsthand account of what happened in Qaanaaq. The media was worse, but the novelty eventually wore thin, and their attention waned, chasing the next scandal or tragedy that satiated their appetite for ratings.

Opportunities rolled in, and I weighed two that sparked my interest. One was a dig in Dakahlia, a sector northeast of Cairo twenty minutes from the Mediterranean. Egyptian archaeologists had uncovered a cache of stone tablets chiseled with uncharacteristic hieroglyphs that had them baffled.

Charles was all about it. "Cracking that mystery. Wouldn't that be a real feather in the university's cap?"

The idea of feathers gave me goose bumps. "It sure would," I said.

The other came from professor Harbi. Political tension has eased in Western Sahara, and a six-month tenure slated to begin in November at Rekeiz Lemgasem appealed to my interest.

"I'm going to Rekeiz," I told Charles in early August.

He released a sigh. "Your decision is final?"

"Yes."

"Is there anything I can say to change your mind?"

"No, Charles. And I'm going home next week."

"To Pangnirtung?"

"Uh-huh."

"A trip down memory lane?"

"Unfinished business," I said.

I discovered Qikiqtani Quests had a chartered flight booked out of Halifax, which would fly me directly to Pang. Boarding the ATR-42 turbo prop at Stanfield International, eleven rowdy Scots occupied the craft for a trek to the mountains. That left the twelfth seat for me. The airbus brimmed with equipment and excitement; the pandemonium fuelled by the Scots' thumb-nosing gesture defying the airline's non-alcohol policy. The three-hour trip was a melee of debauchery and laughter, the laughter being my only participation in their shenanigans.

When the plane kissed the runway, the Scots boiled from the craft, sorting through their backpacks, ah-ing and ooh-ing at the place I'd spent a lifetime trying to escape: Slipping past their glee, I ambled towards the terminal, then stopped. Something had changed. Boats bobbed in the harbour like coloured icebergs, and the aroma of fish entrails wafted in pockets of breeze shifting down from the fiord. Beyond the hamlet, purple saxifrage daubed the moraine, a craggy chin jutting defiant against the onslaught of countless Arctic winters. I crouched, pressing my hand to the ground. Cool. Firm. Welcome.

Inside the terminal, a voice hailed over the boisterous din. "Chulyin!" Michael Koonark bolted across the lobby hollering to the travellers, "Everybody pack your gear into the green van."

"My God, Chulyin." Michael gripped my shoulders while his eyes poured over me. "Are you here to stay?"

"For a while. I'll be going back to Toronto in October."

"Come to Odin. You've got plenty of time. We can catch up on all the exciting news. You know how much action happens in this place," and he laughed.

"Thanks Michael, but I'll pass. I just need to chill for a few days."

"What could be more relaxing than sharing quality time with a bunch of drunken Scots?"

"Case in point. I'll leave that to you."

"Let's talk when I get back. I'm so happy to see you, Chulyin," and he mashed me with a bear hug. A peal of laughter cackled outside the terminal. "Duty calls."

Cutting across the runway, I slipped into the pathway north of the airstrip. Walking left, then right, and at the end of the dirt road my childhood home, perched above the narrow tidal basin where I'd danced with my mother a lifetime ago. The gate, repaired and freshly painted, had a latch and spring installed with new hinges. Passing through, it clicked shut. No squeak. The door was unlocked, and I walked in like I'd done a thousand times as a little girl.

Expecting stale air and layers of dust, the place was orderly and fresh, windows open and the smell of the sea rolled in like an accommodating host.

Stacked neatly on the table were Aanaq's sewing instruments and a pair of unfinished mittens. Immediately I noticed it—the absence of violets. Window ledges were vacant and the tables, usually crowded with her garden, uninhabited. Hanging above the kitchen counter, Jesus, peering down, keeping a watchful eye over the stove and breadbox, populating his field of vision.

By the window, her chair. It was one of four, a set Anun had purchased before my birth, but it was the only one she used. Anun and I would try to trick her, shifting the chairs about, but she'd press her hands to her hips and calmly tell us to move it back. It was armless, and half of the upholstery pins had loosened, allowing the batting to leak out. The red velvet had lost its nap, the pile worn shiny, and the weight of her years pressed valleys into the faded cushion.

Sitting, I eased into her absence. Beneath the mittens were the tools of her labour, a sewing kit of bone hooks and needles stored in a hollowed caribou antler. Closing my eyes, I pretended she would be there when I opened them, telling me about mittens or Fox or her sister speaking from the moon, full and silver.

But when I opened my eyes, my only companion was Jesus, peering down in perpetual sadness. Lifting from the chair, I walked to the image and removed His forlornness from the hook. "No more Tuesdays," I said, placing the photo in the drawer and sliding it closed. Voices drifted up from the harbour and bells from the fishing boats tinkled on eddies, shifting the kitchen curtains.

The latch on the door clicked and in blew Fearney.

"Chulyin," he squealed like a little boy.

"Who did you expect?"

"Not you, that's for sure." He stood frozen in the door frame. "When did you get here?"

"Just now."

Tears welled in his eyes and without another word, he propelled himself at me, squeezing me so hard my spine cracked.

"Easy boy. You don't know your strength."

"I can't believe you're here," squeezing again, this time with a little less vigour.

"You're the one keeping up the house?"

"Yup. Here most every day. When I'm not working."

"You found yourself a job, did you?"

"Sure did. Qikiqtani. I'm kind of the Jack of all trades. Taking care of the boats, painting, all the mechanical stuff. I got this thing for fixing motors."

"And cleaning houses."

"Just seemed a shame to let things go. Besides, I wanted to keep it clean for when you came back."

"You knew I was coming back?"

"Sure. Eventually. This is your home."

"I guess you knew more than me."

"Hey, I got to show you something," and he grabbed my sleeve, leading me out to Aanaq's tupiq. "Close your eyes."

"Really?"

"Close your eyes," he insisted, leading me into the tupiq. "Ready? Okay—now."

Fearney had transformed the tupiq into a botanical wonder. African violets, rows and stacks of them, a multi-tiered forest of green under canopies of lights dousing the tupiq in a cornucopia of pinks and purples and whites, and every combination in between.

"Incredible," I said, spinning, trying to take it all in.

"Those," he said, pointing to a tray with blossoms of double layered petals. "Temperamental. Took me a couple of months to get them to bloom."

"Looks like you can fix more than motors. Fearney, this is amazing."

"Your Aanaq did all the work. I just brought them all out here and made them more comfortable."

Weaving through the trays of pots and snaking through the levels of lights, Fearney had constructed an intricate irrigation system set on timers to water the violets based on the soil's dryness.

"Where did you learn to do this?"

"Mostly from Aanaq. Books. And Father McMurtry helped a bit." A motor clicked and the lazy flow of water dripped from tubes clipped onto the edge of each pot. "Look at this," and I could see excitement in his face. "Aanaq tried cross-pollinating different plants but never made it work." He led me to a small group of violets isolated from the rest, and carefully, with the tip of a pencil, pointed to a swollen lime-green pod. "Look at that. The pistil. It's pregnant."

"Aanaq would be so proud of you."

"Thanks, Chu. She taught me a lot. Said all I had to do was keep trying and be patient."

"Fearney, I think you're shaman," I said. "Only a shaman could do something like this."

He laughed, nervous, flattered. "I did what I was told. That's all. There's no magic in me, that's for sure. I give them what they need and the lights do the rest."

"There's more magic in you than you could ever imagine."

We strolled back to the house, where I caught up on all the news from Pang. How his mother had passed shortly after Aanaq and that his wife was expecting their first baby. When I had returned for Aanaq's funeral, I hadn't realized he'd married, and I apologized. He told me not to worry, that I had enough of my plate, never mind thinking about somebody getting married.

"I want to show you something else," he said as he was preparing to leave. "I hope you're not mad. It just seemed the right thing to do."

He walked to the kitchen and pulled an envelope from under the plates, handing it to me. It was Ms. Stevenson's letter. "I watched you that day when you ran up by Mount Duvall. You were so upset. I thought it best to leave you alone. After we met at the dump and you went home, I fetched it. And I promise. I never opened it. Seemed pretty private. I hope you don't mind I did that."

The envelope was dirty and torn at the edges. I brought it to my nose, smelling the earth and the ghost of Ms. Stevenson's perfume.

"Thank you."

"Well, I have to get back. This baby is coming in a week or so and I catch a problem if I'm away too long." He rolled out the door, then turned one last time before he faded down the lane. "Oh yeah. It's a girl. And we're calling her Chulyin."

* * *

I scheduled my trip to Odin for mid-August, earlier than when Anun and I traditionally made our hike, but I didn't want to interfere with Qikiqtani's schedule. Michael assured me I would have the mountain to myself, and any expedition would be well into the park by that point.

When I closed the door to my childhood home, I wondered if I would ever return. My heart said yes, but there was an undercurrent of sadness telling me this was a last goodbye. Pushing through the gate, I heard no argument from the hinges, and the spring clipped the latch shut. A period at the end of a sentence. An episode of my life.

Fearney met me at the dock. Michael had arranged for him to escort me up the fiord to the base camp. A tinge of annoyance tickled my gut. I had envisioned a solitary boat trip, but stilled my irritation knowing I'd have plenty of opportunity to be alone. This was no time to be insensitive to a kindness extended my way. Fearney sensed my need for quiet. Planting myself on the bow, we chugged deep into the fiord, and it wasn't until Aulatsivik Point was in our wake he broke the silence.

"What happened Chu? In Greenland? I watched all the news and stuff. Most of it doesn't make any sense. And I don't care much about it. The news. What happened to you?"

Mountains fell behind the stern, his hands gripping the wheel, staring straight ahead.

"I had an epiphany."

"A what?"

"A change. A shift in how I see things."

"Like your Aanaq? She saw things different."

"Kind of. But this is—hard to explain."

"Are you shaman?"

"No. I don't know. Maybe."

"Does Raven talk to you anymore?"

"No."

"Are you glad?"

"Yes, and no. Yes, because she doesn't interrupt me anymore. I can think straight with no interference. No, because I feel like a piece of me has been cut out."

"That's sad."

"Yeah. But new things always come to fill the hole. Like this. You and me. Here on the water between the mountains."

He nodded. "I think I get it. Do you remember the night you came for dinner at our house?"

"How could I forget? My knuckles are still sore from your old man cracking them with his fork."

"Before you showed I was in the bedroom. With a pistol in my mouth. When I heard your voice, I put the gun down on the floor. It seemed so silly to do something like that. Off myself. Besides, I had to protect you from Freddy and his assholes. You did that for me, Chu. When we were kids. You filled that hole." Suddenly, his eyes were saucers. "Turn around. Quick!"

A pod of belugas blitzed the boat, splitting in half, two torrents of white breaching through the surf, soaking us in foam and spray. They disappeared as quickly as they arrived, swallowed in the wake, heading for the open water of Cumberland Sound.

"I don't care what happened in Greenland," he said. "I'm just glad you're home."

Fearney was a tiny speck on the horizon before I turned my attention to Odin. Overlord, Ulu, and Gauntlet peaks greeted me as I began into the valley. Anun called them his three siblings. "That's Buniq—Sweet Daughter, Miki—Little One. And Sangilak—Strongest of all," he said, pointing to each mountain. "Never fails. They're always here when I show up."

Clouds rolled in and the temperature dropped, a fog drifting in from the sea crawling up the valley floor. Michael warned me; the braid plains had shifted because a deluge of pent-up water had emptied from Tumbler glacier. "Stick to the inuksuk," he said, and I was grateful, following the markers through the loose terrain. The sun eventually burned through the veil and I rounded Crater Lake, its seaward shore torn by the torrent released from the glacier.

An hour later, I reached camp, a secluded enclave isolated from the main trail, about a hundred metres above the valley floor. Michael had thought of everything; tent erected, firewood stacked nearby, a cache of food and a box of extra cartridges for my rifle. I sat with my back to Odin, basking in the full glow of sun, peering into the lowland, the river snaking through the cotton grass and swathes of heather. A group of caribou grazed, making their way north to some portion of the island known only to them.

(Hello Anun. I'm not angry anymore.)

This was his mountain. Anun dwelled in every chink and crevice, and I was just a privileged guest. Eyes within the stone foraged the valley, searching, finding me the way they did when I was a little girl. Wordless. Knowing. Odin detected me now, Anun's eyes peering through the cracks and shadows shifting in the sunlight, tilting west and over the edge of a world beyond the sight of either him or the mountain. I lit a teepee of wood Michael had prepared and nestled in for the night.

Out of the corner of my eye, I spotted her. Still, like the rock itself, unblinking, waiting to be discovered.

Fox.

A snap from the fire sprayed sparks into the twilight, and she vanished.

* * *

I struck out from camp early the next morning. The moon and sun were trading places, passing the baton just below the horizon like relay runners racing into the next phase of day, leaving the sky sapphire for those brief moments when neither sphere existed. Below, Windy Lake nuzzled between Odin's toes. Glancing one last time, I started the climb along the mountain's steep southern ridge, on high alert for Fox. She'd visited in an early morning dream, coaxing me to get the journey underway, a brush of her tail pulling me into wakefulness. In the light of dawn, there was no sign of her. "If Fox does not want to be seen, you will never find her," Aanaq had told me. "She is master of disguise." Yet there was a ticklish awareness that her eyes scrutinized my every step, and when I turned my head to catch a shift amongst the rocks, it was only the wind or shadows playing tricks.

At noon, I came to the place of the black stone. All that remained was a brown smudge, summer lichen encroaching on a shallow bowl that had housed the rock. A chip broken from the ziggurat, a Foundling found, and whisked away to the in-between place where Fox and Aanaq spied from the mountain. I hopped into the centre of the impression. No light, no swirling mass spiralled to the heavens, just a solid crucible cradling me in Arctic tundra. No Fox, no Raven. In fact, not a single creature attended my journey—only the wind gossiping in the heather kept me company under the watchful eye of Odin.

I continued in silence. At one point, a layer of fresh scree caused me to tumble twenty metres, but I scrambled up and made it to the crossing of solid rock that led to the plateau, the spot where Anun had fallen. Michael had predicted my arrival. A tent with provisions waited for me at the base of the cliff, a stack of firewood and another box of shells with a note on top; 'in case you forgot'. I lit the fire and prepared some tea. There I waited for the moon.

They traded places just before five, the sun submerging in the west, the moon full and brilliant, breaking the twilight left behind in the wake of fading light.

I sat where I had found him. A sharp stone marked the spot where his leg shattered, and I pressed my back into the cliff, hoping.

I implored the dusk. "I'm here. Say something. Anything."

Aanaq came on a shaft of jewelled moonlight, spilling silver over the oasis of my fire.

"Will you come with me?"

I reached out my hand and we rose above the mountain, into the realm of stars, drifting toward our sacred repository of ancestral souls. Anun sat amongst them at a vast table laden with caribou, the hunt successful, celebration in the air. He carved the beast, doling it out, and no one was hungry, filling them with glee. Then he saw me and he opened with a great peal of laughter. "Look who it is! My beautiful niece."

Aanaq squeezed my hand. "Go to him."

He was flamboyant, playful. "I was wondering when you would come."

"I…"

"No words?" he said. "Never thought I'd see the day." And the entourage roared with laughter. "Come. Sit." An ice chair was beside him, Foxes and Ravens chiseled into the crystals, overlain with hides of caribou and furs of polar bear. "You've done well since we parted."

"Anun, I'm sorry."

"For what? This is no time for misgivings. This is time for reconciliation. I have a gift." Fumbling in the pocket of his anorak, he removed a pouch, offering it to me. "This belongs to you, bringer of light."

Receiving the favour, my fingers yielded to the pouch, tracing the outline of Raven sewn on the supple hide. The darkness from the igloo reappeared, and from it, Taktut. "Return this. Return it to its rightful place."

I unravelled the leather strand, securing the pouch, and emptied the contents into my palm. Suvulliik. Brilliant, charging the sky with light. I reached forward and replaced the star in the heavens, its head hanging low.

A rustle from the unknown guests surrounding the table, their infinite faces metamorphosing to runes, the runes of the ziggurat, then melting like a snowflake on a child's tongue into the star guiding the dawn.

Moon shone from Aanaq. "Does Suvulliik hang its head?"

"Yes, Aanaq."

"It's time to begin a new day."

LEXICON OF INUKTITUT WORDS

AANAQ:	grandmother
ANGAKKUQ:	a powerful shaman
ANORAK:	coat
ILIMMAQTURNIQ:	a spiritual journey through the air by a shaman
INUKSUK:	a stone landmark or cairn
INUKTITUT:	Inuit first language
KALIRRANGIT:	sound of runners of a dog sled riding over snow
NANURLUK:	a giant mythical polar bear spirit
NUKAQ:	young sister or girl, same sex
PANA:	traditional Inuit snow knife used for cutting blocks for igloos
QALLUNAAQ:	non-Inuit (singular)
QALLUNAAT:	non-Inuit (plural)
QAUMANIQ:	the light of a shaman, inner light or seeing
QUILLIQ:	soapstone lamp fuelled by animal fat
NAKURMIIK:	thank you
AKSARNIRQ:	aurora borealis spirit sky dwellers
SILA:	spirit of wind and air, the essence of breath and life
SOOLUTVALUK:	mythical raven with one wing
SUVULLIIK:	constellation of 3 stars—Arcturus, Vega and Murphid
TUPIQ:	shaman tent
TUURNGAIT:	plural of tuurngaq
TUURNGAQ:	a shaman's spirit guide